A Texan's Honor

Also in The Heart of a Hero series

by Shelley Gray

A Texan's Promise

A Texan's Honor

Book 2 of the Heart of a Hero series

Shelley Gray

 Abingdon Press fiction
a novel approach to faith

Nashville, Tennessee

A Texan's Honor

For Kelley

Acknowledgments

An author never writes a book completely by herself. I'm thankful for my editor, Ramona Richards, for her notes and help to make the novel better. Thank you and thank you again for your research help on trains in the 1870s. Thank you to Julie Dowd for her incredible help with promotion, and to all the folks at Abingdon for bringing this series to life.

Mercy and Truth are met together;
righteousness and peace have kissed each other.
—Psalm 85:10

" . . . That's nothing's so sacred as honor
and nothing so loyal as love!"
—Epitaph on Wyatt Earp's tombstone

1

Kansas

January 1874

The barrel of a six-shooter was cold against Jamie's temple. As the iron pressed on her skin, a chill raced through her body.

She should've kept her wool cloak on.

She thought it certainly was amazing how in the most dire circumstances, a body resorted to concentrating on the most basic of things. The gunman pressed the barrel harder against her with a shaky hand. Jamie winced and her fear crept up a notch. Closing her eyes, she waited for the inevitable. Tried her best to recite the Lord's Prayer. Surely, that's what God would want her to think about during her last moments on earth.

"Put that gun down, Kent," one of the men ordered from the other side of the train car. "There's no need to start firing on defenseless women."

Her captor wasn't in the mood for advice. "Shut up, McMillan. The boss might think you're somethin' special, but we both know you ain't none better than the rest of us." Reaching out with his free hand—the one not pressing the firearm to her temple—he took hold of Jamie's arm. Wrapped five thick leather-gloved fingers around her elbow and tugged.

Jamie bit her lip so she wouldn't cry out.

Kent noticed and grinned.

Across the aisle on the floor, one of the six men trussed like turkeys looked away.

"I'm just saying we've got no cause to start killing hostages," McMillan said as he stepped closer. His tan duster glided over the planes of his body, accentuating his chest and the pure white of his cotton shirt.

"I ain't killed no one today. Not yet, leastways."

"Don't start now. You heard what Boss said," McMillan said, stepping close enough for Jamie to see faint lines of exhaustion around his eyes.

Jamie found it almost impossible to look away. The man—McMillan—spoke so quietly. So calmly. Like he was speaking of the bitter cold temperatures outside. Or the snow covering the ground. In fact, he looked almost bored, holding his Colt in his right hand and scanning the rest of them with little curiosity.

As though none of them counted.

Jamie blinked back tears as she tried to stay as still as possible. But it was hard, because the train was still moving.

As panic, grief, and a thousand other emotions engulfed her, Jamie wondered why the Lord had placed her on this train with a band of outlaws. Both her parents had succumbed to influenza just two months ago. After selling everything she owned, she boarded the train in Denver and planned to continue traveling east on the Kansas Pacific toward Kansas City. Her future? To go live with her maiden aunts until she and Randall—her aunts' favorite neighbor and her very recent correspondent—decided matrimony was in their future.

However, from the time she'd boarded, the journey had been difficult. She had little extra money, so she was in the second class coach along with everyone else who couldn't afford to travel more privately in first class. No one had needed to tell her that traveling in third class was not an option. Only poor immigrants traveled that way—and it was certainly not safe for a lady traveling alone.

Of course, now it looked like second class wasn't safe either.

When she'd first boarded, she'd noticed that the inside of the car smelled much like the scruffy men surrounding her. However, none of the men had been overtly disrespectful, and soon most ignored her as they fell into brief slumbers.

But somewhere near the border of Kansas and the Colorado Territory, everything changed. When the train had slowed around a bend, a group of men on horses had approached, their guns blazing. The engineer had braked hard, creating a sick feeling of inevitable doom. Moments later, the train screeched to a stop. Passengers in the two front cars were forced off, one by one, onto the frozen expanse of barren landscape.

Jamie had just gotten to her feet when the man who held her grabbed her with a gap-toothed smile. "Oh, no, sweetheart. You're not going anywhere. We're gonna need you."

With another screech, the train had rolled forward, picking up speed. Jamie had been forced to stand by his side as other bandits came in and separated six men from the others like culling calves. Now those six were tied up and pushed to the floorboards.

She was forced to stand in front of them with a gun pressed to her head, pulled into an awkward embrace by the most evil man she'd ever had the misfortune to meet.

Waiting.

The train rocked some more, and Jamie stumbled as her knees locked. Desperately, she reached out to the seat next to her—anything to keep her balance. For a split second, the iron separated from her temple, freeing her from certain death.

Then, with the next sway, her captor slid his arm higher on her taffeta-covered arm, yanking her closer. As her head snapped with the motion, her delicate skin tapped against the ice-cold barrel. She cried out.

"Stay still and stay silent!" Kent yelled.

One of the six hostages gasped and then fell silent as another man cocked his Colt and leveled it on him.

"Easy now, girl," Kent said, his voice laced with triumph as he forced her closer still. Now Jamie was completely pressed against his side, close enough to feel the other six-shooter fastened against his hip jutting into the soft fabric of her black mourning gown—close enough to feel the heat rolling off his body and spy the unmistakable light of anticipation burning in his eyes.

Though she closed her eyes, his presence surrounded her still—his breath beat a rhythm against her neck, causing chill bumps on her skin.

The train was practically flying along the tracks now, gaining speed as they headed across Kansas. And with it, her hope was fading fast. There was little hope of standing as still as the outlaw wanted her to, and even less of a chance that she would be able to control her fear completely.

She was going to die.

Jamie—Jamilyn Ellis—closed her eyes and tried to pray once more. But this time, the words she searched for were not filled with beautiful poetry passed down from generation to generation.

No, this time her prayer was far more clumsy and desperate. *Please Lord, if this is what you have in mind for me, give me a quick death. Would you please? I'm trying really hard to be courageous but I'm just about out of bravery.*

With a grunt and a whoosh, the connecting door to the passenger car opened. The fragrant aroma of an expensive cigar filled the car, ultimately bringing a bit of a reprieve from her captor's rank smell. All went still as the door closed behind a well-dressed man as he surveyed the lot of them.

With his expensive turquoise silk vest, neatly trimmed ebony mustache, and slicked-back hair, he had an air about him that spoke of power.

Instinctively, Jamie knew that the gang's boss had just joined them. All the gunslingers around her seemed to take a step back.

When he stood still, taking in the scene with obvious distaste, Kent's grip lost some of its strength. Moisture beaded his brow as his body began to shake. The cool barrel bobbed against her temple, reminding her in no uncertain terms that she was at his mercy—if he had any.

Jamie forced herself to breathe as her captor's tremors increased, and the leader stared at her with the greenest eyes she'd ever seen. She blinked, thinking that the color reminded her of the meadow in early spring, when everything was fresh and new and full of hope.

Time seemed to stop.

"Kent, what are you doing?" the leader asked, his voice as smooth as velvet. "We don't treat ladies like that. Release her. Now."

Her captor's response was instantaneous. However, the moment she'd become free of the man's harsh grip, Jamie felt her knees give way.

At the same time, the train chugged around another bend. She strived to retain her precarious balance, but it was no use. The nearest seat was just out of her reach, and the man standing next to her was not anyone she'd ever willingly touch.

As if in slow motion, she wobbled. Struggled, gasped. The stays on her corset were tight. She was losing precious oxygen. Dizziness engulfed her.

Suddenly, two strong arms and the scent of bay rum and mint surrounded her, the muscles like iron. The touch reassuring and surprisingly gentle. "Easy now. I've got you," the man—McMillan—murmured, so quietly she was sure she'd only imagined such kindness.

Turning her head, she met his gaze, then froze at his impassive expression. His touch might have been light and easy, but there was certainly no sympathy in his expression.

"Sit down," McMillan ordered, this time speaking more loudly.

Awkwardly, she let him guide her to the nearby bench. Didn't struggle as he helped her sit down. She clumsily adjusted her skirts as she'd been taught years ago, the action so familiar and automatic she hardly realized she was doing it.

For a split second, he glanced at her hand on the taffeta, then slowly lifted his gaze, stopping when their eyes met. His ice-blue eyes, lined with gray, were as chilly and disturbing as the deep waters of Cascade Lake.

Shivers claimed her as the last of her hope dissipated into the cold confines of the icy train car.

"Everything all right, McMillan?" the leader asked.

"Everything's fine." McMillan shifted his stance, edging closer, as if he was shielding her with his body.

But surely that couldn't be.

Nerves kicked in again as her pulse raced. Shaking, Jamie attempted to inhale properly, but her body fought the action. She couldn't catch her breath, couldn't grasp any air. Panic overtook her as she tried to sit still, tried to breathe.

Immediately, the gunman turned and took hold of her arm. "Breathe," he commanded. "Settle down and breathe slowly."

But no firm directive was going to be of much assistance. Her lungs felt frozen. Almost immobile. Still panicked, she gripped his arm, attempting to get control.

But instead of a gentle touch, he closed his fingers around her wrist. "Calm yourself or I'm going to strip you here and slice the ribbons of your corset."

His voice was little more than a thin whisper, but Jamie had no doubt that he meant every single word. Closing her eyes, she concentrated on breathing.

When she followed his directives, his lips curved slightly. "Good girl," he whispered.

But surely she'd imagined that softening.

The door opened. Another bandit entered the car, this one dressed completely in black, from his felt Stetson to his denims, to his boots and duster. Even his eyes and hair were dark.

"Everything's under control," he said, his voice gravelly and deep. "The brakeman isn't going to stop until I tell him to."

"That is reassuring," the leader murmured, as formal as if he were dining at the Brown Palace. After checking his gold timepiece, he slipped it back into his vest.

The man in black motioned toward the men tied up. "You want me to deal with them?"

"No. We're going to keep this group here for the time being."

After surveying the lot of them, the man in black nodded and stepped to the side, leaving the rest of them to decipher the boss's meaning.

The man standing next to her tensed. "Even the woman?"

Jamie felt the leader's cold gaze settle on her. Forcing herself to keep her gaze fixed firmly on the clasped hands in her lap, she began to pray. *Oh, Lord. Please don't let this be my time. Not yet.*

"Especially the woman," the leader finally replied. "She might prove useful in the future."

As Jamie processed those words, struggled with the awful images of what the bandit meant by that cryptic remark, one of the men tied on the ground spoke. "Why are you keeping us? Why me? I haven't done a thing to you, and I sure don't have any money."

Kent laughed. Unable to help herself, Jamie glanced his way again. Though he wasn't nearly as muscular as the man standing guard over her, he seemed the most dangerous. There was something in his constantly moving eyes that seemed shifty.

The curly-haired hostage on the ground didn't seem to have any qualms about egging Kent on, however. "Whatever grievance you have can surely be diverted. Violence isn't the answer."

"Might be."

But instead of being cowed, the hostage gained confidence. "Sir, I demand to know what you intend to do with me."

"*Demand?* You demand?" Kent smiled. Slowly pulling his Colt .45 out from a worn holster on his hip, he ran his thumb lovingly along the silver handle. "You demand to know? Is that a fact?"

Jamie's breath hitched as the hostage sputtered. "I'm only asking . . ." Pure fear tainted his voice now.

"Here's a hint," Kent quipped as he raised his gun and pulled the trigger.

The sound reverberated through the train car as a circle of blood formed on the man's chest.

Jamie's eyes filled with tears as she tried not to look at the man's wide, vacant expression frozen in surprise.

Beside her, McMillan cursed under his breath.

Hardly a second passed before the boss stepped forward and slugged Kent—hard. "That was unnecessary," he bit out, as Kent's gun slipped from his hand with a clatter.

Kent tripped backward, finally ending against the wall. As he obviously did his best to remain on two feet, a dazed expression colored his face, mixing with the bead of blood forming on his lip.

Then the man in charge glared their way. "Deal with that."

Without a word, McMillan, the man who'd come to her aid, walked over and picked up the pistol from the floor. Offering the weapon to the boss, handle first, his voice was rough. "Sir?"

He waved a hand at the weapon. "Keep the gun. But dispose of the body."

McMillan pocketed the weapon, and the leader cleared his throat as he faced the remaining five men tied on the ground. "Gentlemen, since you're so curious about your future, perhaps I had better explain your situation. You are now my hostages."

The leader's mouth twitched as similar looks of shock and fear flashed across the restrained men's faces. "I need this train. And I need collateral." He looked around the compartment, taking in each person's features with such cold calculation that Jamie knew he probably never forgot a face.

The oldest of the hostages, an elderly gentleman who looked to be almost seventy, blinked in wonder. "What are you talking about?"

"There's something much more valuable on this train than you all. The first car is loaded with the rewards from the latest silver strike out of Cripple Creek. I mean to keep ahold of it. Unfortunately, the law won't see it that way. So I've sent out a telegram stating the rules to Mr. Sam Edison."

He paused as the name registered with the hostages. Even Jamie knew Sam Edison was the man currently in charge of the U.S. Marshals. It seemed his name was always mentioned in the papers.

With another smile, the leader continued. "I was fairly clear in my instructions. As long as no one tries to blow us up or interfere with our progress, you all get to live. But if the law tries to impede my goals, I'll shoot you myself and order your bodies to be tossed out as evidence of my displeasure." Lowering his voice, he added, "I promise, I will do this without the slightest hesitation."

The elderly man's eyes narrowed. "Who are you?" he asked quietly.

Jamie waited for him to get cuffed for his insolence. But instead, the question seemed to amuse the leader.

"I am James Walton, of course."

As the elderly man's eyes widened in recognition, Mr. Walton flashed a smile. "Please don't tell me you haven't heard of me . . . or my business partners."

There was a new awareness in the elderly man's gaze. "I've heard of you. Of course I've heard of you."

Jamie could only be grateful that she was sitting on the bench. The Walton Gang was notoriously dangerous and extremely successful. Yet, for all of their villainy, more than one news rag had painted them—especially their suave, cigar-smoking leader, Mr. James Walton—as heroes of a sort.

In some corners of the area, they were. Everyone knew most lawmen only took the jobs in order to keep three meals in their bellies.

In contrast, some said the Walton Gang took money from the most corrupt and spent their spoils on a whole plethora of things—from their infamous hideout to orphanages.

Word was that no one quite understood them but that everyone knew one thing: they were dangerous and as cold-blooded as they wanted to be. They were as unpredictable as a blue norther.

They killed and plundered and they never, ever, looked back with regret.

It was becoming evident that the passengers were all completely at the gang's mercy. And that Jamilyn Ellis was the only woman on the train.

2

Everything about this job was a mistake, Will McMillan thought as he hooked his hands under the dead man's arms and yanked him out of the train car.

The poor idiot's hands were still tied in front of him, as were his feet. Getting him anywhere was like lugging around a sack of potatoes. Why in the blazes had he decided to talk so much, anyway?

If he'd just kept his mouth shut, Will wouldn't be having to do this. And if Boss trusted Kent more, Kent would be the one disposing of his handiwork, instead of Will.

As he continued to tug, blood seeped from the gaping hole in the man's chest and dripped to the floor, leaving a trail that he'd feel obligated to mop up as well, if only for the woman's sensibilities. It was obvious that she was barely holding on.

War was painful and life was hard. He'd learned that at a young age. However, no lady should ever have to step over a trail of blood—not even if she was a hostage.

The dead man's denims caught on the edge of a bench. With a grunt of distaste, Will lowered the poor soul's shoulders, walked down to the man's feet, and pulled the snagged cuff from the metal bar. All the while, he fought to keep his expression neutral, though he felt the harsh pull of disgust. He'd killed before, but never like this. When he'd squeezed his trigger, it had been in the throes of battle or in self-defense.

Kent's vicious need for bloodshed and his complete disregard for human life were difficult things to get used to. All waste was.

But perhaps that was a good thing. Will knew he would be a far different man if he were able to comprehend killing for pleasure.

Russell, the newest member of their crew, scurried up beside him. "Want me to do this for ya, Will?" he asked in his usual youthful eagerness. "I don't mind."

Though a part of him would have liked to push the duty off his shoulders, Will shook his head. Any weakness on his part would be seen as a liability, and he couldn't afford that.

Besides, Walton had told him to take care of the body, and he'd question any deviation from his directives. "I've got it," he said, giving the dead man another tug. Ultimately, he wrapped his arms around the man's midsection and hoisted him out to the train car's opening. For his efforts, more blood seeped onto Will's midsection, defiling his broadcloth.

And ruining the very last of his patience.

Taking care to keep his expression impassive, he tugged again, continuing forward to the empty train car. There, he would store the body. Every man had the right to a decent burial. Eventually.

With care, he laid the man down against the far wall, where he'd be out of the way. In the silence and privacy of the car, he closed his eyes and said a quick prayer over the body.

Just as Will was pulling a fresh shirt from his bag, Russell rushed forward, all five feet four inches of him, full of questions. "You're changing? Again?"

"Shirt's ruined," he said as he pulled the stained shirt down his arms. Unlike many of the men in his company, he wore no thermal wear under his shirt, preferring to keep his body free and loose.

For a brief moment, Russell's eyes found the four-inch jagged scar that ran across the left side of Will's chest. They then darted to the circular mark marring his hip, and the many other scratches and scars decorating his torso.

Will didn't shrink away from the boy's gaze. His body had been abused during the war and had been wounded too many times to count ever since. He was an ugly mess now—something no woman would ever find attractive.

But he was better off than the man lying at his feet, so that was something, he supposed.

When Will stared right back, Russell quickly turned to the slain hostage. "Will, how come you didn't toss him out? Boss was expectin' that."

Unwilling to give his reasons, Will shrugged. "Boss asked me to remove the body. I did."

"But—"

"We can't just go around tossing dead people off of trains," he said sharply as he quickly buttoned his broadcloth and tucked it in. "It will just get the law riled up." It was also just plain wrong, Will knew, but he refrained from saying that because his faith was his business and no one else's.

In addition, Russell was too young and naive to contemplate so many shades of gray. Shoot, even Will wasn't sure what was right or wrong sometimes.

Anxious to move on, Will asked, "Now what's going on with the hostages?"

"Oh, they're still just sittin' there on the floor." Russell chuckled. "After Kent killed this man and Boss told them who we were, they look a whole lot less ornery."

Will hoped so. The longer they stayed seated and quiet, the better chance they had of living. "And the woman?"

"She's sittin' on one of the seats. Scout's watching her."

Will heaved a sigh of relief. He trusted Scout Proffitt. If he was watching the lady, she would have a chance to leave the train with her virtue intact. "Those men, they're going to need water soon."

Russell screwed up his forehead. "Boss won't care about those men getting thirsty, Will."

"It's good business. If they're watered, they'll be easier to manage. Go get them some. And see if you can find something decent for the lady to drink out of. She's gently bred."

Russell's brows lowered, along with is voice. "I don't cotton with getting a woman involved. It don't seem right. She looks like she could be somebody's sister. Or sweetheart."

Their hostage did look like all those things, and more. With her golden hair and light brown wide-set eyes, she looked like an angel.

And her skin . . . Will's fingers had brushed against her throat when he'd unfastened the top button of her dress. It had felt soft and supple. Clean and smooth. Too fine for a man like him to touch.

"She's dressed in all black, too," Russell added, just as if Will wouldn't have noticed her form-fitting black taffeta. "She must be grieving for somebody."

Will was sure she was. Unbidden, a memory of his mother wearing black for his father surfaced. The harsh hue had drained the last of the color from her skin, making her seem even more delicate than usual. "Most people are mourning someone right now. Life hasn't been easy for some time," he said more sharply than he intended.

Russell nodded automatically, then looked toward him and paused, chewing on his bottom lip. "That woman—she looks real scared, Will."

For a moment, Will contemplated painting things just a little bit rosy. After all, Russell was young. Barely seventeen. Too young to be with the likes of them.

Or perhaps not. Will knew Russell had killed a man for attacking his sister, and would kill again if asked to.

"She'd be a fool not to be scared."

Russell paused, then blurted, "I think Kent wants her. He keeps looking at her like she's a treat."

Will started. The idea of Kent ever touching that girl's skin, ever hurting the woman, made his skin crawl. "He won't touch her. Not if he wants to live."

Pure relief entered Russell's eyes. "You'll make sure of it? Hurting men is one thing, but a woman like that . . ." His voice drifted off, obviously fearing he'd said too much.

Will was tempted to berate Russell. It was expected, after all. There was no room in the Walton Gang for soft hearts or tender emotions. But for the life of him, he couldn't do it.

Russell's worries echoed his own, and his vulnerability made Will recall other days, days when things like futures were important.

"I'll make sure Kent doesn't touch her. I agree with you. A woman like that shouldn't be defiled like this."

Russell said nothing more, but visible relief flowed through the boy.

Will turned away so he wouldn't have to give any more promises he didn't believe. Without another word, he returned to the hostages. As third in command, it was his job to make sure orders were obeyed and Walton's almighty directives were

followed. He'd played the enforcer time and again with ease—
never regretting the force he'd had to use. Over time, he'd
even begun to expect to use his muscle to bend people to his
bidding. He never looked back, either.

He was still standing—unlike many of the poor souls who'd
lost their lives during the war. Actually, he figured he'd lived
too long to have regrets.

But the sight that greeted him made his heart threaten
to stop. Instead of sitting under Scout's watchful eye, Kent
had his arms wrapped around the woman and her cheek was
bruised and swollen. He was laughing as he was obviously trying to claim a kiss.

The five remaining hostages looked on with various shades
of pity and distaste. Manny, the only other Walton Gang
member present, was leaning against the wall, watching with
a glazed expression.

When she pulled away from him again, Kent cursed and
slapped her hard.

Anger coursed through Will as he watched her head snap
back. Striding close, he grabbed Kent by the shoulder and
pulled him away. "Enough."

Kent stilled under his grip, true wariness in his eyes. "Hell,
no. She's mine, McMillan. This ain't no concern of yours."

It took everything he had not to pull out his knife and slice
Kent's throat. But it wasn't his place to discipline the man.
Besides, no matter how much he disliked the things Kent did,
the job he was hired to do was more important.

Instead, he grabbed Kent's collar and shoved him hard.
Finally free, the woman half fell, half scrambled back to the
bench.

Once he was assured she was settled, Will turned to the
outlaw. "If you touch her again I will kill you," he promised.
"Right here. Right now." To his shame, he almost hoped for

the opportunity. Kent was pure evil, and it chafed Will to be in his company.

"Now you've decided to stop playing?" Kent said, his voice full of bravado as he used the name they'd all given him on account of his quiet nature and quieter ways.

Will had never liked the moniker. He thought it disrespectful to men of the cloth—because he was as far from a good man as he could likely get. "Don't call me that."

When he fingered the Colt at his side, Kent's face paled.

Behind them, the woman was crying. He heard her quiet attempts to stifle herself, and those attempts nearly broke his heart. And made his temper flare. His job was hard enough without having a woman involved—why the heck hadn't Walton let her leave?

As the tension in the compartment thickened, Kent finally stepped back.

"Will? Will, what do you want me to do?" Russell asked from the doorway. "Do you still want them watered?"

Still keeping his eyes on Kent, Will nodded. "Yeah."

"And the woman?"

Will hesitated, then relaxed when he saw Scout join them. "I'll take her into the next car and get her something myself."

Russell's eyebrows rose, but thankfully he didn't argue. From his position by the window Kent cussed under his breath, then stilled when Will eyed him.

Scout, looking as unruffled as ever, crossed his arms over his chest. "Go on and take her out of here. I've got everything under control."

Will nodded then approached the girl. To his dismay, she flinched when he was in striking distance. "Easy now," he murmured. "I won't hurt you."

He waited a moment, then motioned her to her feet. "Let's go now."

As silent tears continued to fall, the girl stared at him in dismay.

Behind him, he heard Scout clear his throat. Will couldn't guess if it was from impatience or if he, too, had been struck by the sight of an innocent woman in need. But he did know that some things needed to be done. Needed to be done, no matter how hard they were or how badly they hurt.

Waiting and worrying didn't make things easier.

"Come on now," he coaxed, keeping his voice easy and gentle. "Get to your feet and step forward. That's all you can do."

Little by little she scooted forward, then at last got to her feet. Gripping the woman's elbow, Will guided her away in a mockery of manners. He kept her close by his side as he guided her away from Kent, past Scout's watchful eyes, and beyond the line of men who were their hostages. Beside him, the woman stepped quietly but with clumsy, heavy steps. Obviously, she was in shock.

When she stumbled, her breath catching as she continued to cry and struggled to breathe, once again fighting the constraints of her corset, Will gave in to his impulses and picked her up. Holding her with one arm under her knees and another around her shoulders, he pulled her close. After what seemed like forever, she relaxed. Suddenly, she was light and feminine in his arms, her skin and muscles soft and pliable against his own.

She smelled like a lady. Smelled like fresh spring and hope and everything he used to dream of having, before the war had broken his character and the choices he had made removed any other options.

Too afraid he was going to say something he'd regret, Will kept his mouth shut and strode forward. Before he went through the passageway, he paused, then took care to flatten her skirts before stepping through. She had to shift slightly as he did, pressing against him for the space of five seconds. Long enough for him to imagine that she was his, that he was holding a woman for another reason other than taking her hostage.

Once they arrived in the next compartment, he loosened his hold, afraid to scare her any more than he already had. Tremors coursed through the girl's body but she stayed silent, too.

For a brief moment, Will thought about saying something to reassure her—but all told, there was truly nothing to say. Nothing of worth. Nothing she'd believe, anyway.

Only when he pulled the compartment latch closed behind him did he put her down, his knees bending slightly as he carefully set her feet on the floor.

Yet still, she wobbled. Unable to help himself, he kept an arm around her slim shoulders to help her get her bearings.

But instead of leaning toward his touch, she stiffened. Reminding Will that he was nothing to her except a source of terror.

Berating himself, Will took two steps backward.

There was a new sense of fear emanating from her, and Will cursed Kent for that. The Walton Gang was a group of murderers and thieves—but they didn't prey on women. Until her.

She still looked so lost, so—a chill coursed through him. Had Kent done something more than grab her? Will tried to recall just exactly how long he'd been in the other train car with the hostage's body.

"Miss?" he asked roughly. "Miss, are you all right?"

Turning to him, she blinked. And he cursed his mouth. Of course, she wasn't all right. How could she be? When she swayed, he stepped forward, intending to catch her.

Well, in truth, to try and comfort her, as crazy as that was.

But as if the thought of his touch was too much to bear, she jerked.

He stilled.

Then watched as she trembled, then finally sank to her knees like a stack of cards.

Shaking violently, she curled into a ball, finally giving in to violent tremors and deep, heartbreaking sobs.

Will started to kneel at her side, tempted to reassure her. Tell her that he would protect her virtue. Promise her that he would never touch her. That she'd be almost safe.

But since those assurances felt so wrong, he did the only thing he could. He reached into his back pocket, pulled out a worn bandanna, and tossed it on her lap. Finally, he turned away and let her cry in relative privacy. That, he supposed, was the least he could do.

3

After too long, the tears finally stopped coming. Jamie swiped her eyes with the side of her hand, wincing as she touched her swollen cheek. Finally, she sat up, staring across the compartment at her captor.

The man stood with his back to her. As tall and stoic as a redwood. Just as unbending.

Hesitantly, she picked up his discarded handkerchief. Too distraught to care if it was dirty or clean, she dabbed her face and got to her feet. All right then. She'd had her moment of hysterics. It was time to gather her courage and move forward. Whatever the man did to her, she would endure.

She had to. Surely she hadn't survived the war for nothing? When she glanced at the man again, Jamie noticed he'd turned around and was staring straight at her.

"What's your name?" he asked. His voice was steady and smooth. So different from the frightening coarseness of Kent's.

For a moment, she considered lying, then wondered what good a lie would do. She was trapped, and would most likely be killed or violated or beaten. She might as well be herself when that happened. "Jamie. My name is Jamie Ellis."

A black eyebrow arched. "Jamie? That's a boy's name."

"It's short for Jamilyn," she explained, wondering why she was bothering to explain. "It was my great-aunt's name."

After a moment, he spoke. "It's . . . it's a pretty name, Miss Ellis." His words were stilted. Almost like he was unsure how to compliment a woman. As if he wasn't sure what to say.

For a split second she was about to thank him. Then she remembered where she was, and who he was: her enemy. Clumsily, she got to her feet.

When he didn't approach, didn't try to grab her, she pressed her luck and took three steps backward.

The man, standing as still as a deer in the glade, merely watched her. His perceptive gaze seemed to catch every tremor of her body. See every flaw.

No, it was a closer connection than that. It felt as if he could practically read her mind. Read too much of it, anyway.

Yes, he was that intent on her. And for some reason, that made everything seem even worse. All her life, she'd wanted to count for something. Instead, she'd been the daughter her father hadn't wanted. The child who'd survived when her two older brothers had died while fighting in the war. The reminder to her mother of all she'd lost.

Ever since her brothers had passed away, she'd practically raised herself. As the years went by, her parents had retreated further into themselves, moving often. She'd become shy and almost timid, wishing for a man's regard but too reserved by nature to accept any man's attentions. How ironic—now that she finally was the center of a man's attention, it was because she was his victim.

"Are you going to kill me?" she asked.

Surprise flared in his eyes before he visibly tamped it down. "No."

That answer worried her. Death, she wasn't afraid of. Everything else? She was terrified.

Her knees started to knock. Fearing the worst, she forced herself to face head-on whatever was in store. "What are you going to do to me, then?"

Looking her over, he tilted his head to one side. "Well . . . first off, I thought I'd tend to your face."

Though her cheek burned and her right eye was surely swelling, she dipped her chin. "There's no need."

"I think otherwise." Pointing to a spot on his cheek, he said, "You've got some blood on your face. The pistol barrel must have scratched you somehow. . . ." Before she could respond to that, his voice turned weary. "Ma'am, I know you don't trust me. Furthermore, I know you don't want to trust me. However, I promise that I only brought you in this compartment to keep you safe."

"Safe from the other men?"

He nodded. "From the other men. Safe from Kent."

She knew who Kent was. The thin man who felt like he was all sinew and muscle. Who'd grinned as he'd run his hand down the stays in her corset, then along the curve of her hip. Who had slapped her twice and had looked like he wanted to do far worse things.

"I don't think I'll ever be safe again," she murmured.

"You will. Don't fret, Miss Ellis."

Don't fret? Not worrying wasn't even a possibility. But as she glanced at him again under her lashes, something clicked inside of her. She knew liars, and he wasn't one. Not yet, anyhow.

For a moment, Jamie was tempted to trust this man. She wanted to believe that there was someone on this train who was decent. But just as quickly, those daydreams fell to pieces. After all, why would a man be with the Walton Gang unless he was pure evil?

He was still looking at her without much expression. Standing in that relaxed way of his—with his feet spread shoulder-width apart, his bearing relaxed—that seemed to show he was ready to move in a second's urging.

Or not.

Actually, he acted as if he could stand in the same position all day.

She wasn't nearly that lucky. The train's motion kept her unsteady. Fear made her legs shake and her blood run icy cold. Frantically, she looked around, hoping to grasp hold of something, but nothing was in easy reach. And she was afraid to move.

He noticed. "Perhaps you should sit down," he urged. "If you take a seat, I'll help you wipe your face." His eyes stayed on hers, looking far too compassionate, given his line of work. "You have to admit, wiping the blood off . . . it can't hurt."

Gingerly, she did as he bid, then held herself as still as a statue as he quietly dabbed at her cheek.

Neither of them spoke a word. There was no need, not really. She didn't seem to have any words left in her head.

And Mr. McMillan? Well, he seemed too intent on her cut to speak.

The brief moment of contact ended with both of them releasing sighs.

Then he straightened. "I'll go get someone to fetch you some water."

"You can't get it yourself?" She ached to be alone, if only for a few minutes. Then she could relax her guard; she could give in to her urge to lower her head and close her eyes. Just rest her eyes for a time.

"Eager to be alone, Jamie Ellis?"

Hearing her name on his lips was startling. Knowing he'd read her thoughts frightened her. "I won't escape."

"You haven't even contemplated escaping?" A thin strand of humor entered his voice when it was obvious he spied the telltale flash of embarrassment on her cheeks. "Ah. I was right."

"I won't escape," she said again.

"Miss Ellis," he drawled, sounding almost bored, "I suppose I should tell you that there's nowhere to go. Your only other option is to leave this earth, and you're too pretty for that, don'tcha think?"

His words held such finality, his presence was so big, she feared him. Reaching out, she grabbed the top of a wooden bench as he approached.

Something flickered in his eyes. Impatience? "I am not going to hurt you, understand? Jamie, I want you to try to trust me, even if it's just a little."

"I can't."

"You should. I'm the best thing you've got going."

"I can't trust you. You . . . you're part of the Walton Gang."

"That is a fact. However, I have no interest in hurting you. I don't prey on women."

Which meant he thought someone else was going to. "Like that promise means anything?"

"I keep my promises." His blue gaze flashed before hardening, as did his voice. "Now sit back down before you fall down."

She sat.

When he seemed satisfied with that, he walked to the doorway and called for someone to bring a glass of water. Then he strode to the bench across from her and sat down too. After a time, he spread his long legs out a bit in front of him, his denims dark against the burgundy leather.

Moments later, the young man, whose cheeks looked like they were still covered with peach fuzz, entered with a glass of water. "Here you go, Will."

Her captor took it. "Thanks." Still staring at her, he said, "Russell, what's everyone else doing?"

"Mr. Walton is resting. Kent and Scout are with the hostages."

"Good enough. Tell Scout I'll continue to stay in here."

Jamie felt Russell's speculative gaze flutter over her before he nodded and left.

Only when the door latched behind them did the man hand her the water. "Drink."

Half afraid her shaking hands would betray just how afraid she was, Jamie held the glass with both of her gloved hands and sipped. The water felt like heaven on her tongue. It soothed her parched throat, bringing a blessed relief. Anxious for more, she drank again, gulping the water so fast she coughed.

All the while, he watched her. "Careful. Don't drink too fast," he warned. "You'll choke."

Jamie looked at him curiously. What kind of a bandit was he? What kind of a man? "Your name is Will?" she asked, hating that her voice still sounded so tentative.

"It is. Will McMillan."

"Mr. McMillan, you need to free me."

"I'm afraid I can't do that."

"You could. I won't say a word. I won't even tell anyone where I was."

"Jamie, just because I'm here with you, making sure you aren't beaten or violated, doesn't mean that I'm softer than any of the others." His eyes narrowed. "You'd be a fool to think that."

"I didn't think you were soft."

"Drink."

"I don't want any more."

He sighed, looking completely aggravated. "Why is it that women, no matter who they are or where they are, never fail to be contrary?" Before she could refute his words, he looked her over. "Why are you on this train anyway? Where were you headed?"

His use of the past tense scared her. It was becoming increasingly obvious that the odds of her getting off the train were slim to none.

But she tried to play along. "I'm going to Kansas City to live with my aunts." And because she was old enough to have a trio of babies attached to her skirts, she added her secret. "My aunts have a neighbor whom I've been writing to."

His lips twitched. "You've got yourself a correspondent, do you?"

"It's more special than that."

"Let me guess. . . . He's a man who's just perfect for you."

"Yes. His name is Randall. We've been writing."

To her dismay, his lips twitched. "A Missouri man, hmm? Taken to letter writing?" His voice held more than a note of derision. "What's he like? Handsome and gentlemanly?"

"I've never met him," she admitted, suddenly feeling childish. "But I have received four letters. He's—um—anxious to meet me."

"I imagine he is."

Again, his amusement grated on her pride. "Why are you smirking?"

"No reason." He shrugged. "I'm sure he's everything you imagine he is. After all, he survived the war."

"He didn't fight," she blurted before she thought the better of it. It wasn't any of this man's business.

And for that matter, what did it matter if a man had fought or not?

Of course, she knew the answer. It mattered. Of course, it counted for a lot.

Pure confusion crossed his face before he visibly pushed it down. "Why not?"

"I don't know." But that wasn't true. Aunt Millicent had written that Randall had been too sickly too fight. But the thought of telling this man—who was all muscle, hard planes, and emanated power and competence—felt like a betrayal.

"Well, I hope to heck you find out."

"Mr. McMillan. Watch your mouth."

Up went that eyebrow again. "You're held hostage on a train car, on the way to meet some kind of yellow, sorry man in Missouri, and you're worried about my mouth offending your tender sensibilities?"

Crossing her arms over her chest, she turned away. He was right; she was a captive. She needed to worry about survival, not rules and manners. Though she hadn't forgotten her worries, for a moment she'd pushed them to one side.

With a sigh, she heard him stand up and walk to the other side of the car.

In the faint reflection of the glass, she saw him sit down near the doorway. Perhaps he was going to leave her alone now?

She leaned her head against the back of the bench and closed her eyes. She prayed for comfort and for the angels to protect her.

Selfishly, she prayed for her soul and that her death would be relatively painless. She did so fear pain.

Minutes passed. Little by little, she fell into a dazed sleep.

Then the door opened.

"McMillan, what are you doing?" a deep, husky voice asked. "Russell says you're intending to keep the woman in here for a while."

"I answer to James Walton, not Scout Proffitt."

That man—that "Scout" she'd seen earlier—was *Scout Proffitt?* Startled, Jamie turned to see Will get to his feet just as the newcomer turned her way and stared.

And Jamie realized she was looking at yet another famous outlaw, fresh from the dime novels and penny papers. Scout Proffitt was standing not three feet from her. Dressed completely in black from head to toe. Just like all the papers said.

And with eyes as empty as a barren creekbed.

When he turned to her and stared, Jamie's heart sunk and the tremors started again.

The dime novels and reports might have been 99 percent exaggeration. They might have made up stories about his looks or his way with a gun.

But it was now obvious that at least 1 percent of their stories was all fact—Scout Proffitt was a killer.

And as he glared at her without a breath of compassion in his very dark, very scary gaze, Jamie knew she was about to die.

4

Scout Proffitt was tired. Bone tired.

He was tired of being on a train, tired of dealing with fools like Addison Kent, and tired of doing his best to bridge the gap between James Walton and the rest of the Walton Gang.

Being second in command was a thankless existence. Truth be told, even being a part of this motley crew was a difficult thing. The other men weren't like him. They were either too young, too green, or too dumb.

Actually, there was only one man Scout was reasonably comfortable with, and that was Will McMillan. He was quiet and had a semblance of a conscience—something Scout hadn't thought he would find to be an admirable characteristic in a person, but he did.

Unfortunately, now even Will was doing his best to be contrary. Instead of doing what he was supposed to do, the man was hell-bent on taking their lone female hostage and sequestering her away in a compartment by himself.

And, by the looks of things, Will was content to play babysitter—leaving Scout to deal with five shaking, whining hostages; a too-young boy named Russell; Kent; and the elegant heartlessness of their boss.

Tired of their foolishness, he strode into Will's train car. "You need to bring her on back, McMillan. I want her with the rest of the hostages."

But instead of complying or looking cowed, Will stood up and raised an eyebrow. "That's not going to happen."

"I'm giving you an order."

"Are you?" There went that eyebrow again. "Because we both know Jamie is better off in here with me rather than getting mixed up with the others," Will said slowly.

Jamie? Will was now calling this woman by her first name? Scout's temper snapped. "That's not for you to decide."

Will stepped in front of the woman, as if he were protecting her from Scout. "Are you really going to start telling me what to do? What to think?"

The other man's quarrelsome tone took Scout by surprise. Usually his manner was as calm and still as the air after a snowstorm, and just as frosty. By Scout's recollection, nothing disturbed Will—not Indian raids, not a hanging posse, not the threat of starvation. Usually, the man took it all in stride.

But just now . . . he was different somehow. Bordering on belligerent. Acting like he was spoiling for a fight.

Maybe he was, too. "It's my job to tell you what to do," he bit out. "It's my duty to make sure you follow orders."

After staring at him for a good long minute, Will lowered his voice. "Look at her, Scout," he practically whispered. "You know I need to keep her apart from the rest of the men. You and I both know what's going to happen if I don't."

Reluctantly, Scout glanced at the woman again. She was sitting on a bench, staring at her hands clenched in her lap.

Obviously trying not to meet his gaze.

There was no denying it; she was a pretty thing. Dressed in an old, out-of-fashion, black taffeta gown, she should have looked like a crow. Instead, the stark color only accentuated her pale pink skin. And her obvious mourning made him feel a sort of tenderness he'd been sure he'd given up years ago.

But her hair, now that it was falling out of its combs and pins, was long and as curly as he'd ever seen. It was a shade of gold he'd only seen in Kansas during summer, when fields of wheat covered the countryside and blew in the breeze. It was beautiful—there was no other word for it.

It was eclipsed only by her brown eyes, wide and tinted with flecks of gold. And as innocent as he remembered his sister being. Well, the way they'd once been before Yankees had come to their farm and taken everything they'd ever wanted.

As if she could no longer ignore him, the woman raised her chin and stared. Seconds passed. Pure fear entered her eyes, giving him no doubt that she recognized his name, or at least sensed his reputation.

The look she threw his way told a million stories, the least of which was that she'd read about him and half expected him to pull out his Colt and shoot her dead without taking the time to blink. In short, fear emanated from her.

Her breath hitched.

McMillan noticed and narrowed his eyes. "She's mine," Will said quietly. Too softly for the woman to hear.

The way Will spoke was unnerving. It implied ownership; almost a relationship. It was a purely male territorial thing and as foreign to Scout as weakness.

Quickly he darted his gaze back to Will's. "I don't want her."

"I mean it. I won't have her harmed."

Scout was stung. He might be good with a gun, but he'd never been an animal. "I don't want her hurt either."

"Good."

"Honestly, McMillan, settle down." As the woman leaned closer to Will, evidently seeking his protection, Scout raised his voice. His intention was to raise her guard again. Because one thing was for sure—the little fool was in trouble if she relaxed even for a second.

As he'd half hoped, fresh tears formed in her eyes and any last bit of color that lit her cheeks faded in a flash.

Next to him, Will cursed.

Tired of looking at the woman, tired of thinking about his past and all the things he should've done but never had, Scout turned his back to the girl and focused on business, such that it was. "We're about a hundred miles from Dodge City, but Boss thinks we might get stopped before then. When the train stops, we need to be prepared. There's a good chance U.S. Marshals are going to be there waiting. And Boss is going to be itchy. He doesn't want anything to happen with that silver."

"I know."

McMillan's voice was clipped and tight. Irritated. Which made Scout wonder if his mind was on their job or on the woman.

So, although it felt a bit unnecessary, he explained things a little more clearly. "When we stop, things are sure to get dicey. We're going to need to be ready for anything. You can't be watching the woman, understand? You're going to have to tie her up."

"I will not."

"Fine. I'll do it."

"No one will be tying her up."

Though the woman had now turned so pale she looked like she was going to pass out any minute, Scout pushed forward. "We can't risk her getting in the way," he countered. "And we sure as heck can't risk her running. If she escapes, we'd lose our last bit of leverage."

Pain and a flicker of animosity flared in Will's gaze. "If we let her go, it might not be a bad thing," he said slowly, like he was measuring every word before he spit it out. "Maybe we should offer to deliver her to the Marshals in good condition. It might give us some control."

"It won't. All that would do would allow the Marshals to feel like they can use all the dynamite they want on us. Next thing you'd know, we'd be blown to kingdom come."

"Not necessarily. We'd still have hostages."

"A bunch of sniveling men, one so old he might as well be dead." Scout paused for a moment, reflecting on just how much trouble those men had been. They seemed to constantly need to be watered. And then make stops to the lavatories. If he'd been in charge, they'd have been put out of their misery hours ago. "Besides, men don't count. We both know that."

Looking Will over, Scout scoffed. "What's going on with you? You going soft on me?"

"I'm not soft. I just don't like using women. Especially women like her. She's an innocent, Scout."

Remembering his sister, remembering the Yankees and their filth, he shook his head. "Not anymore."

"I haven't touched her."

"It don't matter if you've touched her or not. Everyone's going to think you have. And even if none of us lays a finger on her, that girl is going to be marked for the rest of her days by this."

The skin around McMillan's mouth whitened. It was so obvious he was holding back his words.

Scout respected that, but he respected his past even more. "Will, you listen to me and know I'm speaking the truth.

She's not innocent anymore. You've already ruined her. *We've* already ruined her. Get that through your head."

"She's not ruined. It's not too late. We can still let her go."

"You know it doesn't matter what you want or think. Boss says we're keeping her." Scout let that sink in, hoping that was the end of things. Suddenly, he was anxious to go and get out of Will's head. The things he was talking about disturbed him. The things he was thinking about made him wish for other days. Better memories. A different future.

Standing there in that train compartment, he was starting to wish he wasn't quite so ruined and worthless.

After a good long minute, Will crossed his arms over his chest. "If she's staying, she stays with me then."

Scout was tempted to argue, just so McMillan wouldn't ever think that it was okay to ignore direct orders. But he bit off his temper. No matter what, he sure didn't want to be responsible for the girl. The boss would just forget about her, and the others were no match for Kent if he wanted her bad enough.

And Scout knew he did.

"Fine. Keep her here with you, at least until we get to Dodge." Looking at the girl again, he shook his head in disgust. Women were nothing but trouble, and he wished Walton had let her go hours ago. But because Walton was banking on some poor U.S. Marshal or sheriff in Dodge or Salina or Wichita having a tender heart where a woman was concerned—and therefore not blowing them up—they had to keep her.

Now, blast it, he was going to have to deal with the woman screaming or carrying on and Kent getting too anxious where she was concerned.

"But listen to me close. When we stop, you better be ready to follow Boss's orders. Because if you don't, I'm going to be forced to see that you do."

Will McMillan's gaze hardened, but he nodded. "Understood," he said.

The affirmative made Scout breathe a little easier. Will didn't go back on his word. "All right then. . . ."

He hesitated, and glanced toward the woman again.

She was now making no secret that she was listening to every word they said—well, at least every word she could hear.

She was also making no secret of the fact that she didn't trust him, and was half scared of him too. Her expression was carefully blank. She was sitting stock-still, her back straight enough to have a ruler attached to her spine. Actually, the only movement he saw in her at all was the lone tear trickling down her cheek.

As he watched it paint her pale skin, for one small second his heart softened. A woman like that was special. Fine. But that wouldn't do. He had no time for tender emotions. Shaking off his pity, he strode out of the train car again, breathing easier the minute he was free of her. With any luck, it would be hours before he had to look at the woman again.

5

*W*ill couldn't deny it. He breathed easier the moment Scout Proffitt exited their compartment. The man was decent enough—well, decent enough considering he was a hired killer—but the fact of the matter was Scout was a dangerous man.

A very dangerous one. The tales of him shooting just about anyone for enough money weren't all fabricated. Will had witnessed him do it many a time.

It was also known that he had no patience for women. No one knew why that was, but time and again men had described how they'd watched the gunslinger's usual easygoing nature turn frosty the moment a woman batted her eyelashes his way.

And though Jamie hadn't been anything but scared and tentative, Will had worried for a moment that Scout would aim his revolver at her heart just so he wouldn't have to look at her a minute longer.

Scout had that kind of reputation.

As the air cleared in their compartment and a small, peculiar semblance of normality returned, Jamie exhaled. "I thought he was going to kill me," she said.

He couldn't help but look her way. That pretty voice of hers drifted toward him like a shining light in the darkness. And just like a beam of light, it drew his attention to her like none other.

"He didn't," Will finally replied, hating his cool tone but unable to squelch it. He needed to keep himself firmly under control. Otherwise she was going to get under his skin.

"Do you think he will soon?" She clutched her hands together so tightly they looked fused.

Unbidden, thoughtful, sweet reassurances threatened to erupt from him. Just as if he didn't know any better. Just as if he didn't know any better than to trust a "good" woman. It would be kind to lie to her. To let her think that there was still hope somewhere in the world. Or at least on this train.

But he hadn't been kind for a very long time. "No," he said harshly, finally turning to look at her.

She flinched, and a new wariness filled her eyes. The fear that had left her reappeared. Will felt a momentary regret, and even almost considered softening his reply.

Then, like he'd learned to do, he tamped the urge down. Platitudes didn't come easy in his line of work—or in life. Believing in false hope didn't make things better; it only made accepting the truth harder to do.

Because of that, he dealt with facts. And with what people told him to do. That was what he knew.

But it obviously wasn't what she was used to. Her mouth pursed and the telltale tears that she had been trying to hold at bay threatened to fall.

Had a man ever been so surrounded by tears? Frustrated by the emotions he was feeling, he said, "No one's going to kill you anytime soon."

Well, not if he could help it, anyway.

Her eyes widened as she caught hold of the word "soon" and gripped it hard. "That 'anytime soon part' doesn't make me feel any better."

"It wasn't supposed to. You should be nervous. And you shouldn't believe a thing any of us tell you."

"Then why are you even bothering to talk to me at all?"

Oh, but she was cheeky! "The fact is, Jamilyn, you're our hostage and your very life is in the hands of a few desperate men. We can't sugarcoat the reality, and I'm not even of a mind to try."

"Obviously not."

He heard the note of disappointment in her voice and he felt bad. But there wasn't a thing he could do, because she needed to be afraid.

It was safer for her that way. What he didn't feel like sharing was that some of the men on the train had been a very long time without a woman. And that there weren't any dividing lines in their minds about "good" women and sporting ones.

For men like Kent, she was breathing and therefore available for the taking, and that was all that mattered.

But perhaps Jamie didn't need the harsh truth spelled out for her. Little by little, her bravado evaporated, leaving her looking smaller and even more innocent.

And leaving a trail of guilt piercing his heart.

"I can't believe this is happening," she rasped, visibly holding back tears. "I can't believe I boarded this train in Denver thinking that the worst part of the trip would be going hungry. Now here I am, afraid I'm not even going to be alive this time tomorrow. This . . . this all feels like a dream."

Will said nothing. After all, there was nothing to say. She wasn't in a dream, and no matter how much she cried, there wasn't a thing anyone—even he—could do about it.

"If Scout Proffitt intends to kill me, I hope he does it soon," she said as her tears dried up.

"Scout won't kill you today." Not until he was told to, anyway.

Time passed. Maybe it was five minutes. Maybe it was twenty. Leaning with his shoulders braced against the metal doors, his body rolled with the train's motion. The frosty air outside seeped through the steel structure, threaded through his coat, and chilled his skin.

She shivered, though whether it was from the dropping temperatures or the situation, he didn't know. "That gun-slinger, he was sure a whole lot different than I thought he'd be," she said after a moment. "The papers made him sound ugly and coarse. And loud too. He didn't seem like any of those things."

Thinking of the outrageous stories spun up around the killer, he shrugged. "You're not the first to say that. Proffitt seems to catch a lot of people off guard. He was different from what I'd expected. He's calmer, more thoughtful too." He stared at her hard. "He's not all bad, but that doesn't mean much, not really. Fact is, he's still as dangerous as a pickax in a gold strike."

"You're not making me feel better," she said with a bit of sarcasm.

And that little bit of spunk was more impressive than most things he'd seen in months. Against his will, he crossed the aisle and sat across from her again. It was too cold to lean against the metal any longer, and he was sick and tired of standing anyway.

And, to his irritation, he was tired of the tense silence that filled the air between them. It had been so long since he'd been in the company of a good woman. So long since he'd been around any female who made him think of his precious, silly sister Bonnie.

Maybe because of that, he spoke. "When I first met Scout it was in a gambling house in Lubbock, Texas. I was sitting with Mr. Walton and Russell, just taking a break."

Remembering why they'd been so tired, Will added softly, "We'd been riding hard for three days straight and I'd thought my a—I mean, my backside—was never going to feel the same."

When Jamie giggled softly, Will let his cheeks relax enough to almost smile. "Anyway, we were sitting there, quenching our thirst and what have you, when in came Scout Proffitt. He strode through the entrance like he owned the place. And he was dressed from head to toe in black, just like always."

As if it had been only yesterday, Will shook his head slightly. "Looked like a pallbearer, really. The whole room went silent once word got around of who he was."

She leaned forward. "Then what happened?"

"He walked, ever so slowly, to a table nestled in a corner. Without a word, he just stood and stared at the two men sitting there like they were in his way or something. After three seconds, one of the men apologized for existing on this earth. Then, before you could blink, the pair of them scampered off."

"And then?"

"And then Scout took the chair, sat with his back to the wall, and asked for a whiskey. Even said please and thank you to the bar girl." Will shook his head at the memory. "It was plumb amazing. I thought I'd seen most everything during the war, but never in my life had I seen a person act like he deserved the world."

Jamie looked almost thunderstruck. "Is that when you met him?"

"Uh-huh. Before I knew it, Mr. Walton was smiling at him and pressing his palm. Doing his best to convince Scout to join our outfit. Never thought he would."

"Why was that?"

"He doesn't need the protection of a gang. At least, I didn't think he did." Will shrugged. "But I guess he'd been having trouble sleeping." Noticing her confusion, he clarified. "A man like him can never rest if he's alone—someone is always eager to take him out. He wanted us around to watch his back." He shrugged. "That was a year ago. He's far more serious than I thought he'd be. The dime novels made him seem like he was always happy," he mused, half to himself.

Jamie's eyes were now as big as saucers. "The papers say he's a horrible man. He's done horrible things."

"Oh, he has, and don't you forget it. Of course, we all have," he blurted before he could stop himself. For a while, he'd tried to excuse his escapades by blaming the heat of the battle. Or extreme fatigue. Or hunger.

Or the fact that a man could only take so much cruelty and bloodshed before he did things too.

As flashes of a family in Alabama threatened to surface, Will tamped them down. It was far easier to concentrate on someone else. "Scout is fairly quiet. Keeps to himself," he said. "And for all his reputation and the fact that he can draw a pistol faster than just about any other man alive, I've never seen him be openly cruel."

So far, Will hadn't heard of a single person who doubted Scout's ability to draw quickly and lethally. No one who'd ever seen him draw would forget his lightning speed.

But there was also a lingering sadness about the man that had come as something of a surprise. Will hadn't expected the gunman to have even the slightest lick of a conscience. Of course, with that softness came a bit of an edge to the outlaw's personality. He had just enough of a devil-may-care attitude that not even their boss had been able to break.

Actually, instead of attempting to break Scout Proffitt's hard exterior, their leader seemed to give him wide berth. Will found it easy to do the same. He would speak with Scout but not completely trust him.

He would never do that.

It wasn't hard. After all, Will had learned early in life never to depend on the people closest to him. Trusting people who said they loved or cared for him had led to a whole lot of heartache.

More than one scar on his body proved that trust only led to pain and ruined expectations.

Frustrated by the latest direction of his thoughts, Will looked back to the girl. She was sitting as still as a corpse, and had her arms wrapped tightly around herself. Her posture and bearing reminded Will that she had been gently brought up. Her shivering reminded him that she was clad in only a pitifully thin black gown. Not even a wool shawl covered her shoulders. As he stared at her, he spied the faintest of tremors, reminding him that it was cold on the car. Terribly cold, and there wasn't much they could do about it either.

So, though he was rusty at conversation, he attempted to divert her attention. "So what do you do, Jamilyn Ellis? When you're not traveling to Kansas City to meet your Randall?"

Her eyes flashed. "He's not 'my' anything. And why do you keep calling me Jamilyn?"

He thought it was pretty. He liked how it was feminine and light. How the syllables felt on his tongue. "It suits you. Better than a boy's name does, I'll tell you that."

One golden eyebrow arched. "You think?"

"I know." Pushing a bit, he asked, "That man of your aunts', what does he call you?"

"We've never spoken face-to-face."

"I know, but what does he call you when he writes?" he amended. "Jamilyn, what does this Randall call you when he writes you his letters?"

"He calls me Jamilyn."

Even the cool air couldn't fan the flames rising in her cheeks. "You see? It's a good name."

"It's what my aunts call me in their letters. They don't care for Jamie either."

"And what do your parents call you?"

She paused, then shook her head. "Nothing. Ever since my brothers died, they don't call me anything."

Will was struck dumb. She looked so prim and proper—she was so very innocent—he'd assumed she was the type of girl who'd had a slew of people who'd fussed and pampered her. He'd even imagined she had a loyal pet, maybe even one of those silly, useless dogs.

But the distant expression on her face told him a whole different story.

He thought about pressing her for more information, before pushing aside the idea. After all, her past didn't really matter. It wasn't like he'd ever need to know much about her. Even if Scout didn't shoot her dead, even if Boss decided to let her go free, it wasn't like she'd ever cross his mind again.

So he stayed silent. At first her muscles were bunched. Obviously, she was waiting for him to ask her more. But when he didn't, a curious look of confusion crossed her face. Almost like she was disappointed he hadn't pushed her.

She nibbled her bottom lip for a spell like she wasn't sure how much information to give him. Her resistance amused him. And made his heart go soft.

She reminded him of his cousins, the silly girls who used to worry so much about their manners and their words. But there was something more about her that he couldn't resist, too. Maybe it was her bone structure. She was finely made and a good eight inches shorter than himself. And pretty too. Truly delicate and lovely. There was an aura of innocence surrounding her, foisting brief images of his past to rush forward. Faint memories slowly filtered in. Hazy recollections of life before the war. For a brief moment, he felt warm again. Almost whole.

Then, with a blink, he remembered everything that had come between then and now, and pain rushed forth. He was tempted to share some of that. To tell Jamie about his life. How he was once so different.

But, of course, he couldn't say such things; it wouldn't be right or proper, or whatever was appropriate at the moment. So he held off his thoughts and focused on her.

"Why do you look at me like that?"

"Because you're pretty."

"What?"

"Come now. Your parents might have ignored you, but surely the your mirror hasn't."

To his surprise, she still looked confused. So he pressed, though it wasn't his business how she thought about herself. "In any case, I'm sure the men in your area have told you how they felt."

"No one came near me. They were afraid. . . ."

"What are you saying? Has no man told you sweet things before?"

By her pause, he knew she was weighing the pros and cons of answering him. "No," she finally said. "No one ever has."

He was surprised. In other circumstances, he'd have tried to court her. Or at least done everything he could to be in the same room with her.

"Why not?"

"Before my brothers went off to war, they were protective. Then, all the men were gone." For a split second, a worry line formed in between her brows. When she shook her head, it vanished. "Mr. McMillan, did you fight in the war?"

"I did."

"For a long time?"

"For as long as I could. I joined up when my father got killed."

"Is that why you turned to this? Because of the war?"

The war had changed him. It had made him do a lot of things he never would've dreamed of. But more than that, the war made him dream of things that he couldn't escape from during those long hours in the middle of the night.

But the war wasn't why he was on the train.

"No," he said at last.

When Jamie leaned forward slightly, obviously anxious for him to give her more of an explanation, he turned away.

His reasons for being here were secret. If Jamie knew, it would only do her harm and make her more scared.

And for some reason, he was in no hurry to make things any worse for her. All he wanted to do was keep her safe.

If he could. *I have become like broken pottery*, he thought, remembering a favorite verse from the Psalms. Where he was once whole, he was broken.

But not completely ruined.

6

For a time, back when she was small, Jamie had carried a doll. Her mother had made it out of a flour sack and had sewn on two black buttons for eyes. The doll had had a red gingham dress like Jamie's but no hair.

At first, Jamie had only found fault with the doll. She didn't like it being bald. She wanted there to be a pretty smile. And, of course, it was a sad comparison to the dolls in the catalogs at the mercantile. The more she compared, the more she was aware that the doll was nothing like a "real" doll, and had told her mother so.

Mama had been disappointed by her criticism, and had told her that. It had been a terribly selfish way to behave, considering her brothers were out fighting the Yankees.

Jamie had known that. But it hadn't stopped her from offering her disappointment frequently and with more than a touch of a whine.

Then, the strangest thing happened—she grew to love that misshapen, too-soft little doll. One afternoon, she named it Jo, just because she'd gotten tired of carrying around a no-name toy. And wouldn't you know it? Soon Jo was the best thing she'd ever had. She was comfortable and soft and her lack of expression meant that anything was possible.

Jamie hadn't meant to cling to that doll. But cling she did. And though her mother never said a word about it, Jamie figured she had been really pleased about her change of heart.

Looking at the man sitting across from her, Jamie wondered about her change of heart too. Suddenly, Will McMillan didn't seem as dangerous or as evil as he once had. Suddenly, she didn't look at his hands with fear, worried that he was going to grab at her clothes or slap her silly.

A few hours ago, she'd stopped bracing herself for his advance. Stopped tensing up beside him, preparing herself for pain. Over the day, she'd begun to notice things about Will. Like how he never raised his voice to her. How he was quiet but solid. She'd liked how he was around Scout Proffitt, too. He'd been calm but had held his ground. Never cowed.

She couldn't imagine too many men acting like that in the famous killer's presence.

So little by little, Jamie found her muscles easing when she was near to him, just anticipating that he would protect her from everyone else. Once she'd almost smiled at something he'd said.

All of this worried her. She should know better. Surely, she should behave better. Perhaps she couldn't trust her judgment any more now than she could when she was small. He was her enemy and she needed to remember that. After all, her brothers—God rest their souls—had been good men. Brave men. They'd died trying to preserve everything their family had believed in.

What would they say if they could see her being almost agreeable to a member of the notorious Walton Gang?

It truly didn't bear thinking about.

But that said, she kept finding herself wondering about Will, and found herself wanting to know him better. More than a time or two, she'd caught herself thinking that he was handsome.

How could that be?

Maybe her mind was filled with all things Will because he wasn't currently by her side. A little less than an hour ago, the train had come to an abrupt stop. The moment it had, he'd left her. He'd threatened to tie her up, but when she'd told him that she knew there was nowhere as safe for her as the place she was currently sitting, he'd left her in peace.

Warily, she sat on the bench, her eyes on the connecting doorway, waiting for the sound of his footsteps. And—Lord have mercy—bracing herself for the inevitable. Surely the rest of the band wouldn't let her stay out of the way for so long.

With a creak and a whoosh, the door opened. She sat upright, eager for news. But instead of the one man she was slowly starting to trust, it was Scout Proffitt.

Her blood chilled, and though she hadn't imagined it possible, she got even colder. Her tremors started up again, coursing through her without stopping, each one tougher to hide than the last. Locking her knees together, she glanced his way.

Obsidian eyes met hers. "Ma'am."

His voice was as scratchy and husky as ever. The look he gave her demanded an answer, or at the very least, a response. But no matter how hard she tried, Jamie couldn't think of a single thing to say. It was like a ghost had traipsed into her head, erasing everything there. Leaving her feeling as blank inside as the walls around her.

But instead of finding fault with the way the cat had gotten her tongue, the outlaw's gaze turned amused. "I guess you realized I'm here to take a turn with you."

To take a turn? She flinched in fear.

"Don't get all excited," he drawled. "I still don't aim to hurt you." He waited for a reply. But when she only stared at him, her mouth frozen, he chuckled. "You really should settle down if you can." He pushed the brim of his black Stetson the slightest bit upward, though whether his intention had been to see her better or for her to see him she didn't know.

To her surprise, he took a seat right across the aisle from her and propped one black boot over an opposite knee. "So, how are you doing? Is there anything you need?"

"You can let me go."

He laughed. "Never pegged you as a woman with spunk. You must be feeling better. Finally."

Though his words weren't scary, his dark gaze was. "I'm sorry," she sputtered. "I didn't mean to make you angry. . . ."

"Oh, I'm not angry. Say whatever you want; it won't matter. The fact is, no matter what you want, there's no way I can let you get off this train." He grimaced. "It's probably a good thing anyway. It's cold out. You'd freeze to death."

"Freezing would be better than being here."

"You only say that because you've never witnessed a man freeze to death." His gaze shuttered. "It ain't pretty."

Just then, she noticed he was holding a man's overcoat in one of his hands.

When he saw what she was looking at, he held it up. "I thought you might want this. It's wool. It should warm you up a bit."

Just as she reached for it Jamie noticed a dark stain across the sleeve. Her hand dropped. "Whose coat was that?"

He shrugged. "I didn't ask the man's name. Don't usually ever ask anyone's name." He flashed a smile. "Other than yours, of course."

"Is it from a man who . . . who died?"

"Is that a problem?"

"Of course." Jamie wasn't sure where the words were coming from, but she now couldn't have stopped herself from talking to him if she'd wanted to. "I can't wear a dead man's coat."

"Why not? He can't use it."

"But it's not seemly. It's not Christian."

"Being Christian don't have anything to do with keeping warm, ma'am." His voice turned oily and derisive. "Let me give you an education. Everyone dies sooner or later. People who survive learn to make do with what's left. Even if you burn this it ain't going to make the dead come alive. Believe me, I know."

"But still—"

"Jamie, he's gone. Now do you want it or not? It's not going to get any warmer. And I'll tell you right now, this is as good an offer as you're going to get." After a moment's pause, his voice lowered. "And it's a far sight better than the things some of the other men have in mind for you to keep warm."

Pure fear coursed through her. Her mouth had gone dry and her mind went blank. Suddenly, there wasn't a thing in her brain.

He chuckled. "Cat got your tongue?"

With effort, she shook her head and held out her hand. "Thank you, Mr. Proffitt."

As if he'd just won an inner battle, his face softened into a semblance of a smile. He nodded. "You are very welcome, Miss Ellis. I'm happy to oblige." And with that, he set the wool into her hands.

A man's unfamiliar scent tickled her nose. Knowing the man was dead, she paused.

"The wool still works. Use it."

His honey-infused voice held a strong thread of steel, reminding her that Scout Proffitt was certainly not weak and probably never had been. And he most certainly wasn't used to giving suggestions.

No, he'd told her to do something. As kind as it was, it had been a command. Only when he watched her wrap the coat around herself did he blink.

She stood up and slipped her arms through the scratchy fabric. And though the fabric smelled of a stranger and was far too big, it also was blessedly thick. Almost immediately, the extra layer of fabric insulated her skin. Little by little, the chill that had overtaken her dissipated.

A flash of a match was followed by the sweet scent of fine tobacco that permeated the air as Scout lit a cheroot and inhaled. Inexplicably, the scent of the cigar calmed her nerves. For a moment, she simply sat and watched Scout finger the thin cigar, take a puff, then slowly exhale.

He glanced her way. "I swore to myself that as soon as I could afford it, I was going to never be without these. It was a good day when I bought my first box."

Jamie wondered why. It seemed to her a strange thing to look forward to having. However, she kept her thoughts private. Scout Proffitt's wants and needs were certainly none of her concern.

When the cheroot was just about halfway gone, he stood up with a sigh. "I suppose it's time we moved on. You and me are going to take a walk now."

"What? Why?" She liked being apart from everyone else. Plus Will had promised her he'd keep her safe.

"Ah, so you can talk." Humor lit his eyes as he stood up. "Here's the deal, sugar. We're going to go see the others. Mr. Walton is curious about you."

"And Mr. McMillan?"

One eyebrow rose. "I imagine Mr. Will McMillan is waiting for you with bated breath. Come on, now." He reached for her hand to help her from her seat.

But she ignored the proffered hand and got to her feet unassisted.

"I'm not good enough for you to take my hand, huh? Guess I should've expected that." Just like that, his expression went flat. He gripped her elbow and pulled her forward.

There wasn't a single reason for the next words she said. "It's not that," she blurted. "It wasn't that I didn't think you were good enough."

"Then what is it?"

"I . . . I'm not used to being around men. I'm not used to being helped. I don't know how to accept that help."

He blinked. "You don't? A pretty thing like you?"

"When my brothers died, my parents became reclusive," she explained, though it was hard to admit and certainly none of his business.

"Some would say that's a good thing," he said after a moment's pause. "Some would say that you being sheltered like you were was fine news, indeed."

While she pondered his statement, Jamie tried not to flinch when he curved his hand around her arm. His fingers cut through the thin fabric of her coat and dress and dug into the soft skin of her upper arm. She bit her lip so he wouldn't know. As he pulled her across the car, through the rickety connection to the next, Jamie did her best to keep up with him, hoping that if she stayed close enough, he would drop his hand.

But he didn't. He simply tugged, the remains of his cigar still in his mouth. The heady scent of tobacco surrounded them, and Jamie knew she would now only associate that particular smell with the train and bone-crunching fear.

Scout Proffit never looked her way as they crossed into the next car. But he did pause. "Word of warning to you—I'd keep that pretty mouth of yours closed and your eyes forward. Except when Mr. Walton speaks to you."

"I don't understand why he would even want to talk to me."

"It don't matter, Jamie."

"But—"

With a hint of aggravation, he shook his head. "Miss Ellis, don't you understand? It never matters what you think in Mr. Walton's company. All that matters is what he wants."

As that last phrase spun in her head, he turned around again and started walking.

Still within his grip, Jamie followed him—more confused than ever. By turns, Scout had been almost gentlemanly and almost violent. She shivered as she followed him into the last car, then stood and tried to get her bearings as she was greeted by a far thicker cloud of cigar smoke and the musky smell of men and fear. Right away Kent whistled low.

Though she kept her eyes averted, she couldn't prevent her body from trembling.

To her surprise, instead of pushing her forward, Scout pulled her closer to him, his grip tight—serving as a reminder of his words of caution. "Don't you forget what I said," he murmured. "Listen, nod, and agree. Things will go easier that way."

She had intended to look only straight ahead, but unable to stop herself, she glanced toward the wall.

Now, only three men gazed back at her. Their mouths were gagged and their wrists were bound in front of them. The space where the old-timer had been was empty, save for a stain of red. When one of the men's eyes widened, then looked at her with contempt, Jamie knew he'd spied her coat.

But even if she could, she wasn't sure if she would give it up now. The extra layer not only provided warmth but an added layer of protection from the men's prying eyes. She felt safer with it on.

That knowledge made her skin crawl. What kind of person was she becoming?

"Ah, Miss Ellis. How kind of you to join us," Mr. Walton said from the corner of the train.

Warily, she looked to the man in charge. He was smoking a cigar, lounging back on one elbow. One foot was propped on the seat in front of him. He looked to be in complete repose, sitting as if he was in a comfortable drawing room—or maybe even in a men's club or a fancy hotel lobby.

Then she noticed his expression. His lips were flat and his beautiful green eyes were alert. Cold. She felt his gaze slowly run the length of her body.

In response, she ached to turn away, but Scout held her elbow firmly. "Don't move," he said under his breath, so low she couldn't even be sure that he'd said anything at all.

In case he had, she willed herself to stand still.

"You may release her arm now, Mr. Proffitt. She's not going anywhere." He chuckled. "I can promise you that."

Immediately, Scout's fingers loosened and his hand drifted away. Though it made no sense, she suddenly missed his touch. His hand had been warm and his grip solid. Perhaps it was because by now she knew what to expect from him. She didn't know what to expect from Mr. Walton.

"Now, Miss Ellis, I trust you have been comfortable in our company?"

She nodded, the movement making her head feel like it was made of wood.

Scout, though he was no longer touching her, was standing close enough to let his displeasure be known. Obviously, he was not pleased that she hadn't followed his advice to a T.

However, it seemed to be enough for Mr. Walton. After puffing on his cigar once more, he said, "I'm so glad. Will here was telling me that you hail from Colorado Territory. Is that right?"

She nodded again, wishing she could locate Will but couldn't see him. She ached to stand up and look around the compartment, but she didn't dare disobey Scout's orders. As the seconds passed, she realized the man really had been looking out for her best interests. "Yes, sir. I lived in Denver. My parents moved there from Texas after the war."

"And now you're headed to Kansas City?" His question was phrased flat, like a statement, making her wonder if he knew far more about her than she could ever guess.

But there was no reason not to tell him the truth. "Yes, sir."

Mr. Walton brought his cigar to his lips, inhaled, then blew out a billowy cloud of smoke. Jamie found herself shaking as she watched the smoke dissipate into the air, quietly evaporating into nothing.

Behind her, she heard the hostages shifting. Beyond them all, wind whistled along the steel walls of the train.

After another moment, he said, "I'm sorry to say this journey hasn't been quite as comfortable as I would have hoped. The weather is difficult at best. Then, of course, we had a terrible miscommunication with the engineer of this train. It seems he needed some convincing about how serious I was in my intentions to keep the silver." He shook his head in sorrow.

"I'm sorry to say, he gave his life for this train, which *is* a rather sorry little story." He sighed dramatically as he tapped the end of his cigar on the end of a table. "The truth is that he should have never doubted me. I don't prevaricate. Ever. It was a shame that poor man had such a difficult time understanding that, don't you think?"

He'd killed the engineer.

Jamie's head felt frozen. She was too afraid to nod, too scared to speak.

He glanced at her, seemed to find comfort in her terror, and then puffed on his cigar again. "I don't believe his brakeman will doubt me now."

The air filled with tension as he gazed at her again. "Now, though, at least you have a coat." He smiled slowly. Obviously goading her to make a response.

But Jamie didn't know what kind of response to make. Still frozen, her mind went back to the scene of Kent shooting the innocent man, ripping off his coat, and tossing him out of the train.

All she was sure about was that she needed to hide her revulsion, both of the coat she was wearing and for the men in front of her.

The atmosphere grew thicker. Tense. Before long, Mr. Walton gave up all pretensions of looking amiable. Instead, his green eyes flashed annoyance and his jaw tightened. Two seconds later, he popped two knuckles. The sharp cracks sounded like rifle pops in the still silence, making her shiver all over again. "Miss Ellis? Are you going to grant me a response?"

Her mouth went dry.

"Talk," Scout murmured from behind her back, his mouth so close she could feel the heat of his breath against her skin. "Talk. Now."

But she didn't know what to say. She was frozen. Panicked. Her mind a void.

"Do it," he muttered, his voice still low but with a forceful edge.

"Yes, sir," she finally said, feeling like a puppet. The truth was, she wasn't even sure what she was referring to anymore. Holding her breath, she half waited for him to yell at her. Or to command her to remove the coat.

Mr. Walton flashed his teeth. "How nice to discover you are inclined to converse. At last."

"Yes, sir. I'm sorry," she said hurriedly. "My father never liked to me to speak to men. I'm afraid I don't have much practice."

Scout grunted.

Momentarily appeased, Mr. Walton smiled. "I find that charming." After puffing his cigar again, he continued. "Now that our conveyance is stopped, it seems that a group of U.S. Marshals have come to investigate."

"Yes, sir?"

"Normally, these men wouldn't be of concern to you, I know. However, I'm afraid someone who we very kindly let go has gone and told those men that there is a woman in here. You."

"Yes, sir?"

"This is a problem." His voice hardened as a look of pure venom entered his voice. He paused.

Jamie's mouth went dry as a feeling of foreboding flickered through her.

Mr. Walton didn't disappoint. "Miss Ellis, because the men know you are on board, they are naturally concerned for your welfare."

Once again, he waited for a response. Once again, she had no idea what to say. "Are they?" Her heart quickening, she wondered if she was about to be freed.

"Indeed. I'm afraid they think the worst." He lifted his hand and examined his nails. "But we are not animals. Not a one of us has mistreated you, have we?" He paused. Stared hard at her.

Feeling weak, she shook her head. "No, sir."

"Very good. I'm glad you see my side of things. In any case, I'm afraid it is now necessary that you be seen."

Scout's breathing hitched.

"Seen?" A whole wealth of images festered in her mind, but unfortunately, none of it made sense. "I'm . . . I'm sorry I don't understand."

Beside her, she could feel Scout's impatience with her grow. With some surprise, his words of warning filtered to her brain again. She wasn't supposed to offer opinions.

Afraid to look his way but unable to stop herself, she glanced toward him.

Scout's mouth tightened and his entire body seemed to radiate disdain.

But fortunately, Mr. Walton didn't seem too dismayed about her speaking. With a motion of his right hand, he said, "Miss Ellis, McMillan is going to take you to the back of the train. He's going to open the back latch. You are going to go stand on the miniscule balcony for a full three minutes." His voice lowered.

"Listen carefully. You will not do anything except stand still. You will not attempt to signal anyone. You will not fight Mr. McMillan. You will not even think about leaving our hospitality. If you do, Scout has orders to shoot you. And trust me, he will. Do you understand?"

"Yes, sir."

"You'd better." Looking toward Scout, Mr. Walton smiled. "See, here's the thing about Scout Proffitt. It doesn't matter to a man like him if you are a woman or how you were bred."

Almost kindly, he added, "Life and death mean the same to him. Humanity means nothing to him. He's a killer. A very good one. But that's all he is."

Beside her, Scout's body might as well have been forged from steel, he was standing so still and straight. Pure venom radiated from him directly to the boss.

With a bit of a shock, Jamie realized that she felt sorry for Scout. Ached to set the record straight. To tell Mr. Walton that there was more to the man beside her than the ability to shoot lethally.

But that would be a mistake. Any compassion that she'd earlier imagined had lurked inside Scout now seemed to be long gone. His eyes were blank and his lips were set in a hard line, as if anger burned right below the surface.

Mr. Walton seemed oblivious to it. "Miss Ellis, do you understand?"

She was frozen in shock. Though she'd been warned not to, she glanced in Will's direction. His expression seemed frozen in stone. Not even an eyelash flickered.

Mr. Walton's eyes narrowed. "Was there something I said that you didn't understand, that you are unable to comprehend?"

"Speak," Scout ordered under his breath.

Like a puppet, she followed directions. "Yes, Mr. Walton. I mean, no, Mr. Walton. I mean . . . I understand."

"Very good. If you continue to do what I say, I might be very pleased with your company, my dear," he said, his voice low and dark. "I might be very pleased indeed. And that means you might just survive our acquaintance. And we would all like that, yes? I've never been fond of harming women and children."

Afraid Scout was going to nudge her again, Jamie nodded. And spoke directly from her heart. "Yes, sir. I would like to survive our acquaintance very much."

A moment passed. Two. Beside her, Scout seemed so tense that Jamie felt sure a stiff wind would split him in two.

Then Mr. Walton laughed. "You have spunk. Good for you." His lips curved into a smile as he looked at her, then immediately hardened as he turned to Will. "Take her on out, McMillan. Take her out and show those Marshals what we've got." Flickering over her form, he added, "Don't forget to remove that new coat of hers. I want every man to have no doubt about what he's seeing."

Without a word, Will nodded, walked to her side, and wrapped one hand around her arm. When he motioned her forward, she obediently stepped forward, all the while wondering if she was walking out to a certain death.

7

$\mathcal{T}$aking care not to bruise her delicate skin, Will McMillan wrapped his hand firmly around Jamie's arm as he escorted her out of the crowded train car and on to the next one. Behind them, Scout Proffitt followed slowly and steadily. Dressed in his usual black, he seemed like an apparition from the worst sort of nightmare.

Will gritted his teeth. He didn't think Scout had hurt the woman, but he must have done something.

Things between them seemed different now. Each seemed skittish around the other. Fear was radiating from Jamie's body like the sun, and Scout was glowering more than usual. And looking at her with more compassion.

As Will continued to guide her toward the end of the train, he cursed the situation. How in the world had things gotten so out of hand? He'd been with the Walton Gang for almost two years now. In that time, he thought he'd seen just about everything. Bloodshed. Robberies. Weaklings tossed away and forgotten.

But until this day they'd never been ones to take advantage of females—especially females who were innocent. He'd signed on for his own reasons, not to scare defenseless women half to death. Worse, by the looks of things, little Miss Jamilyn Ellis was on the verge of a nervous breakdown. Her arm trembled under his touch and her skin was so white that Will was certain a light wind could blow her down.

She certainly did have a fair amount of gumption though; he'd give her that. Though she was pale and her lips were pursed tight, she walked by his side without making a peep. By his estimation, few women were able carry on like that. Most he'd known had been far more fond of dramatics and tears.

Finally, they stopped at the door to the platform at the back of the caboose. "It's almost time. Are you ready, Jamie?"

"I am." Her caramel-colored eyes, so warm and pretty, met his. "I'm just supposed to stand outside, right?"

"Right. All you have to do is stand there, and don't say a word."

When she nodded to show her understanding, Will fought the urge to give her a reassuring smile.

He couldn't trust her. He could only imagine that she was guileless. Because if she decided to act up or escape, he wasn't going to be able to be responsible for what would happen next. If Scout didn't shoot her dead, he'd be forced to do anything he had to in order to get her back.

Even if it meant hurting her or worse. It was either that or ruin his reputation. And no matter what, he couldn't afford to let anyone think that he was less than a full-fledged member of the Walton Gang.

As Jamie steeled herself, Will held onto her arm with one hand, then reached out and grabbed the lever to the door with the other. The door's handle was cold to the touch, reminding Will just how bitterly cold and windy it was outside. "All right now," he murmured. "We better get you out there."

She took one step forward.

"Hold on. She needs to take off the coat," Scout ordered from behind them.

Will turned to him in surprise. "It's freezing out there. She'll catch her death."

"No. She'll catch her death if she gets shot."

Under his hand, Jamie's trembling intensified.

Will narrowed his eyes. "She's frightened enough—she doesn't need you making things worse."

"McMillan, you know Boss wants her standing in only her dress. Are you refusing to follow orders?"

"Of course I'm not. It's just that I've got a brain, you know. It's as cold as—"

"She's wearing a dead man's coat," Scout interrupted. "From a distance, some of the Marshals might even get to thinking she's a man. Might get trigger-happy. It needs to come off."

Will thought there was no way any man looking at Jamie's form was going to mistake it for anything masculine. She was a tiny thing. Petite, yet curvy too. Remembering how she'd felt when he'd carried her, Will knew for a fact there was little angular about her body.

However, he wasn't going to push. James Walton had issued his orders, and no one had ever made the mistake of thinking that the gang was a democracy.

Well, they didn't make that mistake twice.

Just as important, Scout seemed more dangerous than ever at the moment. His gray eyes looked even closer to black and his manner was even more surly than usual.

"Jamie, that coat needs to come off for a time," he said.

Still in the open doorway, Jamie didn't meet his gaze as her shaking hands unfastened four buttons. She then slipped the heavy wool from her shoulders, revealing her black gown once again. Though it should have made her look less beautiful, the opposite was true.

And in that minute, Will knew Scout's orders had had merit. The gown made her small waist look tiny and the bustle and petticoats made the gentle flare of her hips more pronounced. She was everything feminine that men dreamed about.

She was everything he'd ever fantasized about.

"All right. Let's get this over with."

Immediately, a fierce cold breeze slapped them in the face, making his eyes water. "Step out and stand still until I tell you otherwise."

She raised her eyes to his. "You'll be here too, right?"

Her words softened his heart and nearly made him weep, there was such trust there. "I'll be right here. I'm not going anywhere."

She stepped forward, standing with both feet on the platform.

Will was right behind her, his hands loose and easy, ready to reach out and grab her the moment she was in danger of losing her balance.

When Jamie rested her hands in front of her, Scout issued another order from the portal. "Nope, that won't do. Miss Ellis, you keep your hands behind your back. If you even attempt to make a hand signal, you'll regret it."

To Will's surprise, Jamie turned to Scout and glared. "I won't make a hand signal, Mr. Proffitt. Believe me, I have no wish to die today."

Then, with the cold wind blowing hard enough that it made a man think he was on a ship in the ocean, Jamie continued to stand unassisted.

True to her word, she kept her hands behind her back, even though not being able to hold on to the railing was truly a difficult thing for her. Big gusts of frozen sleet slammed them from the north. Her body rocked with the motion. She swayed, obviously attempting to keep her balance.

Behind Will, Scout cursed.

After two more seconds, Will couldn't take it anymore. He stepped out and walked to her side. As the Marshals looked on and Jamie trembled, he stepped closer. Angling his body right next to her, and a little behind, he used his body for support.

Or, perhaps, he was trying to offer her comfort, such that it was.

As she steadied a little and the wind bit into their skin, freezing the points it could touch, Will rested one palm flat in between her shoulder blades.

Which, if he thought about it, had to be just about the saddest, most pathetic attempt at gallantry he'd ever used in his life.

✍

It was all Jamie could do not to scream or cry. Or leap. Beside the train, at a good twenty paces away, six men on horseback stared at her from their spot on the tracks, effectively blocking the train's way. Their Winchesters were cocked, and their expressions were filled with so much contempt that Jamie felt they were already judging her and were finding her wanting.

When she dared to meet their eyes, one of them cursed. She was barely aware of Will's presence, but still was grateful for it. It was bitterly cold, and with the wind and flecks of ice swirling and whipping around them, Jamie knew she'd never felt more vulnerable in her life.

The cold winter elements made her taffeta dress feel as thin and insignificant as tissue paper. Bits of snow and ice flicked her face, stinging her cheeks and making her eyes water. Immediately after, her ears started to burn.

And still, she was forced to continue to stand.

"Who are you?" one of them called out.

Will had already made it very clear that she should definitely not speak. Teeth chattering, Jamie looked to him for guidance.

With some surprise, she realized she now practically had completely given up trying to think for herself. It was too risky—the goals and rules seemed to be mercurial. People who were too confident were pushed or shot or derided.

She feared for her life too much.

Or perhaps she was just too cold.

"Girl? Can you talk?" The closest Marshal called out, his red handlebar mustache matching the sneer in his voice.

She hadn't expected this. For some reason, she'd imagined the lawmen would be more mannerly. Kinder, or at least feeling sorry for her considering her situation. Was no man full of kindness anymore?

"Girl?" the man yelled again.

She turned to Will again. "What do you want me to say?"

After gazing at the Marshals again, the man behind her nodded almost imperceptibly. "Talk."

"Girl?" the Marshal called out. "Girl, start talking to me or else I'll be forced to remind you which side the law is on."

As loudly as she was able, she stated her name. "I am Jamilyn Ellis."

The man in a tan hat and a silver star pinned lopsidedly on his duster looked at the others before turning to her again. "Are you part of the Walton Gang?"

Shocked that he would even think such a thing, she shook her head violently. "I am not."

One of the men muttered something to the others. They laughed. Though she couldn't hear their conversation, their tone sounded vaguely slimy. Making her wonder what was ever going to happen to her. Would she ever feel safe again?

Behind her, Will's body tensed.

For one breathless moment, she ached to say something else, if only for the opportunity to defend herself. All she'd ever done in her life was do what her parents had asked of her, and then nursed them until their deaths. She'd been dutiful and boring, but always respectable. The way the men were looking at her said in their eyes she was anything but that. "I . . . I'm not part of the gang," she called out. "I'm a hostage. I was traveling by myself and taken hostage." She gathered a breath, hoping to come up with a way to let the Marshals know how innocent she was, when finally the men stilled and gazed at her again.

"Miss Ellis?" One of the Marshals called out. "Are you being held against your will?"

"Yes! Yes, of course!" She almost laughed. Here she was, standing in the shadow of two gunmen, freezing in the winter air, and shaking for all she was worth, and the riders below actually wanted to know if she was a hostage or not?

"She's our hostage," Will answered. "But she's unharmed."

Another rider got closer. This man wore a gray Stetson and what looked to be a buffalo-hide coat. But there was a hint of derision on his face. As if he'd lived too long and had done too much.

His gaze on her felt like an oily mark, staining her with shame.

"You ain't hurt her yet, McMillan? She's been willing?"

Jamie gasped as the man's reference sank in.

"Stay quiet," Scout ordered from the doorway.

"You wanted to see her. Now you have," Will called out.

"Now I know why you don't mean to give her up," one of the lawmen said, his voice thick with sarcasm.

Jamie flinched. She heard everything unspoken in the man's tone. Obviously, he thought she'd been used. For a brief moment, it was on the tip of her tongue to protest against their darker thoughts. She didn't want anyone to think that she'd been violated—or worse, had let herself be used without a fight.

But of course she didn't say a word. Even without Scout's warnings, she now knew better than to trust any of them. Maybe not even herself.

So all she did was shiver and try to keep her balance and keep her eyes almost unfocused so she wouldn't see too clearly how the men were looking at her.

The inspection seemed to draw out for the longest few minutes of her life.

"How many hostages are there?" one of the younger members on horseback called out. "Have they killed any of them?"

"Hold on—" Will called out. "You know I'm not going to tell you that."

"Not you, McMillan. I want her to speak."

Jamie felt herself crumbling. This was becoming too much. She didn't know what to say, what not to say.

Luckily, Will's voice saved her again. "You know she can't tell you that, either!"

"I know we want more information! Girl, how big is the Walton Gang now? When did you board? Where is the silver? Which car? How have you stayed alive?"

Each question, punctuated with derision, felt like a slap.

By now her skin was damp and red and numb. Her balance was precarious at best and her vision was becoming blurred by tears she couldn't seem to stop.

She opened her mouth, but no sound came out. Sure enough, she was frozen. Oh, Lord in heaven, what was she going to do now?

To her amazement, it was Scout Proffitt who came to her rescue. "I'll deal with them for a bit, ma'am," he said, surprisingly kindly. "You've done your part." Looking to Will, he said quietly, "Take her inside, but don't go far. I've a feeling we're going to have to bring her out again."

Jamie needed no further invitation. She tried to turn but her feet gave out. Before she knew what was happening, Will had scooped her up into his arms.

She was so grateful for his presence, his body heat. So grateful to be out of the elements and out of the men's prying gazes that she let herself relax against him.

Just for a moment.

Quickly, she pulled away from Will and stepped through the partially opened door.

Seconds later, Scout followed her inside. Though his expression was as impassive as ever, he didn't look as angry. Without a word, he handed the coat to her. Then to her surprise, he looked beyond her to Will, who was still standing outside.

Almost shamefully, she slipped her arms into the sleeves and securely wrapped the edges around herself.

"Funny how you get used to things, huh?" Scout said. "Less than hour ago you would hardly touch the coat. Now you can't pull it on fast enough."

As that sunk in, he crossed to the latch and opened the door wider. "Come in, McMillan. We've done what was asked."

Jamie watched Will turn and close the door behind him. And stare at Scout. "What's wrong? You didn't trust me out there?"

"Let's just say I don't trust anyone," Scout said before walking back to the rest of the group. "I'll tell Boss that you both did what you said you'd do."

And with that, he left.

Still shivering, Jamie stared at Will. "What just happened?"

"You showed yourself to a pack of U.S. Marshals, that's what."

"What good did that do?"

Will shrugged. "Probably not much. Mr. Walton wants some leverage. He thinks a helpless woman might assure we don't immediately get blown up."

"The man in front didn't seem to think I was too helpless." Remembering the leering way he'd looked at her, she shivered. "Actually, he seemed as bad as some of the men here on the train."

Will leaned back against a post. "Some?"

Jamie couldn't deny who she was thinking of. "Kent."

For a split second Will's eyes softened with compassion before turning flinty again. "Jamilyn, we're all bad."

"Even you?"

"Especially me. A man doesn't get to be my age without having regrets, and I have more than most." Looking at his right hand like it belonged to someone else, he shook his head. "I've done things that would shock you."

Right away, her mind drifted to imagining the very worst of things. What had he done? Murder? Thieving?

Did she even want to know?

"What's going to happen to me, Mr. McMillan? Am I about to be used?" Her cheeks heated at her words. Goodness, couldn't she ever learn to speak plainly? Though her mouth had gone dry, she forced herself to say the words. "Am I about to be raped? Killed?"

"I hope not," he said after two beats.

"Hope?"

"I've long since given up trying to predict the future." His gaze flickered over her, as if he was pushing all the bad thoughts away but not really succeeding. After swallowing, he murmured, "Now, let's try to find you some place warm."

Getting to her feet, Jamie followed him, though deep down she knew the search would be futile. There was no way she was going to be warm again.

Not while she was on the train.

Not when she was in these men's company.

Not when it was very likely she wasn't going to live to see the light of another day.

8

*W*ell, that whole look-see hadn't done a lot of good, Scout decided.

Instead of being ready to let them move on, the lawmen just kept making more demands. As he stood next to the window, the leader of the Marshals kept talking like they were at a social gathering.

"Give her to us, Walton!" the U.S. Marshal called out, loud enough to wake the dead. "A woman on board is of no use to you."

As the hostages on the floor squirmed, Scout watched his boss slowly shuffle with nimble fingers a deck of cards before carefully setting an ace of hearts on the table.

For the last fifteen minutes, the routine had been the same. The lawman would yell for the woman's release, the hostages would turn hopeful, and James Walton would deal another card. It wasn't a good combination. The Walton Gang had never been known for patience, and their boss, though well groomed, was no better than the rest of them.

Sooner than later, blood was going to be shed. The only thing that wasn't certain was whose it was going to be.

From outside the car, the Marshal barked yet another command. "Walton? It's time you showed yourself. You're running out of time."

"Doubt that." Boss chuckled as he drew a two then a four of hearts. "We're at the advantage. We're inside while they're braving the elements on horseback."

"It's cold out there," Scout agreed. Hours ago, the light snow flurries that had been teasing them had finally turned to a decent snowfall. Now inches of fluffy powder blanketed most everything that couldn't take cover. Though the temperature wasn't terrible—most likely it wasn't even twenty degrees—it still made for a difficult wait on the back of a horse.

Actually, it made things downright miserable. He knew—he'd done it more times than he could count.

"Give us the woman!" the voice blared. "You don't want to add her death to your conscience."

Boss's fingers paused. "I hadn't planned on killing her yet. Had you, Scout?"

"No sir, I hadn't."

As a king was drawn and joined the other cards, Russell shifted nervously in front of the line of hostages. "Mr. Walton? I think the Marshals have gone and surrounded us."

"That so?" Boss picked up the cards again and shuffled. "Hmm. Maybe they've got more men out there than I'd previously thought." Abruptly, he raised his head and stared at Scout. "Where is she?"

"McMillan still has her in the caboose."

"Do you think we ought to give her up?"

Scout knew his answer didn't matter much. Their gang was nothing close to a democracy. James Walton would do whatever he wanted, whenever he wanted.

But still, he spoke his mind. "I don't know."

"Why not?"

"I've never liked the idea of using a woman for my interests." Scout didn't particularly trust the Marshals outside, anyway. The Marshal in charge didn't look any different from the outlaws he was supposed to chase.

It convinced Scout that their lone woman hostage might not be any safer in the law's hands.

"Is that right?" A flash of humor entered their leader's green eyes. "Even you have limits as to how far you'll go?"

"Even me. Besides, the woman seems to be a fragile sort."

"Kent would say she's ripe for the taking." His lip curled in disgust. "Is that what McMillan is doing? Taking her?"

"I don't believe so." Privately, Scout knew Will McMillan was doing his best to protect her from the rest of them. Not only from their baser instincts, but from the danger and ugliness that surrounded their actions.

Their life wasn't pretty, and it was downright ugly if one took the time to examine it closely. Their rough way of life, combined with the pain it brought, made even the most decorous of men turn into people their mothers would be ashamed of.

"I think you're right." Boss's hands stilled as his lips thinned. "McMillan's never been one to abuse women, which is fine with me. We do still have some standards, you know."

"Yes, sir."

"I don't want her blood on my hands."

"No, sir."

Mr. Walton glanced up at him sharply, obviously thinking that Scout was being sarcastic. He wasn't. He agreed with everything his boss was saying.

But more important, he knew better than to argue. There were ways of staying in line, and then there were ways of staying alive.

Pushing the cards to one side, Boss lit a cheroot and breathed deeply. "None of this is going like we'd planned. We were supposed to get the bankroll and move on, not get stuck in this godforsaken snowstorm with a woman on board. And now we're surrounded by the U.S. Marshals, and the fool engineer decided to be a hero. . . ." He exhaled harshly, sending a stream of smoke across the table. "I didn't plan on this, Scout. How did this happen?"

"I'm not sure." That was the truth. So far, this job had been nothing but terrible and littered with problems—the girl being the worst problem of all.

Jamie Ellis was too pretty and too innocent to be stuck with the likes of them. And though a small part of him felt sorry for the woman, his conscience wasn't virtuous enough to actually insist she be let go. The only way he'd been able to stay alive was to put his needs and wants first. Always.

"If we give the woman up, the Marshals will still come after us," Scout said pragmatically. "They want that silver, but I have a feeling they'd blow us up within minutes of claiming that woman."

Mr. Walton tapped ashes on the floor. "Reckon so? Even with the bankroll on board?"

Scout nodded. "They'd have nothing to lose. Fact is, there's a big enough bounty on our heads to make the bankroll seem small. Shoot, they'd make almost that much with our dead bodies and have the notoriety that comes with it."

Cool eyes studied him before picking up the cards again. "I'm thinking that as well. We can't give her up. And if McMillan keeps her away from Kent and the others, she'll be relatively safe." Raising his voice, he said, "That's what we'll do. We'll just sit tight and wait them out. We have bourbon. That's really all we need, right?"

Scout needed a clear head more than the numbing effects of whiskey. However, he kept that thought to himself as he got to his feet. "Do you want me to say anything to the Marshals?"

"No. If you show yourself without the woman, they'll kill you dead. They have not one lick of compassion. Go tell the men to cool their heels. If things get worse, we'll toss out another hostage."

"Yes, sir."

Scout turned away. Weighing on his shoulders was the reality that his days in the Walton Gang were numbered. He was bored, and he chafed at answering to another man. When they got off this train—if they ever got off this train—he was going to disappear. James Walton might be disappointed, but not much else. Scout had joined him on his own, and they'd both known that it would be only a matter of time before he would leave them.

That was the benefit of living with a band of outlaws. At the end of the day, all anyone really cared about was his own skin. And that, of course, was enough.

He went to inform McMillan that until further notice, the woman was all his.

✍

"Walton, give her to us. Now," the lawman on the palomino ordered, his horse prancing underneath him.

The man and his three comrades surrounded them. As Jamie watched from her spot next to the window, she wondered why she didn't feel more hopeful.

Instead of looking forward to being rescued, her body quaked at the idea of a different group of men watching over her.

The one man she could see clearly had a thick mustache, a gray Stetson, and a deep, scratchy voice. His movements were precise, like he was used to being in complete control of his body. And everything around him.

She had the terrible impression that he would impart that same hard control over her. For better or worse.

And because he was the law and not a criminal, everyone would expect her to be grateful and to obey. Because he'd saved her.

But that didn't stop the terrible premonition that being looked after by him would be uglier than where she was now.

The lawman spoke again, this time louder. "Walton, hand her over or I promise you, we will not be responsible for our actions. We'll blow up this train."

Beside her she felt McMillan shift and tense. Beyond him, Scout looked bored, but still pulled out his pistol. Neither man looked her way, and for that she was glad. Jamie didn't trust her emotions, or trust how she would react if she was forced to leave the train car and join the Marshals.

So instead of guessing the future, she looked out the window and watched the delicate snowflakes swirl in the air as the men surrounding the train repositioned themselves.

"Getting colder out," Scout said. Just like there was nothing more important to him than the current weather conditions. "Their hands have got to be hurtin' by now."

Jamie wondered if that was true. From the moment their train had stopped in the middle of the Kansas Plains, they'd been surrounded.

She'd heard James Walton didn't trust the Marshals at all, and so though the lawmen had made all kinds of warnings, he'd basically ignored them.

Things had gone downhill fast after that. First, the lawmen had crept closer and had called out enough threats and assurances to make even the most stoic of men quake. Jamie was certainly not stoic. As she listened, she shivered. Eight or ten hours had now passed since the train had been held up. Cold had settled into her bones while stark terror had settled deep into her heart.

With a new sense of certainty, she realized she wasn't going to survive. Either the men were going to shoot her or she would perish when the Marshals stormed the train.

Or, heaven forbid, worse things were in store for her. And she knew she wouldn't want to survive that.

Beside her, Will turned even quieter. He'd long since stopped talking to her. Instead, he'd settled himself across from her, choosing to lean back and peek out the window every few minutes.

Time continued to drag. Her eyes felt like a pound of salt and sand had settled in them. They stung from lack of sleep. But every time her body tried to force her to sleep, her mind jerked herself awake. She needed to stay alert in order to save herself.

If that was possible.

"Walton? Time's running out!"

Jamie's heart clenched. "What are they going to do?"

To her dismay, Will simply shrugged. "Don't know. I've long since stopped guessing what men will do when they're cold and hungry." With a long look at her, he frowned. "Or desperate."

Though it made no sense, for a split second Jamie was tempted to apologize. She had a terrible feeling that Will somehow was starting to resent her being there. And with that resentment came a fear that he was just about ready to do almost anything to get rid of her. Even if it meant using her as bait.

Even if it meant handing her over to the set of six men on horseback around them. In the dark, their bodies looked larger than life and twice as dangerous. As the minutes passed, she had begun to fear them more than the man by her side. Time had taught her that even the most decent of men could do bad things if given the opportunity.

Or if he had the inclination.

"Mr. McMillan?"

"Will. I told you, call me Will."

His voice had just enough impatience in it to make her give in. "All right. Uh, Will. Do . . . do you think Mr. Walton is going to hand me over? Hand me over to the Marshals?"

As the lawmen called out again, their threats even more dire and disturbing, Will stared hard at her. "Truth?"

"Of course."

"No."

She was glad the dim light hid her sigh of relief. "I see."

"I doubt you do. Jamilyn, fact is, you're the only thing that's stopping those men out there from tossing a couple of sticks of dynamite at us and blowing us to kingdom come." After glancing at Scout, who still stood in the background as quiet as death, Will continued. "I promise you this—we're not keeping you to keep you safe. We're keeping you to keep *us* safe. That's it. Don't forget it. You're our ace."

"But the other hostages . . ."

"They're men—men old enough to have seen death a hundred times over. They know what's happening. What's more, they know their fate."

But that didn't change things, she figured. Death and dying surely felt the same at any age. Just thinking about what the future held—or didn't hold—gripped her tight and made her yearn for vanished dreams. She shivered and coughed.

"Look, the only reason we're still stopped is because that blasted engineer's brakeman is next to worthless and the tender is injured. But Russell is shoveling coal and word is that the train will be running again shortly. You should get some sleep."

Jamie noticed that his voice was softer, kinder. That small amount of comfort held her close and lifted her guard. And with that easing, came the fear again. She trembled. "I can't sleep."

"Sure you can." Impatience tinged his voice. "Just close your eyes."

"You might be able to do that, but I can't."

To her surprise, he chuckled. "Yep, I can fall asleep 'bout anyplace, it's true. A body learns to find comfort and rest almost anywhere."

"Well, mine hasn't learned that yet. Besides, I'm too afraid. And I'm too cold anyway."

He looked at her long and hard. Then slowly, so slowly that his knees creaked, he stood up and moved even closer to her. "Lean against me," he said after a moment.

Will's voice sounded rusty and hoarse. Just as if he wasn't used to offering comfort and was even less sure about how it was to be received.

"I couldn't." But even as she said that, she felt the warm heat radiate off his body. Added to that was the thick canvas of his duster, heavy and woolen and luring her closer.

Little by little, her tense muscles eased and the cramps in her legs loosened. Oh, but how did he stay so warm?

Beside her, he shifted. He wasn't looking at her. Instead, he was staring straight out the window. She noticed the muscle in his jaw jump—just like he was holding on for a comfort that he couldn't deny.

Or else he was trying to grab hold of his patience and cling to it.

She wiggled again, trying to get comfortable, trying to get warm but not touch him. He sighed, then snaked an arm out and wrapped it around her shoulders, coaxing her head to rest against his chest. His body was solid and warm. The weight of his arm felt heavy and secure. Holding her tight, but not in a bad way.

In an odd way, she felt more secure, like maybe—just maybe—she was going to have a chance to live a little longer. She shifted again, finally tucking her feet under her skirts.

Next to her, Will shifted again. In her movements, his hand curved a little more tightly, falling to her waist and feeling far too personal. She gasped.

He cleared his throat, just as his hand moved again. "Stop. Just settle now. Relax and try to sleep."

Though she feared being so close to him, her eyelids felt heavy. As she listened to the steady beating of his heart against her ear, her will to fight him fluttered away. "I don't want to be here," she murmured.

"It doesn't matter what you want. All that matters is what you need. Now sit still and stop wiggling so much. A man can hardly think with you moving and squirming the way you are."

The thread of warmth in his voice took her off guard. Warily, she looked his way. "I never imagined you would have much experience comforting a woman."

To her amusement, he rolled his eyes. "Long ago, I wasn't an outlaw. Long ago, I had a sweet sister named Bonnie. She used to cuddle up against me just like this."

A yawn escaped her as hope settled into her heart. Maybe Will McMillan wasn't pure evil. Maybe there was still a good portion of him that would protect her and hold her close. "What happened to her?"

"She died," he said, his voice flat. "Now stop talking and sleep."

Unwilling to fight exhaustion anymore, Jamie finally gave in to her body's needs. Will McMillan was warm, and for the moment, he wasn't hurting her.

He wasn't making her leave the train and go out into the unknown.

And for right then, right there, Jamie knew that was enough. Her body relaxed. The sweet oblivion of dreams captured her then and pulled her under. She finally gave up and relaxed her head against his ribcage.

And slept.

9

$\mathscr{A}$s Jamie's weight settled against his chest, Will shifted slightly and rearranged his arms around her, hoping to make her more comfortable. His movements weren't automatic. Instead, they were more than a little awkward and choppy.

It had been a long time since a woman had rested in his arms—and a very long time since the female had been anyone he cared about.

Actually, there hadn't been anyone since Bonnie. Even her name caused a painful ache to rush through him, reminding him yet again of all he'd lost. And he'd sure as heck not needed any reminding. He'd only mentioned Bonnie so Jamie would drop the topic.

And she had.

He was thankful for that, since he'd been even less eager to talk about the other women he'd known since then. Not that there had been a lot. Easily less than a handful. But each woman in her own way had claimed a piece of his heart—at least for a little while.

Jamie Ellis was his first hostage though.

The realization of who he'd become kicked him in the gut and made his head pound. He'd become someone he hardly recognized. Someone even his mother wouldn't know. Thank the good Lord she wasn't alive to witness his change. Disappointed wouldn't begin to describe her feelings.

Of course, there was little that could convey the complete metamorphosis that his life had taken since he'd been a scared soldier in Arkansas. Surely, it was nothing like the life he'd planned on back when he still looked to his mother's smile for support.

Shifting slightly, Will kicked out his feet and stretched his legs. The worn tips of his boots pointed up at him. He'd worn them so long, and so many hours at a time, it was sometimes hard to imagine what his feet looked like bare.

There was something to be said about that.

As the train continued to sit idly, held captive by a dead engineer, too many demanding lawmen, and a poker-playing boss who refused to back down no matter what the odds, Will decided to take advantage of the quiet and briefly let his guard down. The air around him smelled sweet and almost clean. It was a rare moment when he wasn't assaulted by noise and the stale smell of fear and unwashed men. No, here, wafting upward, was the faint scent of gardenias. It floated toward his nose, teasing him. And with that, it brought a hint of a moment from another time.

Years ago, when Bonnie had been alive, he'd sat on a cornhusk mattress and had held her tight. Pa had been out fighting in the war, of course, and he'd instinctively known that his time to defend the South was coming on soon.

Bonnie had been all of five, and with her twin braids in disarray, she'd lain by his side and had chattered on about the cut on her finger and the mess of bluebonnets she'd seen in the field. The sun had showered a warm ray across their bodies, making Bonnie giggle when she'd spied him stretching his toes to catch the sunny spots.

The sweet, soft memory slammed him with force, almost taking his breath away with its sharpness. He'd plumb forgotten what it had been like to enjoy the pleasure of merely feeling warmth on his toes. And being in the company of a girl.

And smiling? Giggling? Did anyone even do those things anymore? Almost everyone of his acquaintance were shadows of their former selves. Wariness and pain prevented them from embracing frivolity and pleasure.

Time had proved that letting one's guard down meant pain—not pleasure—was around the corner.

Under his elbow, Jamie shifted and shivered. Unable to stop himself, he repositioned his coat about her more securely, hoping to retain a bit more of the heat.

But instead of seeking the warmth of the wool, she curved closer to him, taking obvious comfort from not only his body's heat, but also his person. The sweet, soft curves of her body pressed against his—bringing with it the many masculine urges he'd suppressed for too long.

It had been a necessary thing. The war had been an unforgiving mistress and his current job was far too dangerous. Surely that was why his body and mind were sliding along such disastrous roads?

As if she'd read his mind, Jamie sighed and cuddled even closer. Her cheek lay against his chest, tangled tendrils of her hair mixing with the buttons of his coat. Before he could stop himself, he reached out and smoothed the strands, then caught himself fingering the silky mass just as the door opened again.

Will inhaled her sweet scent as he tightened the burden in his arms. He let his mind drift and dream. Maybe this time things would be different. Maybe this time he'd get to keep the girl—form a relationship with her that had nothing to do with loneliness and doubts and had everything to do with promises and love.

Sweet emotions. Silly ones, really. But even men accustomed to pain and regrets deserved a flash of hope every once in a while. Surely, even a man like him.

The jarring click of the door opening brought him back to reality. Will's hold on Jamie loosened as he faced the intruder. "Yes?"

"Russell has somehow figured out how to run the train. He and that idiot are firing up the engine now."

"Lord have mercy," Will said. "Wonders will never cease."

"Faith is the substance of things hoped for, the evidence of things not seen," Scout quoted.

Will blinked. "I didn't know you knew the Bible."

"I know it. I just rarely quote it," Scout replied. "However, the occasion felt warranted."

"You come in here to tell me about Russell?"

"Nah. I came in here to let you know that the boss has been asking for you."

"Right now?"

His gaze darting from Jamie's position to Will's errant fingers brushing her cheek, Scout shrugged. "He could probably wait a minute or two if you wanted." Below them, it sounded as if the train was coming to life as the wheels began to gradually turn. Then, slowly, the train fell into motion, inching forward. Gathering speed.

"Guess we're on our way again."

As if seeing Will so tenderly holding Jamie embarrassed him, Scout looked down at his boots. "Looks like it."

"You look worse than usual. What's going on?"

"We've lost another hostage."

Well, that was one way of putting it. Will felt chilled as he met Scout's direct gaze. The muscles in the gunfighter's neck moved. They were the only sign that perhaps everything hadn't gone as smoothly as he had hoped to convey. Briefly, Will pondered the pros and cons of asking for details, then decided against it. It didn't really matter who killed the hostage. Or why.

Fact was, a death couldn't be undone and he'd long since given up trying.

"I see," he finally said.

The tic in Scout's cheek jumped. "I doubt it. I, for one, don't understand a lick of what's been going on inside of this miserable train. Fact is, everything and anything is going poorly on this job, McMillan. You and I know enough to know that things aren't going to get better with time, either."

"I know." Scout was right. There was a feeling of incautious desperation around them that seemed to weigh them all down. "And I'm tellin' you what. That girl—that girl you're holding too close—she's trouble."

"Our bad luck isn't her fault. She's the innocent in all of this."

Scout shrugged. "Doesn't matter. She's making everyone act strange and peculiar." Looking even more agitated, Scout stuffed his hands in the front pockets of his denims, as if he were trying hard to keep his emotions in check. "Something's going to happen to her, you mark my words."

Scout's words had credence, but Will thought he was overreacting too. "I've yet to see Mr. Walton use and abuse a woman. Especially not one of gentle birth."

"I've never seen that either. But I've seen the others with women hostages before." A bleak, cool, vacant look appeared in his eyes. "They're getting restless. Fact is, Will, the other men ain't going to wait much longer to get their hands on this girl."

Even thinking about such a thing made Will see red. "They'd have to get through me first. And I'd shoot them dead before I'd let them touch her. She'll be safe."

Scout pressed his lips together but refrained from commenting. "And one of the men surrounding the train was Blackstone. Do you know him?"

"No," Will lied.

"I've seen him rape and pillage in a way that would put a carpetbagger to shame."

Blackstone wasn't Will's supervisor. Sam Edison was. But Blackstone's reputation was well known. More than anything, he had a reputation for achieving results. Will had never thought much about how the man had gotten those successes. "Did you witness it?"

The tic jumped again. "I witnessed the aftermath in Austin once. He threatens women . . . and has been known to make good on those threats."

"But the men in his company—"

"Oh, those men will do their best to convince Blackstone to leave women alone. But sometimes, what they say don't matter."

Will didn't doubt Scout's words. In these times, sometimes the only bout of decency and sanity depended on the day and the time. All of them were capable of murder and thieving. All of them were capable of doing their worst with anything available. And all of them had. He knew he had. Shoot, even one of the heads of the railroad was in cahoots with the gang.

That was the whole reason he was there—to bring him down.

But suddenly his duty didn't seem nearly as important as the woman in his arms.

After weighing his options, he blurted, "What do you suggest I do with Jamie?" No way was he going to give a hint to what he was thinking.

A full minute passed. It was obvious that Scout was as unused to disclosing his private feelings as Will was. Finally, he folded his arms over his chest and stared hard at Will. "Truth?"

"Truth."

"McMillan, you need to do what you need to do. Soon. Do you understand?"

Slowly, Will nodded.

Looking curiously relieved, Scout nodded. "Good. If you care about her as much as you act like you do, you need to do it soon."

There it was. But still, he was too smart to trust too much. "Do you have a stake in this?" Could there be a reason Scout was practically telling him to take Jamie and run?

"Do I have a personal interest?" Slowly he shook his head, his eyes lighting up with misplaced mirth. "Not so much. Not enough to risk a bullet hole. But I have enough of a sense of right and wrong to look the other way if you take matters into your own hands."

After a pause, Scout added, "Maybe even to encourage some others not to ask questions or look too hard."

"Why would you do that?"

"Why?" A lopsided smile appeared. "Let's just say I've taken to having a soft spot for a woman in black."

"So you're favoring the color and not the woman?" Will asked wryly.

"I'm not favoring it," he amended. "Sometimes it's enough to know that she's been through enough. You know?"

"I know," Will said softly.

In his arms, Jamilyn sighed then opened her eyes. He knew the moment she spied Scout because she stiffened and pulled away from his embrace like his body was on fire.

Scout cleared his throat, his voice once again becoming as remote and cold as the desolate land outside. "You'd best get going, Will. Boss is going to be wondering what you're doing if you don't hurry. I'll watch your hostage."

Jamie trembled.

Will knew there was no choice. He'd been sent for. Jamie gazed at him with wide, frightened eyes as Will stood up. "You'll be safe here," Will said over his shoulder as he walked to the portal. "Safe enough."

Catching Scout's eye, Will made his decision. "Safe enough until I come back."

Scout nodded.

The decision had been made. And as Will walked back to the train car of men, he wondered why he didn't feel a single shard of regret. Instead, all he felt was anticipation mixed with the sensation that he was about to do what was right.

That was something he hadn't felt in a very long time.

10

After checking in with James Walton, Will returned to Jamie's train car and let Scout leave. Then he looked at Jamie and cursed fate.

It had finally come down to this moment. And though he was as sorry as could be, Will knew beyond a doubt that he no longer had a choice. If he didn't get Jamie off the train as soon as possible, she was going to get violated or killed. Most likely both.

In his worst moments, he feared he'd even have to watch.

Pure agony coursed through him as the probable consequences swam in his mind. They were only going to have the clothes on their backs. No horse. Only one set of guns. And no food or water.

When Will pulled Jamie off the train, they'd be in terrible danger, with both the men from the Walton Gang and the Marshals hunting them.

They would shoot to kill, most likely him first. Then Jamie would be at the mercy of men who had none. It would take everything he had to evade both groups, and that was assuming Jamie would willingly be by his side.

Of course, she wouldn't be. When she wasn't in the depths of an exhausted sleep, Jamie feared him—and with good reason. He'd held her against her will and would have shot one of the Marshals right in front of her if the situation had necessitated it.

And all of that wasn't even taking into account the bitter cold and unceasing snow that seemed determined to blanket them. If he couldn't keep Jamie warm and dry and alive, not even the most grandiose of schemes mattered a whit.

She would die and her soul would be on his conscience.

No, most likely she would fight him every step of the way, even going so far as to try to run from him.

The idea made his blood run cold. What would he do if she fought him? Tie her up?

Though the idea pained him, if it meant keeping her alive Will knew he would do it.

With a feeling of inevitability that now seemed an integral part of his life, Will realized he would do whatever it took to keep her safe, even if it meant forcing her to hate him. Even if it meant causing himself pain, even sacrificing his life.

It was time to do something he could be proud of.

All he could do now was wait and plan and look for his chance.

"Will? What do you think is going to happen?"

Jamie's voice was sweet and tentative and scared. Of course, she had every reason to feel that way.

"I didn't know you were awake."

"I just woke up a little bit ago." After another yawn, she sat up straighter. "The train's running again."

"It is." Keeping his voice detached, he added, "If you're ready, Mr. Walton wants to see you, that's all."

"I'm afraid of him." A sheen of pink colored her cheeks when he looked at her curiously. "I mean, I'm afraid of all of you. It's just that . . ."

"You're afraid of some men more than others."

She bit her lip and nodded.

"I understand." Then, though he shouldn't reassure her, because, after all, who other than God knew what their future held, he said, "Jamie, I can't promise you much, but I will promise you this: no harm will come to you while I'm here." Not if he could help it, he added silently.

"Why?"

"You're too good a lady to die on a train full of no-good men."

"Is that what you are?"

"Yes."

Getting to her feet, she stepped forward. "Always?"

Will thought back. Tried to remember another time, a time when he was almost innocent. Almost good. Surely there'd been a time? "No, not always. But for a long time."

"Then what makes you different?"

Ah, she was a smart woman. For a moment he was tempted to tell her the whole truth about himself. That although the company he was keeping marked him as no good, he *was* more than that.

A whole lot more.

But even the walls had ears, and he certainly didn't trust anyone. "Maybe one day, I'll get the opportunity to tell you," he said quietly. "For now, though, you need to come with me. We can't tarry much longer."

To his surprise, she touched his arm. "Will, if Mr. Walton wants to . . ." Her throat worked as tears sprung to her eyes. "If he means to use me . . . or plans to let Kent use me . . . kill me first, would you?"

He was so shocked, he stared at her, struck dumb. "Jamie, nothing is—"

"I mean it," she blurted. "There was a woman, a woman living across the street. She'd been . . . hurt." Shaking her head, she stared at him directly. "She had been raped and beaten by a band of soldiers, and she was never the same. Her brother said she hardly slept, and when she did, she was plagued by nightmares. I don't want that. I don't want to survive after that."

"Mr. Walton doesn't have that in mind." At least he hoped not.

"But Kent does. And I fear some of the others do too. Maybe even those Marshals who were surrounding us."

"Marshals wouldn't do that." Though as he remembered what Scout said, he knew he was being naive. There would always be men who wouldn't hesitate to take advantage of an innocent woman.

She laughed bitterly. "You act as if you know something about men that no one else does. I saw their looks, Will. They may want me free, but they already think you men have done their worst. And I have the terrible feeling that Mr. Walton wouldn't be opposed to using me as bait if things got desperate."

She was right, of course. If it came to a matter of living or dying, he knew most every man there would use her in order to survive.

That was how it was done. It was always how it had been. "I promise," he said.

"You'll do it? You'll shoot me dead?"

"If that's what you want," he lied. Because he knew he couldn't do that. Just the light touch of her fingers made him yearn to hold her close and never let her go. With that in mind, how could he extinguish her life?

"Let's go before Mr. Walton sends someone to retrieve you."

A slight tremor rattled her fingers, then with the briefest of nods, she turned and started walking.

He was shamed to realize that she now understood how things worked.

❦

James Walton was sipping whiskey when they entered. "McMillan, I was worried you'd gotten lost on the way here."

Beside her, Will stiffened. "No, sir."

"Miss Ellis, I hope you are still being treated well."

"Yes, sir," she said, because, really, there was no other choice.

Looking at the formidable man who all the other men on the train visibly feared was extremely scary.

Struggling not to let her fear show was terribly hard. But the fear was inevitable. No man there would expect her to be calm.

She was more frightened than she'd ever been in her life, and just as afraid of the stark, sudden sense of peace she felt when she was in Will McMillan's company. How could she bring herself to trust a man who was a hired killer?

Was it merely that she trusted the devil she knew more than the one she feared?

Pointing to a bright red stain marring the oak trim, Mr. Walton frowned. "I'm sorry to say that yet another one of our guests had to leave us."

Tears sprang to her eyes and fell to her cheeks. She winced as Will dug his fingers into her arm, signaling her to stay quiet and strong. However, Jamie couldn't hold back the tears any more than she could stop the train.

When Will glanced her way, his eyes narrowed as he spied her tears.

Without compunction, the tears kept falling, speeding up and staining her cheeks.

"Stop," Will muttered, giving her arm a slight shake for emphasis.

She tried, she really did, but all she seemed capable of was a ragged sigh.

As Will groaned, two other bandits glowered. A terrible chill coursed through her as she realized that her days were at an end. Though every functioning part of her brain told her to hush and be quiet, she knew her will was not her own anymore.

And right then and there, she began to shed big, noisy sobs.

"Jamie? Jamie, please stop."

But instead of leveling a revolver at her temple, Mr. Walton looked pleased. "Yes, it is a shame, isn't it? And here we showed you to the lawmen, too." Frowning slightly, he looked toward the window. "It is a pity, but I'm afraid everyone is getting restless. This has been a particularly bad trip." He pulled out his gold pocket watch and opened it with a lazy flourish. "And time does move on. Miss Ellis. I do believe something must be done with you." He crooked a finger. "It's time you earned your keep, don't you think?"

She stood, stunned, as the next four seconds floated forward in slow motion.

Will turned to her in shock, Mr. Walton grasped his cigar in surprise, and with a savage curse Kent stepped forward and grabbed her shoulder.

Rough fingernails scratched the tender skin of her neck before clutching the delicate collar of her dress. In vain, Jamie attempted to pull away, but all her efforts did was help him. With a jerk, the collar ripped, its seam tearing apart like newsprint.

Jamie shook as frigid air stung the skin of her bare shoulder. Her tremors increased as she sensed the men's hard gazes settle on her exposed skin.

She knew it was simply a matter of time before her worst fears were realized.

11

$\mathcal{T}$rue pain spiraled through Will's body as Kent began to laugh. In front of them all lay Jamie's bare shoulder, its feminine slope and pure white skin more of a temptation than most men could deny.

This group didn't even try. All eyes were drawn to the fine display, like bees drawn to honey.

Though he grimaced at the silly comparison, the facts remained the same—there were some things a man couldn't ignore, and the pale pure skin of an untouched female was one of them.

Especially for men like them.

Will knew it had been a very long time since he'd seen a woman so innocent and delicate. Although her bare shoulder wasn't all that shocking, the hint it gave of other, more private parts of her body made his mouth go dry. Especially seeing how even he, a supposedly God-fearing man, couldn't resist looking at her.

And imagining more.

In front of them all, Jamie crumbled to the floor. Covering her chest with her arms crossed, she curled into a ball, weep-ing. Against the wall, the three remaining hostages stared. Even their unflappable boss appeared taken aback.

"Git up!" Kent screamed. "If I gotta git you from the floor, I'm going to meet you down there."

Kent's awful words finally spurred Will to action. "Move away from her," Will ordered. "Now."

Kent narrowed his eyes, but glanced at Mr. Walton first. Their leader stared hard at Kent, his expression glacial.

Visibly afraid, Kent stepped backward.

Ignoring them all, Will knelt down and placed his arms protectively around Jamie, retrieving the duster that had fallen and wrapping it around her like a blanket.

When she only cried harder, her body stiff and panicked against his, Will looked up at the man who led them all. "This isn't who we are, James," he said quietly, using Walton's Christian name for emphasis. "This isn't what I signed up for. This isn't who I thought you were."

Anger—and perhaps surprise—flew into Walton's gaze.

Buoyed by that, Will continued. "The Walton Gang hasn't stooped to raping women and children now, have we?"

As James Walton remained silent, Kent scoffed. "What does it matter what we do, McMillan? She's gonna die anyway. We all know that."

The telltale click of Scout cocking his six-shooter echoed in the car. "It matters," Scout whispered. "It matters to me. We're not going to rape any women."

Will turned to the newest speaker in surprise. Though Scout had warned him to take Jamie away, Will had never imagined the outlaw would openly confront Mr. Walton. At least not in front of witnesses.

As Jamie continued to cry and Kent seethed, the smell of their boss's cigar filled the car. Will wondered what was going to happen. Scout wasn't giving their boss much of a chance to recount.

"Shoot him," their leader finally said. "Shoot him or back down."

Will swallowed. Who was their boss speaking of? A hostage? Him?

Eyes cold and completely void of any emotion, Scout leveled the gun at Kent and pulled the trigger.

The repercussions filled the air, shattering the silence while spraying blood and tissue across the floor.

When Jamie's cries turned more shrill, Scout turned toward Will. "Take her out of here."

Will immediately got to his feet. And, seeing how Jamie was in shock, wrapped one arm around her shoulders and the other under her knees. With a sigh, he picked her up and carried her away from the danger and the blood and the humiliation.

Surely nothing in this world could have prepared this woman—this girl—for such a sight. And as he opened the compartment door with one hand, marveling all the while about how light her frame was, Will realized that he would have moved heaven and earth to spare her from this event.

He also knew they were out of time.

Stopping briefly in the next car, he grabbed his knapsack, heavy with two boxes of ammunition and a filled canteen. Not daring to pause, he kept walking.

He opened the next compartment door, stood out on the small balcony, and lightly brought Jamie to her feet. "Put this back on now," he ordered, motioning to the coat.

Without pause, she slipped her arms inside.

"We're leaving. Do you understand?" As if he were speaking to a child, he said, "You can't stay here. Not a minute longer. If you do, you'll die. Or worse."

Jamie tilted up her head and met his gaze. "I know," she said. Her eyes were vacant. Most likely she was in shock.

But if that made her more biddable, he would be grateful for her trauma. His body relaxed with a new sense of purpose.

"I'm going to get you off of here. Okay?"

She nodded.

Of course, what he didn't say were false promises. He didn't promise to protect her, or offer her a pretty future. All he could do was vow to himself to stay by her side.

But perhaps that was enough.

Grabbing her hand and throwing his knapsack over his shoulder, he said, "Look. I know it's dark, and I know this train is moving, but listen to me good. I do believe there's a thicket of trees just to the east of us. At the count of three, we're going to jump off this train, and then we're going to run hell-for-leather to that thicket. Understand?"

She nodded.

"Promise?" Still too worried about the state she was in, he hardened his voice, turning his tone almost violent. "Say it. Say what you're going to do."

"I'm going to jump and run to the woods."

She sounded unafraid, almost like she didn't expect to survive anyway. That, of course, made him feel even more on edge.

But it was too late to go back. Will breathed in. Then, with a mighty exhale, he counted. "One. Two. Three."

And with a yank and pull, Will jumped.

In doing so, he pulled the finest female he'd ever set his eyes on off the train and into his sole protection.

Right then and there he knew his life had just twisted again. Onto a path he had no control over.

Only God knew how he'd keep her alive and safe.

Only God knew where they were headed.

Only God knew how they'd survive.

The last thing he thought of, as the cold air whipped his skin and his past sins flashed before his eyes, was that God knowing was probably enough.

12

$\mathcal{L}$ong ago, Jamie had seen a tumbleweed sweep across the western plains of Colorado. Pushed by the wind, it was turned in every direction imaginable. Each time, it left both a part of its body behind and picked up more debris. By the time it flew out of sight, it had looked battered, beaten up, and ill formed. Decidedly lopsided and used.

And that was exactly how she felt.

The moment they'd jumped off the locomotive, Will had grabbed her elbow. Almost immediately, she'd reached for him, taking hold of his arm just so she could have something to touch. They'd sailed through those few feet toward the ground as two halves of a whole, then fallen with enough force to knock the wind right out of her.

When she forced her lids open, the stars in her eyes mixed with the ones in the night sky and blinded her. She whimpered.

"Hush!" Will cautioned.

Biting her lip, she nodded as she got her bearings as best she could. Her arm burned and stung from the force of his hold on her when they fell. Her knees throbbed from her awkward landing on the hard, frigid ground.

The ground was vibrating from the train's passage. When her eyes cleared, she saw the shape of the train moving on, but she still felt as if they were stranded in its shadows.

What was going to happen to her?

She was sure Scout or any number of men were going to appear from behind a rock, aim their guns, and shoot to kill.

But it was only Will who clambered to his feet. "Come on," he ordered.

When she'd looked around in confusion, he linked his fingers through her right hand and half guided, half dragged her from the tracks and toward the dark copse of trees.

The rest of the short journey to the thicket was a blur of pain. Her right ankle felt sprained; her left elbow felt pulled out of joint. Everything in between felt bruised and battered. And it was terribly cold. Oh, so cold. The frigid temperatures bit through her clothes and skin and snapped at her bones.

But none of those painful physical ailments held a candle to the complete desolation that was weighing in her heart. What had she done? Was being alone and stranded with one outlaw better than being in the company of many on a train?

After pulling her deeper into the brush, Will finally loosened his grip. Without his support, she sank to the ground, wrapping her arms around her legs and tucking her head into her body. Afraid to think, afraid to look, she kept herself in a ball and tried to pray.

But all that seemed to come to mind were regrets. How could she make a prayer out of that to the Lord?

Minutes passed. Maybe thirty. Maybe sixty.

All the while, Jamie half expected to hear the sharp sound of a shotgun being fired. She couldn't fathom that they were actually free. That she wasn't going to have to worry about being accosted or beaten by those horrible men.

No, now all she had to do was worry about one. Doubts rolled into fear, fueled by the dark and a throbbing wrist.

"You okay?" Will asked softly.

Warily, Jamie looked his way. Since he'd ordered her to keep still and quiet, she'd done just that. In the shadows, she'd watched him position his Winchester at his shoulder and keep watch.

"Are you?"

As his question set in, a hasty retort flew to her lips. Just as quickly, she pushed it back. What she was thinking was best left unsaid, because she most certainly wasn't fine. Truthfully, she didn't know if she'd ever be okay again.

So she lied. "I'm okay. You?"

Though only part of his face was illuminated by the glow from the snow, she felt his surprise just as easily as if she'd witnessed his reaction completely. "Good enough," he said, his voice hoarse and deep.

For a split second, the clouds left a gap wide enough for a ray of moonlight to reach their spot. And in that brief moment, their eyes met. Will McMillan's eyes were blue and caring and kind looking—just like he was asking her to trust him.

Jamie felt herself sinking deeper into his world, leaving her former ties and restraints in the past. Worrying about social norms or who was good and who was bad hardly mattered now.

All that mattered was that she was alive. For the moment, that was enough.

The air between them grew tight, almost tangible. Her body tensed as she waited for Will to say something—any-thing—of merit.

But of course he didn't.

Just as quickly as it had come, a blank stare replaced the burn in his eyes, making her wonder if she'd imagined a connection between them at all.

As he turned from her, Jamie scooted her knees up to her chest and tried to think of something to say. But of course there was nothing in her head worth saying. So she huddled into herself and waited.

And then waited longer still.

✍

As Will watched Jamie through the corner of his eye, a thousand regrets filled his soul. What was he doing? What had he done? On the train, he'd agreed wholeheartedly with Scout. It would have been tragic if Jamie had come to harm under their supervision. That worry had slowly filled him, until he'd been sure that there was nothing else he could do except get her away.

But to this? To being outside in the elements in the dead of night? With only him guarding her? With hardly half a plan?

At the moment, Will wished for a cheroot or even the harsh, stinging relief of a shot of whiskey.

Naturally, neither of those vices were available, and he doubted he'd even be able to take another drink anyway— he'd forced himself to stop just six months after the war. The alcohol had merely reminded him of what he'd become. And of everything that he wasn't.

But as Jamie huddled next to him, he knew he was going to have to face some serious truths. One of them was that he was now responsible for Jamilyn Ellis, no matter what. Her life was in his hands, and he couldn't discount that. Even if she was afraid of him.

In the distance, he listened to the last echoes of the train fade away and wondered if Scout realized that they'd jumped. And if he had noticed, what would he do? Would he do his best to keep the rest of the men in the dark, or would Scout show his true colors and double-cross him?

Will was inclined to believe that Scout would sound an alarm. After all, that was what was expected, and though there might be something decent in the infamous outlaw, Will had seen him kill without compunction and lie at the drop of a hat. But then a faint memory entered his mind. He remembered the look of wonder and regret on Scout's face whenever he stared at Jamie. It looked to have nothing to do with lust and everything to do with past aches.

So maybe Scout had kept his word and had stayed silent a little longer. Every moment he waited would increase their chance of survival tenfold.

"Mr. McMillan?" Jamie said softly.

"It's Will, remember?"

"Will, is it safe yet?"

He wanted to tell her that there was nothing safe about their circumstances. She was an unmarried, innocent woman in the hands of a known member of an outlaw gang. The temperatures were hovering at the freezing mark, and they had little food and water, no horse, and no real plans.

But of course he couldn't say any of that. Their circumstances didn't matter all that much. "The train's long gone," he said, knowing that his answer had little to do with her question.

"Do . . . do you think they know we're gone?"

"If they don't, they'll know soon."

She shifted, a small sound of pain accompanying her movements, reminding him of how delicate she was. "How badly are you hurt?" he asked, not even giving her the chance to pretend she wasn't injured.

"I don't know. My ankle seems swollen, but it might simply be sprained."

Or broken. It would just be his luck if it was broken.

Getting to his feet, his muscles screamed. His body hadn't appreciated their jump from the train either. "Let's get you to your feet and then we'll see if we can't find some shelter." Bending down, he reached for her hand.

After a moment, she slipped her hand into his. As carefully as possible, he helped her to her feet. When she stumbled, he wrapped an arm around her waist.

She gasped, then melted into his grip. He pretended he didn't notice how fine her figure was, or how right it felt to hold her. Embarrassed, he covered his feelings with a veil of gruffness. "You okay now, Miss?"

"I'm steady," she replied, showing she too was becoming adept at providing the right answers to the wrong questions. "You may remove your hand now."

With some surprise, he noticed that he still held her, just as if he had a right to. He dropped his hand like she was on fire, then stepped away for good measure. It didn't make a lick of difference though. Will knew he would never forget the curve of her waist and how right she'd felt tucked next to his side.

"Jamilyn, we need to move. It's dark as sin out here, but come morning we're going to be right next to the tracks." He pointed toward the shadow of a valley in the distance. "I'm not sure, but when the clouds broke I saw what looked like an abandoned house over there. That's where we're going."

"What if someone lives there?"

"Then they'll have to give us shelter, I reckon."

"But what will they think? It's late. . . . We have no horse, nothing." Pure confusion colored her voice, reminding Will of how different he and Jamie were. She saw only honesty; he saw nothing but lies.

"Here's what we're going to tell them. You and me, we're married. And a few miles back, our horse turned up lame. We're trying to get to Topeka."

"But—"

The only way they were going to get through this was for him to cut her off and force his agenda to be hers. "There are no 'buts,' Jamilyn. We're out of options and about out of luck. So, get by my side and get ready to lie through your teeth. Because one thing—and only one thing—is for sure. If we don't find somewhere else to be other than in a bramble of bushes next to a train track, we're not going to live to tell any more lies. If some vagrant doesn't shoot us, the temperature will freeze us for sure."

Fear entered her expression once again, reminding them both that they weren't friends. They certainly weren't lovers.

He might have saved her from rape; he might have saved her from certain death; but the fact of the matter was that Will McMillan was her captor and she was his hostage. No matter how kind or decent he was, she was at his mercy.

Sooner or later, his fine idea of getting her off that train was probably going to kill her. They had too much against them and too little in their favor.

Then, without a doubt, her death would be on his shoulders, just like all the others he carried—all the ghosts of his men from the war.

Sure, he might be slightly better than the worst men on this earth, but he was a very far cry from being one of best.

As they started walking, Will wondered if Jamie had realized that yet.

13

"Where are they?" James Walton yelled, looking from one end of the train car to the other, even stopping along the way to stare down at the three remaining hostages. "Where are McMillan and the woman?"

"It's Jamie," Russell murmured.

Oh Lord, have mercy. Scout shifted on his feet, silently willing Russell, the pup, to keep his mouth shut. Not even on his best day did James Walton want to hear information he never asked for.

And this sure wasn't one of those days.

Predictably, Boss pivoted on one highly polished black boot and glowered at Russell. "What did you say?"

"J . . . Jamie," the boy replied. "That's the woman's name."

No, her name was Jamilyn Ellis, Scout thought to himself, and not even a beautiful name like that was good enough for a woman of such worth. The woman was lovely and delicate and seemed so vulnerable that she brought to mind images of his sister Corrine.

Well, Corrine back before the war had begun.

As Russell trembled under Boss's lethal gaze, Scout cleared his throat. "Seems as though McMillan and the woman jumped off the train."

"And you didn't see them?"

"I did not."

"Sure?"

"Boss, if I had, they wouldn't have gotten far," he lied. Because, well, he'd known that Will would get her off the train. In fact, Scout had certainly hoped he would—getting her off was the only way to save the girl.

"Did you know McMillan was planning to take off?"

Not exactly. "No sir, I did not."

Mr. Walton cursed under his breath. "Why would McMillan leave? Try as I might, I don't understand it."

Scout knew their boss was feeling legitimate confusion. In his mind, he was the leader, and it made no sense to him that someone would undermine his authority.

It was a fair assumption. Most men who crossed James Walton's authority never survived to regret their decision.

But Will McMillan wasn't like most men, that much was evident.

And the woman, well, she wasn't like most, either. There was an innocence and freshness about her that Scout hadn't believed really existed. She was sweet enough to make him think of all kinds of fanciful thoughts, things like nights when the stars were bright and the horizon became so vast and huge that it seemed like the Lord had taken a cloth and smudged out all the boundaries of the world.

However, that wasn't the answer Boss wanted. It also wasn't something Scout wanted to think about, much less share out loud. Weak thoughts led men to make mistakes and to a certain, bloody death. "I don't know why he left."

As the train continued to roll forward, Mr. Walton stared out at the distant plains. Where snow didn't cover the ground, the brush and grasses were brown and flat, packed down and dead from abuse. His lips flattened. "No man takes my property and lives."

As Russell's eyes widened, looking on the verge of kindly explaining to Mr. Walton that neither Jamie nor Will McMillan were technically his property, Scout spoke fast and firm. "No sir, they do not."

"Go find them, Proffitt. Get off this train and track them down."

"And then?"

"And then you will make sure that neither will talk again."

Disbelief made him speak before he thought the better of it. "The woman too?"

"Of course. She's not a woman, Proffitt. She's a witness, and therefore dangerous. If she testifies against us, we'll all be hanged from the nearest trees, and that won't do." Cold dead eyes met his. "She cannot survive. Do you understand?"

There was only one correct answer, and Scout hadn't lived this long by being a fool. "Yes sir, I do."

He turned around before anything more was asked of him, and before he caught sight of the dismay that was surely burning bright in Russell's eyes.

Though, of course, what did any of it really matter? If he followed through on these orders, Scout Proffitt would prove to one and all that there wasn't any decency left in his body nor a shred of compassion in his heart.

He'd long since given up being a man of worth. But it was still hard to realize he'd now become someone to pity.

Though he was still breathing, it was become completely obvious that he might as well be dead. He surely was dead inside.

Will hated his death grip on Jamie's elbow. He hated the harsh way he was speaking to her and the way that she trembled at his touch.

He hated that he was contemplating stealing the horse he saw in the broken-down shanty on the side of the cabin they'd sought for shelter, and he wished he was the type of man who wouldn't dream of hurting others if it meant keeping himself and Jamie alive.

But he was.

Fact was, experience had taught him that surviving meant doing a whole lot of things one never considered when the air was sweet and the future looked obtainable. Yep, a man had to do what he had to do. And he needed to get Jamie to Kansas City and contact Sam Edison of the U.S. Marshals—his real boss.

It had been a difficult thing, agreeing for the last eighteen months to secretly investigate the Walton Gang and James Walton's private agreement with Arthur Jackson of the Kansas Pacific. With each passing day, he'd lost a little bit of his humanity. But he'd lived too long and too hard to put his own interests first. What mattered was the reputation of the Marshals, and of course the safety of the people they served.

The plan had been for him not to get in contact until spring. It was too risky to attempt to report any more frequently than every six months or so.

But taking an innocent woman hostage had changed everything.

What he'd hoped to do was tell Jamie the truth about himself. If, at the very least, she knew he was one of the good guys,

Will thought that would go a long way toward making things better between them.

However, at the moment, she was too weary and panicky around him to listen much, and he knew intuitively that she most likely wouldn't believe him anyway.

So he decided to just keep his cover going as long as possible. It was safer for the both of them, especially if anything happened to him. Right now, if a single soul was told that he was undercover, they'd laugh themselves silly before they sliced his throat. Then she'd be even more vulnerable.

As he approached the shack with Jamie by his side, he saw that her mouth was set in a tight line and that pure exhaustion emanated from her body. Again, he wished things had been different. He wished he could be the man she needed—the man he knew he still was under all the layers of lies.

"Someone is in there. A man . . . a man is watching us," she said, her voice breathless. "He's armed."

He'd spied the man a good hundred yards back, when the man had lit a cheroot. However, he'd kept the knowledge to himself. It wouldn't have served any purpose to get her even more uptight and wary. "We are armed too." When he saw her tremble, he tried to soften his tone. "When we get closer, just keep your mouth closed, okay? I'll do the talking. I'll get us through this, I promise."

He stared at her until she nodded.

They were now only about a hundred yards away. It was time to announce themselves. Raising his voice, he called out, "Hello, there!"

The man raised a hand in greeting but still stood at attention. Proving he was no fool.

Jamie half held her breath. More and more, she was scared to death that she'd gone from one horrible situation to something worse.

As they got closer, she noticed that the man wasn't as old as she'd first thought. Most likely fifty or so. He also didn't look like he suffered fools lightly, making her wonder what he would do if he guessed they were lying to him.

Beside her, Will was presenting an expression of embarrassed happiness. "So glad to see you, I don't mind saying. Me and my wife here have been having a terrible time of it."

"How so?" the man called out. His arms were crossed over his chest now.

Well at least he wasn't aiming that Winchester their way.

"It's like this. Horse turned up lame a good three or four miles back. When we were off it, horse got spooked and ran. Now we're stuck with just the clothes on our backs."

"Now that's a shame," the owner of the cabin said.

But Jamie noticed that he hadn't made a single move to invite them in.

"We'd be mighty beholden if you'd let us seek shelter for a bit," Will added, making his voice turn syrupy. "My Jenny here is in a family way and I sure don't want anything to happen to her."

When she started to scowl, Will pressed his palm against her back. "I don't want to hurt you," he whispered. "But I didn't jump off that train just to get a bullet in my head now."

The fear she'd been holding at bay returned tenfold. After a moment passed, she looked even more serene.

"Jamie?" Will hissed between his teeth. "You will look happy now."

Weakly, she smiled. Tried to look a bit bashful.

The stranger pointedly stared at her stomach. "Ain't that something? Congratulations, Missus."

She didn't know what to say. Part of her wanted to blush while the rest of her wanted to stomp her foot and refute Will's claim. But of course she didn't want to die.

Instead, she stared at the man in fierce wonder and felt her mind go blank. Until Will's fingers dug into her shoulder a little harder. "Thank you kindly," she blurted.

After giving them another thoughtful stare, the stranger motioned them forward. "Come in, come in. You're going to catch your death standing there like you are. Come meet my missus."

As soon as the man walked through the doorway, Will leaned close. "Don't think he'll save you, Jamie. I'm your only hope. Don't you ever forget that."

"Believe me, I haven't forgotten a thing."

"And you'll keep quiet?"

"I'm going to do exactly what you want me to do, Mr. McMillan. My brains make up for what I lack in looks."

His eyes widened just before they entered. And she couldn't help but feel a little thrill that she'd finally managed to shock him, before she saw exactly why the man's wife hadn't come outside to meet them as well.

Her stomach knotted as she wondered if things had just gone from bad to worse.

14

The man's wife was terribly ill. The smell of sickness and despair coated the interior, making the air feel thick and claustrophobic. At that moment, Will was tempted to pull Jamie out of there, bathe her in lye, rinse her in fresh water, and promise the good Lord that he'd do whatever it took to keep her safe. Just as long as He would keep her from catching the woman's illness.

Because surely that woman was only going to be getting out of bed one way, and that was to be carried to a grave.

The man shifted awkwardly, obviously uneasy. After a time, he spared a quick, awkward glance their way. "Abigail has the influenza," he said quietly, hardly lifting his eyes from his wife's lifeless body. "That's why I wasn't real eager for y'all to step inside here. Especially with you two in a family way."

Influenza. So it was as bad as he'd feared.

Will swallowed as he attempted to keep his emotions from his face. By his reckoning, influenza had taken more lives than bullets in the war. Once again, he questioned the Lord's intentions. Surely things with Jamilyn were hard enough without adding disease into the mix.

His hostage, however, had no such qualms.

Stepping toward the woman, Jamie smiled graciously, just as if she were in a fancy drawing room and sipping tea out of china cups. "I'm pleased to meet you, Miss Abigail. I'm Ja . . . Jenny Lynn Miller. We're much obliged for your hospitality."

Gradually, the woman's eyes opened. After a time, she focused on her visitor. Soon after, a faint glimmer of a sweet smile lit her face, hinting at the lovely woman she'd once been.

With effort, Abigail shifted, obviously wanting to sit up to greet her. Of course, she was too weak and frail, and her efforts ended almost as soon as they began.

❧

Across the room, her husband bit his lip. "I don't know what to do," he whispered to Will. "I want her to conserve her energy, but she ain't been this happy in days."

Will didn't know what to do either. All he could do was settle for Jamie's sweet example. "Not much we can do," he murmured. "Women are going to do what they want, with or without our guidance."

The man chuckled softly. "If you understand that, I foresee a long and prosperous marriage in your future."

Will smiled back, though he knew his own expression was terribly strained. Too worried about their future and all the lies he was telling, he said nothing. Instead, he focused on Jamie.

By now, she was even closer to the lady and was patting her arm. "Oh, no, ma'am. You mustn't trouble yourself. Please lie back and relax."

Will's heart skipped a beat as he watched Jamie reach for Abigail's hand and clasp it, then lean forward as the woman choked out a whisper into her ear.

"What was that?" she asked again.

The woman arched closer and murmured something, just before her words were disrupted by a torrent of violent coughs. Hastily, the husband rushed forward, covering his wife's mouth with a dingy cloth.

And Will cursed himself all over again.

But Jamie kept smiling, just as if there weren't a fresh smattering of blood on the handkerchief. With a shy look Will's way, Jamie chuckled. "I'll be sure to tell him that. I reckon he'll be right surprised."

Will could hardly hold back. Only with extreme effort did he keep his voice even. "Tell me what, Jenny?"

"That Miss Abigail thinks you're right handsome."

"What?"

Jamilyn laughed, the tinkling sound lighting up the room like a set of piano keys. "See, I told you he'd be surprised."

It was true. Will could hardly contain his surprise. Honestly, Jamie was speaking as if she were in the middle of a tea party, not side by side with an escaped outlaw and in danger of catching disease.

As he stared, his fingers itching to pull Jamie away and wash her hands in lye, their host's expression turned to sheer gratitude. "Oh, Miss. I mean Ma'am, it's sure a pleasure to have your company. My wife hasn't looked so happy in days. I'm Chester. Chester Clark."

When it looked as if the man wanted to touch Jamie too, a tinge of jealousy skipped forward. Striding to her side, Will rested a protective hand on her shoulder. "We thank you for your hospitality."

Jamie looked up at him in confusion for a moment before turning back to the struggling woman. "Abigail—Mrs. Clark—how may I help you? Would you like me to help you with your hair?"

"Yes," Mrs. Clark said weakly.

Will looked on and feared Jamie getting sicker by the second. "Jenny, darlin', perhaps—"

"Don't worry yourself, dear," she interrupted, her expression hard. "This doesn't concern you."

He was just about to remind her of their exact circumstances when Chester laughed uproariously. "We sure know how to pick 'em, don't we? Never could abide a timid woman. Let's go get some wood. It's going to be a cold one tonight."

Will hated even the idea of leaving Jamie's side. But it was obvious he had no choice—and that Mrs. Clark needed some privacy. "Lead the way, Chester. Lead and I'll follow."

✦

An hour later, they were all settled for the night. Well, as settled and situated as Jamie could be in such unfamiliar surroundings and next to a man she didn't trust.

Except for the glow of the fireplace, the interior of the cabin was dark, almost black. The flames sent off a multitude of shadows, so she had to rely on her other senses to help her with her bearings.

Next to her, Will lay on his back. He was resting on top of their covers even though the cabin's interior was chilly.

They were so close that she felt his wide shoulders and smelled his scent. Over the top of them lay Will's duster and an ancient wedding-ring quilt that had seen better days.

But still she was terribly cold.

Mrs. Clark was near the fireplace on the far side of the room. In addition, Mr. Clark had positioned their spot behind the table and chairs, in an attempt to give Jamie and Will privacy.

But instead of feeling more private, Jamie felt more on display than ever before.

All night long, Will had watched her, fussed over her, been extremely solicitous. All under the guise of a caring husband. Unspoken was the warning about saying too much, or even attempting to escape.

Jamie knew Will wouldn't hesitate to resort to violence if need be. Reminding her of just how murky everything seemed to be. Yes, Will was a better man than Kent.

But really, how good was that?

As Chester's snores began to echo through the room, Will sighed next to her and shifted again. Jamie tried to reposition herself with each movement, but it was difficult. Will was a big man, and they were in a terribly small space.

Finally, he settled on his side and faced her. "You okay?" he whispered.

Was she? Well, she was alive, so that was something. She nodded.

He stared at her, his gaze skimming over every shadow on her face. "Are you cold?"

"Yes." There'd been no point in lying about that.

He stiffened. Looked her over some more. Then seemed to make a decision. "May I hold you?"

His voice was low, so low it was barely understandable. However, the look he shot her way was earnest, and as the meaning behind it settled in, Jamie realized he was truly concerned for her. She meant more to him than just a captive.

The idea made a little tingle whip through her body. It had been so terribly long since she'd felt any sort of connection of worth with anyone. The last six months had been taken up with her parents' sickness and death.

And living in that strange, hostile void of grief. She'd practically floated in a haze through each day—wondering what she was going to do. Wondering what she wanted to do.

She'd prayed and slept and tried to remember to eat. And then she'd prayed some more. Of course, never had she imagined that the Lord would send her into the arms of the Walton Gang, and now she was running for her life next to a too-handsome man who was undoubtedly her enemy.

"Jamie? Are you ever going to answer me?" Will drawled, soft and low. "May I hold you?"

May he? The words and the images they spurred brought forth that same old flicker of awareness she was starting to recognize.

Of course, it started to scare her as well. She ached for human contact. But she feared being hurt worse.

And though she was still technically his hostage, Jamie guessed she might still have choices. That just because he offered didn't mean she had to accept. "I'm fine."

"You sure? Sharing body warmth will help us both." He paused. "I know you're chilled."

She was terribly cold. But moving close to him had its own set of worries. She'd let her guard down so much on the train that she'd fallen asleep in his arms. Getting that close to him again felt foolhardy. "I'm fine," she said primly. "I'm fine right here."

Something flickered in his eyes, then he shifted to his back again and stared up at the ceiling. "Try to sleep then. Tomorrow will be a long day."

His words sounded empty and sad. Almost as if he wished things between them were really like their lies. Almost as if he wished things between them were different.

But of course they weren't. The very worst thing that could happen would be for her to start to pretend that she believed in wishes or miracles.

Or that she was ever going to get to Kansas City. Because at the moment, chances were very, very good she was not going to make it.

And her body would just end up alone on the plains like the rest of the hostages'.

Closing her eyes, she asked God to help her. And if He couldn't do that, she asked that He give her peace. Surely that wasn't too much to hope for?

15

After a cursory glance, Scout Proffitt refrained from looking left or right when he entered the saloon. To his way of thinking, surroundings didn't matter all that much anyway. He'd seen the inside of enough saloons to last a lifetime, and if he knew anything, he knew one thing for sure: they were all the same.

The only thing different about this one, located in the middle of some two-bit, nondescript town just west of Dodge City, was that it held information he wanted.

Someone had to have seen McMillan; Scout was banking on it. He was anxious to locate McMillan and the woman, do what he had to do, and then do his best to forget what kind of man he'd become.

As smoky air, heavy with the scent of unwashed bodies, surrounded him, he kept his pace slow and his eyes straight ahead. Back when he'd first started out, when he was greener than spring grass, he'd learned the hard way to never make eye contact with strangers.

A miserable ex-soldier with a bad case of regret had beaten him good when Scout had dared to look too closely at the man's empty shirtsleeve.

Well, he'd learned not to do that anymore.

Now Scout made sure that he was the one who people feared, the one who people barely dared to sneak a peek at. Few men shot the man who kept to himself. It wasn't a rule, but it always made sense. He wasn't the type to pick a fight with men who respected privacy. Life was too tiring and hard for that.

Now, as he walked through the dusty, noisy room, Scout felt his jaw clench. Lord, but he was worn out. Dirty, too. Only duty, not any great desire for vengeance, propelled him forward. Truth was, if he'd had his way, he'd never enter another saloon for the rest of his life.

With every step he took, the scent of dirt and grime and something softer and more lewd seeped into his pores like familiar friends. One by one, the inhabitants looked him over. Considered.

He kept his shoulders back and his face blank. Old lessons piled up inside him and pulled his muscles into compliance. Walk with pride. Don't show emotions. Never show weakness. Don't court trouble.

Pride and instinct kicked in as he realized that yet again he was in control of the situation. He was the one who made things happen. That was how a man like him survived.

And, every once in a while, thrived.

After a pause, raucous laughter from a bar girl rang loud and clear, and the coarse grumbling and conversation from a table of poker players mixed in with it. The sounds blended together and reverberated in his ears, making him feel on fire and on edge. And as those familiar feelings came over him—just like they always did—Scout cursed his luck.

No matter how much things changed, they were always the same too.

When he'd jumped off the train, he'd half expected to be camped in the middle of nowhere, shivering under the moonlight in desperate silence. A part of him had yearned for that as well. He'd be alone with only coyotes to fear. In addition, finding some pain in his circumstances would mirror the pain he felt inside for being the person that he was.

A killer. A coldhearted killer who deserved nothing. Only he would be able to find a saloon so easily.

However, a brief four-mile walk had brought him to the town of Saddlecreek, and his feet into the only place where towns folk who were up to no good congregated.

Continuing to feel more than one person's eyes watching him, he found the most opportune spot to watch the crowd and gave thanks that it was empty.

He took a chair and sat with his back to the wall, his usual spot. Time and again had proved that only with his back against the wall could he be certain no one was behind.

Stifling a sigh, he leaned back and looked around. Waited.

Then, there it was—a prickling at the back of his neck. He almost welcomed the feeling. He breathed slowly as it amped up, signaling a warning that he couldn't ignore and knew better than to ever try.

He knew the feeling as well as he knew how long it would take him to draw with his right hand. Someone wanted his attention, and was determined to get it.

Unable to put it off any longer, Scout finally let himself scan the crowd. As he stared, one by one, men looked away.

He shifted. Waited some more. Then looked into a pair of eyes that were as dark and soulless as any he'd ever encountered. It was a crying shame they belonged to a woman who had to be no older than seventeen or eighteen.

Habit and experience told him to keep his mouth shut and wait. No reason to give himself or his feelings away. She could want any number of things. His body. His skill with a pistol. Or she could be observing him for another man, hoping to use his weakness for another's benefit.

All of those things had happened more than a time or two.

Forcing himself to breathe slowly, he kept his eyelids at half-mast and stayed patient.

Inch by inch, the woman stepped forward.

Her dark brown hair hung in a tangled mass around her shoulders and back. Although it looked in need of a comb and brush, the wildness of it complemented her dark eyes and thick eyelashes. And the bruise on her cheek. Her pale lips parted.

But instead of intriguing him, her expression only increased his uneasiness. Though she was a female, he found his right hand hovering over his Colt. After all, she wouldn't be the first woman to wish him dead.

Across the room, the poker game continued. To his left, the barkeep continued to talk horses with a pair of cowhands bellied up at the bar. Two harlots dressed in faded calicos smiled tiredly at a pair of cowboys still dusty from the range.

But here, right at that minute, time seemed to stand still.

Continuing, the woman crept forward with her bottom lip tucked between her teeth.

His eyes narrowed. "That's close enough, sugar."

As he'd expected, his command was obeyed. She stopped abruptly and seemed to gather her courage.

Scout waited.

Finally, she spoke. "You're new."

"I'm not staying long. Just passing through."

She inched closer. "Where are you from?"

There was a drop of blood now decorating that lip she bit. "Now why would you imagine I'd tell you?"

"No reason. I just thought I'd ask."

"It doesn't matter where I'm from."

He was just about to shoo her away, to tell her almost kindly to move on, but just as if she'd suddenly made a decision, she closed the distance between them. Next thing he knew, she'd pulled out the chair across from him and had sat down. Uninvited.

Which made him good and bothered. He didn't want a woman. He wanted information about McMillan, and he'd bet his last dollar that she couldn't give him that. But his muscles eased somewhat and he leaned back. Braced a hand on the table. "I don't know what you have, but I don't want it."

"I don't . . . I mean I know . . ." Her cheeks pinkened as she sputtered. "What I mean to say is . . . I need your help," she finally said, her voice quivery but solid. A true combination of twin emotions. Hesitation and steel. Promise and fear.

'Course, he wasn't in the mood to give help. He had two people to hunt down. "Sugar, I can't help you."

"But I haven't even asked what I—"

"It don't matter."

To his surprise, his rudeness seemed to give her courage. "I hope you'll reconsider. Or at least listen. If you could." She bit her lip again, encouraging another drop of blood to appear. "I'm desperate, you see."

All that desperation made him uncomfortable. The wild, wary look in her eyes made him remember his life long ago. Made him recall things better left forgotten.

Which, of course, made him angry.

So, he kept his voice hard. "I don't know who you think I am, but I'm not your savior. I can promise you that."

Pushing aside his words, she leaned forward. "There's no one else. You're it."

Further discussion was prevented by the barkeep. "You drinking?" he asked, wiping his hands on the white dishrag wrapped around his middle.

Scout lifted two fingers. "Whiskey for me." And then out of nowhere, he turned to the woman. "What do y'all want?" As pure apprehension licked her features, he clarified himself. "To drink, sugar. What do you want to drink?"

"To drink? Oh. Nothing."

The barkeep rolled his eyes like he knew better.

"Better get something. I'm buying," Scout ordered. After all, he hadn't even wanted to be in her company. He sure as heck didn't want to sit and watch her just stare at him while he drank. When she still hesitated, he offered more choices, just like he was a bartender or some such. "Beer? Water?"

"Could I maybe have tea? Hot tea?"

The barkeep sneered. "We ain't got tea here, Kitty. You know that."

Against his will, a tiny bit of irritation morphed into amusement. "Kitty?"

"Brother's nickname," she said. "Stuck."

"I guess so," he murmured as he looked at her. At her too-dark eyes, so void of hope. At her too-much hair that should have been pinned up. At her too-skinny body that should have been hungry.

At her dress that was too faded. At the dress's collar, which had been hastily mended with the wrong color thread. Several times.

He thought about that. Thought about her seeking him out. And even though he wasn't the type to stick his neck out for anybody, something inside of him clicked. And that's when he knew right then and right there that things had changed.

"Barkeep, find the lady a pot of hot tea," he said softly. When he felt the man's hesitation, Scout raised his eyes and looked right above the man's right shoulder. "I know you've got a kettle in the back."

The barkeep's arms folded across his chest. "And how would you know that?"

"You always do," he said frankly, knowing he hadn't been in a bar that didn't have some kind of stove in the back. "Now, do it." And because the girl looked peaked, he added wearily, "I promise, I'll make it worth your while."

"How so? You going to pay double?"

The man's belligerence grated on his nerves. "Perhaps. Or perhaps if you do what I say, I won't kill you." And with that, he finally looked up at the man. Stared coldly at him, making sure they both knew he wasn't a man to make false promises. Ever.

The barkeep started, then looked at him more closely. All color vanished in his face. "Lord have mercy! You're Scout Proffitt, ain't you?"

If it wouldn't have been so much trouble, Scout would have pulled out his Colt and fired. "Keep your voice down."

"Yessir." The man complied, but his eyes lit up like Christmas had come early. "But . . . you're him, ain't you?"

Scout's only reply involved an impatient, dark glare.

The man's right hand crushed the white cloth in a fist. "I'll get that tea."

"And my whiskey?" he prodded. "Two fingers worth?"

"And your whiskey. Sure." With another awkward look at Kitty, the man turned away.

Leaving Scout alone with the woman again.

If he'd been able to, he would've tilted his head back in frustration. All he'd been wanting was a few moments of peace and quiet before he had to start asking questions.

Now that fool bartender was announcing his presence like an auctioneer and some poor beat-up girl was keeping him company.

She was now staring at him like he was an apparition. "Are you really Scout Proffitt?"

There was no reason to lie. "I am."

She blinked, took a breath, then asked, "Are . . . are the things people say . . . the things people wrote about you . . ." She swallowed. "Are they true?"

He let her stew on that one because the bartender had hustled over with a tumbler half-filled with whiskey. "Tea's a'comin'," he muttered before turning away.

Slowly, he ran a finger around the glass's rim.

It was on the tip of his tongue to lie. Or to let her know that he was probably much worse than anyone could ever guess.

But he was tired of living up to his reputation. "I don't know. I ain't read much about me."

The girl scanned his face. But instead of turning more bleak, her dark-as-night eyes almost filled with hope. "Mr. Proffitt, you kill for a living, don't you?"

It took everything he had not to flinch.

But when he looked into her eyes—he knew that there were now two entities he could never lie to. The first was the Lord. He always knew what he did and why. Now, all the sudden, He was joined by this girl, right there in front of him.

"Yes," he finally said. "Yes, I kill for a living."

As it looked like she was out of breath, he forced himself to pick up his tumbler and take another sip.

And then he waited and watched.

Sooner or later she would talk. People always did.

This time, he would listen.

16

I suppose I should mention that I only kill for money," Scout clarified after the whiskey slid down his throat and burned enough to remind him that he was alive. "I never do anything for free."

"I kinda figured that." The girl looked at him again, opened her mouth, then changed her mind and shifted in her chair.

He knew she was scared.

Part of him suddenly wished he were a different kind of man. The kind who could say his hiring-out days were long gone. That the days of trading cash for a person's life were over.

There was no reason to deny it. Or to attempt to explain that he wasn't all bad. That more than a few times the killing had been in self-defense. Daring to smile, he finally asked, "Sweetheart, now that you know all my secrets, are you still certain that you need my help?"

As she looked at him, a thousand questions in her eyes, the barkeep came, a pot of tea in one hand, the mug in the other. After placing both in front of the woman, he turned back to the copper-coated bar.

Seconds later, he brought Scout yet another glass liberally filled with amber fluid. Feeling like the girl was going to make him need a never-ending supply of the stuff, Scout lifted his tumbler with a wry expression. "Cheers."

As he tossed back another mouthful, she carefully poured her steeping tea into a chipped cup. After blowing on it twice, she closed her eyes and sipped tentatively, as if a cup of tea were a real treat.

He was just contemplating how many times she'd probably mended her ragtag dress, when she spoke. "Mr. Proffitt, there's no good way to ask you what I'm gonna."

"Then just spit it out."

Pressing her palms on the table, she leaned forward. "All right. I want you to kill my stepfather."

Part of his brain wished he was shocked. Surprised. But all her request did was answer the question. The stepfather was the reason for the torn dress.

But just to be sure he was reading everything right, he said, "Why?"

"Does it matter?"

"Not really if you pay me enough. But something tells me you don't got much."

"He beat me."

"That all?" To his way of thinking, that didn't explain the torn dress.

"No."

"Ah."

Her eyes widened as she realized he wasn't shocked. "My brother got himself killed with some rustlers a year ago. Since then, well, it's been just my stepfather and me," she said. Her voice cool and matter-of-fact, she continued. "He's an evil man. Mean."

"And your mother?"

The girl picked up the mug again and stared into the weak brew. "She didn't survive the war."

"I see."

Dark eyes flashed darker. "I don't know if you do. See, he's used me for as long as I can remember."

Used. Pity flowed through him, somehow finding a thin, narrow-winding path to his heart and his conscience. Unable to help himself, he looked her over more carefully. Now that his eyes had adjusted better to the dim light, he noticed the bruises on the delicate skin of her neck. On the smooth expanse of bare skin bordering that torn collar.

Anger for her situation boiled deep inside. Irritation that she'd decided to involve him in her problems nagged him like tiny pinpricks. Hadn't he already told her he was no one's savior?

"Why don't you run?" he asked.

"I don't know where I'd go."

"Away. All you have to do is just go away." After all, that was what he'd done, wasn't it? When he'd realized that he'd missed the war 'cause he'd been too young, when one too many bitter, ruined men had looked at him with derision, saying he had no idea what life was like, he'd run because he'd known they were right.

Yep, he'd run when he'd realized that he was weak.

Then he'd ventured even further into the abyss when he'd realized he would never be the man his father was. And never, ever be the hero his older brother Clayton was. Clayton had commanded hundreds of men, some double his age and had courageously led them into battle. He'd saved innocents, supported the weak, and inspired the brave.

One night when his insomnia had been particularly bad, Scout had looked up into the stars and realized that God just didn't make men like Clayton more than once in a blue moon.

And moreover, the good Lord wasn't likely to waste time on someone as undeserving as himself.

And so he'd taken to wearing only black and made a reputation that could never compete with a soldier's honor and glory. A reputation so dark and ugly that the only way it could be measured with Clayton's was as the complete opposite.

Scout gripped the glass again and brought it to his lips, then was stunned to see that it was empty. Again. He held it up. "Barkeep?"

Sitting next to him, sipping that tea like she was at a church social, Kitty continued. "Mr. Proffitt, see . . . I'm not a man."

"I noticed that."

She ignored his comment. "There's no way for me to make my living unless I want to sell my body."

She had a point—no denying that. But what she didn't realize was that there was still a sweetness to her that paying for a murder would destroy.

Hoping to scare her, he raised a brow. "If you can't give me money, how do you suppose you're gonna pay my fee?"

Swallowing hard, she called his bluff. "However you want me to."

Lord have mercy! Turning around, he begged the bartender for liquid salvation. "Whiskey," he ordered, his voice strained.

When the fool man finally started pouring, he turned back to Kitty. "I'm not going to kill for you. I'm sorry."

"But—"

"Look. If word got out that you hired me, you could be strung up for murder, and dying like that is a painful way to go." She blanched. Exactly as he'd intended for her to. "Sorry," he said again, surprising himself. He wasn't a man to apologize for anything.

At last the whiskey came. Scout picked up the shot like it was his lifeline.

A full minute passed.

She sipped her tea again, the tremors in her hands making Scout half hold his breath waiting for the hot liquid to slosh over the brim and burn her thin fingers.

"I'm sorry too, Mr. Proffitt," she said. After another sip, she started to scoot back. Then the door to the saloon opened and a dark hulk of a man appeared.

"Kitty! Kitty, where the hell are you?" he called out. His voice slurred. Desperate. "I heard you were in here. Kitty!"

To their right, the bartender cleared his throat.

One second passed. Maybe two. The girl across from Scout visibly shook but scooted out her chair the rest of the way and awkwardly got to her feet.

Scout knew the moment the man spied her. His stance became almost rock solid. "Git over here."

All discussion halted in the room as everyone stared. Waited.

Obviously, the scene had been played out before all over town.

It was also obvious that no one had any intention of changing things.

When Kitty stepped forward—one hand fingering the poorly mended collar like she was already preparing to sew it up again—Scout knew he had no choice. Throwing out a hand, he grasped her elbow and halted her. "Sit back down."

When she turned her head to stare at him, complete surprise was in her gaze.

Shaming him.

He lowered his voice until it was hardly more than a whisper. "Do it." She sat back down.

"Girl?" The drunk scanned the area, fixated on her, and trudged forward. "Git over—"

"I wouldn't say another word," Scout said.

"Why the hell not?"

The barkeep behind him coughed. The woman in the chair trembled.

Scout looked at her. "How old are you?"

"Eighteen."

Relief, sharp and cool, flowed through him. "Because this lady isn't your property any longer. She's of legal age."

The guy swayed and smirked. "And what are you gonna do? Stop me?"

Though he hadn't wanted to do this, Scout realized the outcome was inevitable. Blood was going to have to be shed, because sometimes that was the only thing that people paid attention to.

But just as he was fingering his Colt, deciding where to shoot so he wouldn't take out a handful of innocents along the way, the bartender spoke.

"That there is Scout Proffitt, Duke. *The* Scout Proffitt."

Some of Duke's oily confidence slipped away. "That true?"

"Why would he lie?" Scout murmured.

"That girl, she's mine."

"Not anymore." Scout looked around at the whole assemblage. At everyone who knew what wasn't right but hadn't wanted to make things better for the woman sitting on his left.

"Fact is, Kitty here was just telling me she's had just about enough of being yours." He paused then gave in to what surely seemed to be predestined. "I'm going to take her with me."

"You won't want her for long. . . . She'll scratch you."

The sick warning made his stomach turn. Though he ached to tell the man that he certainly didn't want to use the woman, that he had no intention of lying with her, he kept his thoughts to himself.

Instead, he smiled. "I guess I'll take my chances." Eyeing the crowd, he added, "Now, are y'all going to let us get on our way . . . or not?"

"Take her, Mr. Proffitt," the barkeep murmured behind him. "Not a soul here's gonna fight you. If you took her, it would be a blessing."

Scout turned around in surprise. Who would ever speak to him about blessings?

The shock must have shown on his face, because the man tugged at his collar and reddened.

And as Kitty sat there like a stone, listening to every word, the barkeep continued. "She's a decent sort, that girl is," he said, stumbling over every word like they were getting stuck in his teeth. "She could've been better . . . in other circumstances."

The words sounded familiar.

Funny, they were the same ones he'd told himself time and again when he was riding alone and the night was falling. He'd stop and think about his day—and his life—and compare it to Clayton's. He always came up wanting.

That's when he'd known that if things had been different everything would have been better. If he hadn't killed his mother in childbirth, if his pa hadn't died in the war, and if Clayton hadn't followed their father into battle, trying hard to be man enough for two.

If his sister hadn't had to shoulder so much responsibility. If everyone around him hadn't marched out to war then come home different.

If none of those things had happened, maybe he could have been someone to be proud of. Maybe he could have been someone who wasn't so ashamed.

"Mr. Proffitt, take her, would you? I promise, no matter what you do, it will be better than what she's got now."

"I don't prey on innocent women."

The barkeep's eyes darted away. "'Course not. Meant no disrespect. It's just, well . . . if you took her, it really would be charity."

As if of Scout even knew what charity was. As if he still cared.

But what if he did? What if the good Lord hadn't given up on him after all? What if He had put him right in this woman's path all for this moment?

And what if he dismissed it?

It would be a blessing.

Leaning down, he spoke quietly and clearly. "In two minutes, we are going to leave. We're gonna go to your home where you will pack a duffle. And then we are getting out of this godforsaken town. Understand?"

She stood up, a new resolve in her eyes. And something that looked like . . . hope?

After tossing too much money on the table, he took her arm and escorted her through the maze of tables, ignoring most of the gamblers' curious looks. Past her irate stepfather.

When the man looked ready to grab at her, Scout looked his way and smiled, betraying that no matter how much he might try to redeem himself by helping one poor girl, he really was beyond help.

Because at that moment, right then and there, he knew he was itching to kill. He wouldn't even mind taking his stiletto and slicing deep, either. Make him bleed onto the floor, right there in front of everyone.

Fear entered into the man's gaze and he looked down at his feet.

Taking away Scout's opportunity to shoot. "Let's go," he murmured, gripping Kitty's arm a little more firmly, even though she didn't need his grip.

Only when they stood on the street in the cold, dark night did he release his hold. "Are you sure about this? Being with me ain't easy."

For a long moment, she gazed at him. Seemed to be measuring his worth. Probably was wondering how he was about to hurt her.

"I won't touch you," he sputtered. When her lips parted, he looked at her arm. Most likely, that arm sported five fingertip bruises on it. "I mean, I won't . . . I won't disrespect you."

She blinked. Then, to his surprise, she shrugged, as if his lies didn't really matter anyway. "My house is this way."

He walked by her side, thinking how wrong she was. No one knew what bad was until they'd experienced it. Things could always get worse. Always.

He stood outside the door of a humble house with nothing growing in the front yard beyond a few weeds and a month's worth of trash.

She paused, looking a bit ashamed. "I'll only be a couple of minutes," she said, her tone apologetic.

"Take your time. This here, it's nothing I haven't seen before," he murmured softly as she slipped inside.

As he watched her shadows behind sheer curtains, he lit up a cigar and breathed deeply. It was bitterly cold out. The wind had kicked up, stinging his cheeks and making his eyes water. He needed something to take off the edge.

To make him question what in the world he was doing. After all, he was on a killing mission, not a saving one.

Only two minutes passed until she returned again, a stuffed pillowcase in her hand. When he eyed it, she tucked her chin. "I don't have a duffle."

"That'll do. You got a horse?"

"My . . . I mean Duke, he does."

Scout finally let himself smile. "Not any longer. Show me where it is, Kitty."

After a moment's hesitation, she led him to a surprisingly good piece of horseflesh. Whatever the man did to his step-daughter, he seemed to have more respect for a good animal.

After saddling the horse, he helped the girl onto the saddle and settled in behind her. As he expected, she tensed, unused to feeling his body.

"I'm not going to hurt you," he said again. "You don't have to believe me, but it's the truth."

While she thought about that one, he clicked the horse forward out of the ramshackle barn. Out of the weed-ridden yard. Out of Kitty's own version of hell.

"Let's move on now," he said, and almost smiled when he felt her body relax against his, lightly pressing her back against his chest.

They rode in silence. The horse nickered as he motioned it forward, down the street, beyond the saloon, and into the pitch dark night filled with desolate plains. The moon was gone, the stars dim under a curtain of clouds.

But he didn't mind. Neither did the horse. And, by the looks of things, neither did Kitty. As each minute passed, she seemed to settle more easily against him.

As he continued to move west, Scout had a feeling she'd be asleep within minutes, and was thankful for that.

But as the lights from the two-bit town faded into the distance, he realized with some surprise that he'd never asked a single person about Will McMillan. Or about the woman he was instructed to kill.

Somehow—like the hopes and dreams he'd clung to as a small boy—his mission had slipped his mind.

17

*W*ill woke up with a woman curved next to his side. As he gradually became aware of his surroundings, he realized a soft arm was nestled against his and a faint floral scent emanated from her, mixing with innocence and trust.

He scooted back a bit, needing to put some space between the two of them. The distance didn't help. Though the cabin was bitter cold and smelled like death, somehow the woman next to him seemed content. Deep in her dreams, she stretched a leg and then scooted a tiny bit closer. When her toe met his calf, she sighed—just like he'd seen children trust their parents to look out for them.

Mesmerized, Will took advantage of the dim light and stared a little longer. In repose, her breathing was slow and steady. Even. Her lips—so delicately pink and perfectly formed—were slightly parted. Her caramel-colored hair had become loose, liberating itself from its braid. Beautiful strands of copper and gold cascaded over her shoulders along the lines of her pillow and the threadbare quilt.

Just looking at her brought forth a terrible ache for things that could never be. Made him yearn for featherbeds and fresh, hot coffee. Warm fires. For girlish laughter and suppers that lasted too long and had too much food.

For sweetness, even though such things had never been part of his life.

He'd grown up outside of Houston, the adored son of a wealthy family. His father had taught him to ride before he could barely walk, and had taught him responsibility right after that.

Will had grown up knowing he would one day be responsible for their land, their home, and for his sister Bonnie. For Aaron, his baby brother.

Under his father's tutelage, Will had accepted those things as his due. He'd never minded the extra work, knowing that such things came with the gifts he'd been given. He'd been blessed with a good brain, good looks, and wealth. His body was strong and his family was solid.

When he was sixteen, he'd even begun to look around at the girls in his family's circle, mentally cataloging each female, weighing the pros and cons of each one, deciding who would one day suit him best as his wife.

As only an arrogant boy would do.

Then, of course, everything changed. The war came and their father had been gravely injured in his unit's first skirmish. After that, everything in his paper-perfect world came tumbling down. An influenza epidemic swept through their town, killing his brother and sister in one week.

His mother retreated into herself as grief became heavy.

And then the Union soldiers came and made his home—his birthright—theirs. Will and his mother had left in the middle of the night, afraid for their lives, and had ended up in a neighbor's small cabin. The day he turned seventeen, he'd found his mother dead by her own hand.

He'd cast away his immaturity, pushed aside all those gran-diose ideas, and went to war. He'd put his brain and brawn and anger to use, eventually serving under Captain Clayton Proffitt and Major John Merritt.

When the war ended, he drifted for a bit. But when it became evident that his land was ruined and overtaken with squatters, he'd found another home—the U.S. Marshals.

It was a good fit. Eventually Sam Edison, its director, told him he had a unique talent for pretending to be someone he wasn't.

Since his reality wasn't much, he'd dived into the new job with an eagerness that would have been admirable if it wasn't so shameful.

Time and again, he'd posed as any number of losers and thieves. He'd begun to count on others' need to trust in order to gain inside information and ultimately crush the very peo-ple who'd reached out to him.

He was so good at it, he'd even been asked to infiltrate the Walton Gang in order to procure enough evidence to take James Walton to trial.

He never considered refusing the directive.

All those steps had been a matter of survival, and he didn't fault fate. He'd praised God for his opportunities. Gave thanks that he was still surviving, that he was still moving forward. In the back of his mind, he'd wondered why it had all hap-pened. He didn't understand why he'd survived when others hadn't—what purpose his gifts were going to be used for—until he'd met Jamilyn.

From the moment he'd gazed into her velvety brown eyes, he'd known for certain that God had never left him. He'd taken so much, but had gifted him with a beautiful woman worth saving.

And now she was curled up next to him. His responsibility.

The knowledge screamed inside of him, spurring him further awake. He needed to get up and keep her moving. He needed to get her to safety before whoever James Walton had sent to find them got lucky. One thing was certain—Boss would send someone to gun them down. There was no doubt about that. James Walton didn't look lightly upon loose ends.

A quick glance toward the other side of the room confirmed that the elderly couple were still asleep. Good. With any luck, he and Jamilyn would be on their way before they were missed.

Reaching out, he dared to brush her shoulder with his fingertips. "Jamie? Jamie, honey, we need to go."

With a languid sigh, she shifted and rolled toward him, her leg going flush against his, her lips slightly parted. His heart beat rapidly while the rest of him ached to take what she was offering. Blinking, he forced his leg further from her and hardened his voice. "Jamilyn, wake up now."

Her eyelids fluttered open. For a split second, when they rested on him, her expression softened. Wonder lit her gaze, making him think of pretty postcards of places he was never going to see. A wistfulness flowed through him, igniting his imagination.

Then she blinked again, as if she'd suddenly noticed they were sharing a bed. And her wonder changed to fear.

"I won't hurt you," he whispered. "Do you remember where you are?" He swallowed. Then, because she looked so wary, he spoke again. "Do . . . do you recall who I am? And who we're pretending to be?"

Slowly, she nodded.

As a shiver ran through her, Will wished he could have changed so much. But there was nothing that could be said. "How soon can you be ready?"

She shook her head in an obvious attempt to clear her head. "As soon as you need me to be."

"Good girl." Getting to his feet, he leaned down and held out a hand. After a moment's hesitation, Jamie climbed to her feet. He stared at her for too long, took a chance and ran his thumb over her delicate skin, and then dropped her hand. "Let me look outside to make sure everything is clear, then I'll walk you to the outhouse."

Even as a pale flush flowed up her cheeks, she nodded.

Will was amazed by her bravery. Many a woman would have been overcome by now or would have collapsed under the weight of so much adversity. But not this lady. Instead of crumbling, she was standing straighter and growing in strength.

But how could he tell her any of that? She still believed he was an outlaw. And he needed to keep up her fear until the time was right. The only thing worse than her being afraid of him was for the Walton Gang to even have an inkling that he wasn't who they thought he was. If that were the case, Will knew for certain that they would stop at nothing in order to find him—and to get information out of him.

Even, he knew, using Jamie to bend him to their will.

After pulling on his boots, he slipped outside and scanned the area. When he saw no signs of anyone, he guided Jamie outside and walked her the few frozen yards to the outhouse.

Scant minutes later, she came back to him.

To his eyes, she looked pale. "Are you all right, sweetheart?"

Her eyes flickered briefly, as if she'd just noticed that he'd started talking in endearments. For a moment, he was tempted to apologize, though he wasn't sorry. It had been too long since he'd been around anyone who had inspired any sort of tender emotions. The novelty was too good.

Besides, he figured that apologizing would be out of character. At least for her perception of the man he was.

After gazing at him a moment longer, she looked away. "I'm fine."

She was anything but. He couldn't help teasing her. "I'm starting to get the feeling you'd tell me you were fine no matter what the situation."

"It doesn't matter anyway, does it? I mean, it's not like we have a choice about what we're doing. Or what we can do. I'm grateful for your assistance."

Oh, but she spoke so formally. As if they were in her parents' front parlor and he was paying a call on her. Not like the two of them were lost in the middle of a Colorado snowstorm with a half dozen Marshals out for his blood, an old woman dying of influenza, and a set of killers hunting them down like they were their latest prey.

This time he nodded. And brought forth a new severity between them. Calling up lessons learned at his father's knee, he said, "You're right, ma'am. We don't have any choice except to keep moving. That's all that's left to us. Let's go tell these folks good-bye and get on our way."

Her cheeks colored, though whether from their time in the cold or whether she was preparing herself for another hard moment, he didn't know. Instead of speaking, she turned and walked forward, leading him back to the cabin.

When they got inside, he almost smiled. The warmth of the cabin caressed his skin, bringing with it a blessed relief from the cold. Though the pungent odor stung his eyes, the smoky scent relaxed his muscles.

Then he realized they were no longer the only ones up. The man was across the room, kneeling in front of the fire. And looking at Will.

Will cleared his throat. "Sir, we'll be going now. Thank you kindly for your hospitality."

"Such that it was," Chester Clark said with a hint of sarcasm.

Will noticed that he was fussing with a coffee pot and a tin. After another moment or two of coaxing the flames, the man added, "You know, wherever you're going will still be there in twenty minutes. Can I convince you to stay for biscuits and coffee?"

Though his instincts commanded him to get on their way, stronger concerns for Jamie made him consider the invitation. She already looked too pale; he couldn't refuse her a hot meal. "Can you spare it?"

"I can, if you can spare me a few moments and bring in some of that wood you chopped last night. I'm afraid your brawn is more than I've got at the moment."

"I'll stack as much as you want," he offered before he could remind himself to move on.

"Just enough to stack up right here." He pointed to a small two-foot square area, allowing for only a dozen stacked logs.

Will got to his feet. "Will you be all right if I leave you for a moment?" he asked Jamie.

"I'll be fine."

"Obliged," the man murmured. "I'll be grateful for your assistance, and for the company." With a cough, he pushed forward a needle and thread. "I couldn't help noticing that the collar of your dress was torn. If you want, you could put on one of my wife's old gowns for a bit and mend your dress."

Jamie looked at Will with such a look of longing that he couldn't refuse her.

"If you don't care to wear one of her dresses, just stay behind that curtained area for a few minutes," the man said agreeably.

"I'd like to mend my dress," she whispered.

Will nodded, then escorted her toward a dark blue piece of fabric hanging down. The area that it covered was so slim, he'd thought it was a curtain. After standing outside of it while Jamie took off her dress and slipped on the woman's worn calico, he left her to her mending. "I'll be back soon."

Even as he walked out the door, he realized he'd just put himself in an extremely precarious position—at this moment Jamie could be telling them everything. She had no reason to trust him, and every reason to be afraid.

18

*H*ave you been with your man for long?" Chester Clark asked.

Looking up from her sewing, Jamie bit her lip. For a split second, she contemplated telling him the truth. Considered pulling him aside and asking him for help. Thought about telling him everything, confessing her sins.

But then reality set in. This man was no match for Will McMillan. Even if he was a good shot, there was no doubt in her mind that Will could shoot him dead without a second's hesitation.

"No," she said. Then looked at the door again. Half praying that Will would come in right away. Save her from the lies.

He chuckled, his expression easy. "I thought so. You two have that way about you."

"What way?" she was intrigued in spite of herself.

"That way that newly marrieds have." When she stared at him in confusion, he explained himself further. "You know what I mean. . . . It's like you two only see each other. You probably don't even realize it none, but your eyes follow him nonstop. Just like you're afraid he's going to surprise you with something good." Looking at his wife fondly, he murmured, "I've been there a time myself with Abigail."

Jamie couldn't help being amazed by the irony of the situation. Of course she couldn't stop watching. Will like a hawk. She didn't trust him or trust their situation. What's more, she was afraid of him.

Terribly.

Well, maybe that was putting it a little heavy. But she did fear what could happen.

"I guess that's true. I can't help watching him," she said, as she knotted the thread and surveyed the mended collar.

The fix wasn't perfect by any stretch of the imagination. However, it was a definite improvement from the way it had been.

After excusing herself, she changed dresses quickly behind the curtain and stepped out just as her "husband" came in, his arms laden with a stack of wood.

"Seeing a young pup like you loaded down heavy does my old heart good." The old man cackled.

A grin appeared out of nowhere as Will stood up. "I'll go get a few more sticks."

Jamie watched Will leave.

"Where are you off to now?" Chester asked when she sat near him again.

She tried to recall what Will had said. Could she tell the truth? Or not? "Wichita," she replied, though as soon as she said the words she remembered that Will had said Topeka. Panic rocked her as she glanced at the man. Waited for him to call her on the blunder.

But instead of pointing out the discrepancy, he merely nodded. "Nice place. I've been there once myself. Seein' family?"

"No." She didn't know what was there. All she did know was that it wasn't where she was now.

For a moment the man waited politely for her to expound. But when she didn't, he coughed and went back to watching the biscuits. "Coffee, ma'am?"

"Please." When he pointed to a set of metal mugs, she crossed the room to the miniscule kitchen and picked up two. One for herself and one for Will. Without a doubt he was going to need something hot to fight off the outside chill.

When had she begun to think of him as part of her whole?

With a tremor, the old man picked up the pot with a folded cloth and filled the cups. Just as she was taking her first sip, Will came in again.

"These should do it, sir. Don't think there's much more room."

"You've helped so much. Come take a seat. Your Missus got you some coffee."

"Obliged," he said to her, his light blue eyes making her think of bluebonnets once again.

He blew gently on the rich brew. Unable to help herself, she watched his lips purse and blow, slightly startled that he was capable of anything so delicate.

An eyebrow rose, indicating that he watched her, then he turned to the man once again. "Good coffee."

"Got some beans three months ago. My Abigail treated those beans like gold, I tell you."

"On some mornings, it's just as valuable, I think."

"Indeed." He cackled, then grinned with pleasure as he tottered around the kitchen again. "Looky here. Perfect biscuits."

As he grabbed ahold of the pan with the cloth, Jamie was tempted to warn him to be careful. But of course she kept her thoughts to herself.

"These look delicious," Will said, surprising her. Crossing to the man's side, he pulled two of the piping hot biscuits out of the pan and placed them on a tin plate. Then he carried it over to her and placed it in front of her. "Eat."

"What about you?"

"We'll share." And with that, he pulled off half the offering, tore a bite-size section off of that, and popped it into his mouth.

As she watched, a look of pleasure slid into his eyes, telling her that he appreciated the simple treat and that he hadn't had such things in a very long while.

"You ought to eat too, Jenny," he said softly. "There's no telling when we'll have anything so good again."

He was right. Well aware that the man was watching them curiously, she too pulled off a bite-size portion and popped it into her mouth. "This is delicious," she said, attempting to smile easily.

But the elderly man wasn't watching them any longer. Instead, he'd moved to his wife and was gently coaxing her to sit up. A spasm of coughs wracked her body as she scooted into position.

As Jamie noticed again that Mrs. Clark was really little more than skin and bones, she knew that the woman's days on this earth were few. A quick glance toward Will told her he was thinking the same thing.

"Mr. Clark, would you like me to help you? I could help you bathe her, if you'd like."

Beside her, Will stiffened. She ignored him.

A flickering of appreciation flashed before their host's gaze shuttered again. "Thank you for the offer, but you two need to get on your way. And I'm afraid my Abigail won't know the difference."

"All right then." As quickly as she could, she finished the remainder of her coffee and breakfast.

As soon as she finished, Will took her plate, pumped water into the sink, and deftly rinsed the plates and mugs. Then to her surprise, Will stood in front of the man.

"Do you pray?" he asked, his voice husky, seeming to be filled with gravel.

The man seemed flustered by the question, but answered after a moment. "Yes, I do. I mean, we both do."

"May I pray for you? For you and Mrs. Clark?"

"I'd be obliged."

Jamie couldn't hide the surprise she felt. Who was this outlaw who fetched wood, washed dishes, and prayed over strangers?

"Jenny, would you join us?" he asked, holding out his hand.

Obediently, she walked to his side and slipped her hand into his. The moment her palm was surrounded by the rough, calloused skin, a warmth spread through her that was almost unfamiliar. For a moment, she tried to catalog it, attempted to find the source, tried to determine where she'd felt such a thing before.

If she'd ever felt it before.

Then, with some wonder, she gave the feeling a label.

It was *safety*. She felt safe next to this enigmatic man. Safer than she'd felt in some time.

Will squeezed her palm before closing his eyes. "Heavenly Father," he murmured. "Dear, gracious God. We give you thanks and praise."

The warm sensation that was easing through her expanded as Will continued to speak, praising the couple who'd sheltered them. Giving thanks for the food and water.

And wishing Mrs. Clark's journey into heaven would be a safe one, without pain.

With a start, she glanced at the woman's husband. Surely he would find offense at hearing such plain-spoken language. But instead of being offended, the man's shoulders eased. Obviously, he'd been hoping for some of those same things.

Finally, Will squeezed her hand again. "Dear God, I give you thanks for the woman by my side. Please watch over her as our journey continues. It is sure to be hard. Please give her strength to make it through." He paused. "In your name we pray. Amen."

"Thank you." Mr. Clark wiped a tear from his eye.

"We'd best go now," Will said, making her realize that there was so much she had never been around.

Then, he surprised her again when he unrolled a wad of cash. "I need one of your horses."

"Take the gelding," the man replied, accepting the money without hesitation. "He's strong and steady."

Will nodded again, then finally glanced her way. "Sweetheart? We need to go now."

She followed him to the door, pausing to glance backwards at the man who watched them, sitting stoically next to his ailing wife.

He raised a hand, letting her know without words that no words were necessary from her either. She was relieved, because really, there was nothing to say.

With an economy of motion, Will saddled the gelding, an easygoing quarter horse with a lightning stripe along its throat, lifted her into the saddle, then clicked her into motion.

Jamie held on to his waist, giving into temptation and resting her forehead against the hard planes of his back. She closed her eyes as they picked up speed and headed toward the eastern horizon.

Only hours later did she stop to realize that never once had Will asked for prayers for himself. When he turned slightly, clearly checking on her welfare, she asked him about that.

He blinked and replied without a flicker of embarrassment. "I don't deserve prayers."

"Of course . . . I mean, we all do."

"Not me. I haven't deserved them for some time."

When he faced forward, she knew better than to refute him.

Besides, she was having too hard of a time coming to terms with the fact that all of a sudden she didn't think he was all bad—even though he was an outlaw and killed and robbed for a living.

Obviously, she'd begun to change.

It fairly broke her heart.

19

*K*itty was trying the very last of Scout's patience—and he hadn't been gifted with a lot of it to begin with.

Fact was, he didn't like being around the girl all that much. Not because she was difficult—shoot, she wasn't demanding at all. What he found disturbing was how she was *too* easy to be with. Actually, she kept to herself and was so quiet that sometimes he felt like blinking a few times just to make sure she was real and not something he'd dreamed up in the middle of a whiskey fog.

But she was definitely real. And unquestionably different. Indeed, she was like no woman he'd ever encountered before. And those differences were setting his teeth on edge. And for all the wrong reasons too. Kitty didn't chatter incessantly. She didn't ask questions.

She didn't flirt with him, need to constantly go to the bathroom, or complain about the lack of food in his trail bag.

In short, she didn't ask for much, and didn't expect much either. It seemed that if he wasn't molesting her, she reckoned her life was good.

He found her attitude to be fairly disturbing.

After all, from the time he'd set out on his own, just about everyone and their brother had wanted something from him. Most hadn't been afraid to use coercion, pain, or blackmail to make sure they got it, either. After a time, he'd learned not to take things personally. It was just how things were. People wanted what they wanted and were willing to do whatever it took to get it. He certainly had done that a time or two.

In contrast, Kitty's lack of motivation in that direction was slowly driving him crazy. At least, she had last night.

After riding all night, he'd picked an abandoned shack for them to sleep in. He'd stood at the entrance, waiting for her to complain. She didn't.

When they'd entered and the dank smell of mold and mildew and the previous occupants infused the air, he waited for her to wrinkle her nose. She said nothing.

Instead, after cautiously looking his way, she'd stood stock-still while he spread out the dirt and attempted to smooth it. When he lay on the ground, offering no excuses for the hard surface, she lay down beside him without even a moment's hesitation. In fact, the only clue that she was at all at odds with the situation was that her body was tense. At the ready.

And that's when he'd realized that she'd expected him to hurt her. Even though he definitely remembered telling her that he wouldn't.

She'd looked surprised as all get out when she'd woken up beside him, obviously having gotten more sleep than she was accustomed to.

Which made him mad. And because he wasn't all that good of a man, he'd snapped at her. "What has your life been like, girl?"

Instead of crying, she'd simply stared right back. "How do you think it's been, Mr. Proffitt? You know why I found you."

Her no-nonsense way of speaking embarrassed him mightily. "I'm talking 'bout other things."

Crossing her arms over her chest, she lifted her chin. "Such as?"

"What happened to your ma?"

"She took off during the war."

"How old?" She flinched, and he felt bad about that, but he had to know.

"Six."

Though he'd seen more bad than most, he still had been struck cold. "She left you with that poor example of a man?"

"You know the answer already, don't you think?"

Her voice was as empty of emotion as his was when he was about to make a kill. He'd been tempted to imagine she was devoid of emotion, until her eyes betrayed her. Or maybe it was like looking into his mirror image. Hopelessness emanated from her.

And it broke his heart just a little. Even he hadn't been so worn down at her age.

Finally, he answered. "I know the answer . . . but I still have to say that I think it's a crying shame."

She bit her bottom lip and looked away.

"Kitty, what made you come up to me? What finally happened that made you think you'd had enough?"

With a sigh, she replied, "It wasn't what had happened to me. The other night was no worse than any other."

"Then what?"

"It was your hands."

He spread out all ten fingers in front of himself and examined them. "What did you see?"

"Your hands are clean. Your nails are short. My stepfather's hands are never that way. When he touches me, he makes me feel dirty. Marked." Looking away again, she added, "Sometimes I was sure I'd never be clean again."

He swallowed as what she was saying hit him hard. She hadn't hoped for her life to be better with him. She'd simply hoped it wouldn't be so bad. "You thought my hands would be cleaner when they touched you."

"Yes." She looked at him steadily then got to her feet. Without a lick of modesty, she straightened her dress, attempting to shake out some of the wrinkles as she did so. Of course, it was a hopeless task. Only a Chinese launderer was going to be able to make that dress clean again, though it would be easier to throw it out and get something fresh.

"I'm not going to touch you," he said.

"Because you think I'm ugly?"

"You're pretty, Kitty," he replied, not because it was true, but because it was how she could be one day. "I'm not going to touch you because that's not who I am." As his words echoed in their ratty enclosure, he had the grace to be embarrassed. Sure, he'd killed and cajoled and maimed people. He'd even accept money for it. But raping and pillaging? He hadn't crossed that line—at least not yet.

"I'm bad, but that's not all I am," he said finally. "All I aim to do is get you somewhere better than you've been, that's all. Once I do, I'm going to leave you and let you live your life."

Kitty stepped forward and spoke in that frank, no-nonsense way he was beginning to associate with her. "Mr. Proffitt, we may be sleeping on a dirt floor and freezing our tails off, but I can assure you that this is already better. It's already much better." She turned away then and started brushing out her hair.

For a moment he was tempted to ask her what had been done to her. What, exactly, she'd endured. Then he would have a reason to backtrack and kill her stepfather. Maybe, just once, he'd be thankful for his ability to kill.

But he didn't ask a thing. Her problems weren't his business. Besides, no one liked to discuss their bad stuff. And everyone had it. Everyone.

Feeling too close to her, too tempted to bridge the gap between them—and they had no business bridging things—he stood and straightened. There was nowhere to go, but he thought he'd at least give her some space.

But just before he moved away, to give them both more space, more privacy, though there really wasn't any to be had, he heard the rest of what she had to say. "Sometimes, in the middle of the night, I get to thinking that I'm not all bad either. Do you think that's okay?"

After a moment's reflection, he replied, "I think that's the truth. God gives every one of us gifts. All a person has to do is use them."

"And you think I have some of those gifts?"

"I know you do."

She looked at him steadily, truly looking like she was weighing the pros and cons of his words, then shrugged. "I can't think of anything I have that's still decent. I'm afraid your God's going to take one look at me when I show up in heaven and point me someplace else."

His heart clenched. For a moment, he paused. It took everything he had not to walk those three paces, turn her in his arms, and hold her close. Just to give her comfort. As a brother would. As a father would hold a child.

But she didn't know what a comforting touch was like. So he strode away, choosing to concentrate on what an unexpected difficulty she was in his life. That was easier than recalling that it had been a very long time since he'd felt the quiet comfort of another person's arms.

"Mr. McMillan?" Jamilyn said into the middle of his back.

Her hands were resting lightly on his waist as the surprisingly steady gelding continued his journey underneath them.

But though her touch was familiar, her use of his name still grated like gravel on bare feet. "My name is Will. I told you, honey, my name is Will."

She didn't listen, or else she was just as stubborn as he'd been guessing she was.

"Mr. McMillan?" she said again, leaning closer to his back. So much so that if Will closed his eyes he was sure he could feel her warm breath coaxing its way through all the layers of his clothes.

"Hmm?"

"Well, I hate to ask you this, but why did you take me off the train?" Will felt himself stiffen, and he felt her body notice it. "Forgive me," she said quickly, her voice a little louder, a little farther away. "Forget I asked. It's none of my business."

Though he ached not to tell her anything that was in his mind, he knew that wasn't right. She deserved to know.

Of course, he'd thought his reasons would have been evident. So, because it was her business, and it was painfully obvious too, he said, "You were going to be killed. Or, uh, worse."

"Oh, I know that. I knew from the moment Kent grabbed my upper arm and placed that gun to my head that I was either going to be injured, violated, or flat-out killed. I didn't expect to survive. Not really."

"I wasn't going to let that happen."

"That's what I mean. What I'm asking is, why did you get involved? You're going to get in trouble for taking me, aren't you?"

He was going to get killed—after a long and personal relationship with Scout Proffitt's knife. Or, more likely, perhaps a bullet from Scout's infamous pearl-handled Colt.

"Mr. McMillan?"

Her questions—mixed with her formality—were trying his patience. "Jamie, why the heck won't you call me by my first name?"

"I can't. I know you want me to, but I can't do that. I'm sorry, but I just can't."

He closed his eyes briefly, remembering again that to her, he was an outlaw.

"So, will you get in trouble?"

"Yes." He looked out over the plains, toward the west, and gazeded at the majestic mountain chain sprouting up out of the snow in the far distance. The land looked so clean and pristine. With some surprise, he realized any number of men who he'd served with were probably only a day's ride from where they were.

For a moment he imagined taking Jamie to one of their homes. Instinctively, he knew most of them would welcome her with smiles and open arms. Even though he hadn't seen any of them in years—and certainly none of them since he'd taken up undercover work—that was the kind of bond they had. They'd fought side by side and had starved together. They'd buried good men in their company, and women and children who'd gotten lost in the war's path. They were full of an immense ability for forgiveness.

But after the first moments of reuniting, they would realize what he'd become, or at least what they'd thought he'd become. A man like Major Merritt probably wouldn't be feeling as welcoming then. No, he would lay those cool gray eyes of his over Will, over Jamie, and assume the worst.

And because he was unable to remove his alias, he would have to let Merritt believe that.

Jamie shifted behind him. Her hands at his waist relaxed a bit. Though he couldn't see her, he knew she was disappointed and frustrated by his lack of conversation. Feeling like the words were being pushed out of him by someone else, he spoke. "Jamie, you needed to be saved . . . and I was ready to leave. You were a good excuse."

"Ready to leave the Walton Gang?"

He couldn't help smiling as he heard the complete surprise in her tone. "Yep."

"Why?"

Why? Well, the right answer was to tell her that he'd never really been a robber or a true member of the gang. That he now had more than enough evidence to testify against James Walton and make sure he was hanged.

But their future was still too uncertain for complete honesty.

Or maybe honesty had been vacant from his life for so long that he hardly remembered what it felt like.

"I wasn't born robbing trains, you know. I served honorably in the war."

"And then we lost."

Her voice sounded bittersweet, as if it were filled with things that might have happened if fate had intended them to be different. "And then we did," he agreed. The simple explanation told nothing, yet summed up just about everything, too.

"What did you do in the war?"

For a moment he was tempted to dodge the question. Though he knew of some men who never failed to bring up stories about those hard, lean years, he'd never been one of them. But perhaps she'd seen enough bad in her life not to be surprised that his memories were full of bad things, too. "At first, I was what any man was—nothing. Just a greenhorn soldier. But later, I was an officer. I was good at leading people. I became a captain. In Texas."

"That was your rank. What did you do?"

"What do you think? I killed Yankees," he blurted. "Tried to, anyway." Before she could blast him again with her need for more information, he continued. "I rode with John Merritt. He was bear of a man. Ended up marrying a woman real near here. We were stationed in Texas. Fought a lot near Galveston and on the Louisiana border." Even as he named the places, he felt the blistering ache of remembrance. Their time in Galveston had been especially filled with pain.

"I guess you saw a lot of action?"

"Action? You mean fighting?" Was that what it was called nowadays? "We saw a lot of Yankees wanting to put us in our place. We did our best not to make things too easy on them."

"Did you have a horse?"

Will wondered if she really cared or just liked him to be talking so they wouldn't be alone with the silence. "I did. She was a beauty. Black. And as brave as any man I've known."

"Perhaps that gave you some comfort?"

Who asked such things? No one in his life cared about sweet things like comfort and feelings. But obviously Jamie had learned those things somewhere. He wasn't even sure how to respond to it. There had been too few females in his life. And most of the ones he'd encountered weren't fit for company. "I liked the horse," he said shortly.

Again, like she was tethered to him, he felt her disappointment.

And his respect for her continued to grow. Jamie was lovely, and she had a spirit and a fire that was admirable.

And he thought about who he was taking her to—to a man who'd dodged battles and who communicated through old women. "Why would a woman like you be willing to marry a man you haven't seen? Don't you reckon you deserve better?"

"Because this woman wants to make even a few dreams happen—even if what happens isn't quite as sweet as the dreams."

"And those dreams involve marriage?"

"Marriage and children. I want to raise a family." Her voice turning wistful, she continued, "One day, I want to do something of worth. More than simply surviving. Somehow that doesn't seem enough anymore."

Her words struck a chord with him. For the last ten years, surviving had been more than enough. It had been all he'd asked for. But now, he figured she had a point. Perhaps it would be better to have other goals than simply living. "Maybe one day I'll have another dream too."

"You don't have one now?"

"Other than seeing you safely to Kansas City? No. But that's enough. The journey's going to be hard enough, I reckon."

She sighed against him. As she did so, he felt her soft curves against his spine. He imagined what it would be like to be the man who had the right to hold her for real.

Imagined what that fool in Kansas was going to do with a woman like Jamie. Did he even realize how lucky he was? To have a woman who wasn't afraid? Who was willing to ride across the plains with a known outlaw in order to get to him?

He doubted it. Few men were aware of the extent a woman would go to protect what was right.

As she leaned closer and her body loosened up even more, Will realized she was falling asleep. She was trusting him enough to rest.

That made him feel good. Which, of course, made him feel all twisted inside.

After all, she was promised to another, was afraid of him, and only looked at him as something to endure.

He was slowly falling in love. Which was a terrible thing, considering he'd most likely be dead very soon.

20

"Rider coming," Will stated. Just as calmly as if he were commenting on the weather.

Jamie started, almost losing her balance. Immediately, his hand snaked out behind him, grasping her thigh hard. His touch made her jump.

"Easy now," he said, his voice deeper and slightly more raspy than usual. "Settle yourself. I can't help you if you go falling off the horse."

Even though she didn't think she had any more fortitude inside of her, she did her best to pull herself together. "I'm not going to fall off the horse. I'm made of sterner stuff than you give me credit for, Will."

"Listen to you."

"What?"

"Finally, you called me Will. I have to tell you I never thought I'd hear my first name on your lips."

His voice had a smile to it. "Well . . . never's a long time," she quipped.

"So they say."

She gazed out into the distance. At first, she didn't see anything, but then, flickering in and out of the shadows, filtering in, mixing with the dark shadows of the coming night, she saw a faint cloud of dust. Little by little, the information registered. "That's more than one horse."

"I believe so. At least two riders. Maybe three."

"Do you think we'll have to stop?"

"Most likely. I don't see how we won't."

Jamie noticed his voice didn't have a bit of fear in it, more likely a hint of resolve. Of inevitability. As though he knew what was in store for them couldn't be stopped. "Do you think it's someone from the train?"

"No. If it was someone from the gang, they'd be closing in faster. Mr. Walton doesn't like his men to lollygag much. I have a feeling those men are trying to figure out who I am."

That caught her by surprise. "You?"

"Doubt they realize there's a woman sitting behind me." He paused, then his voice grew darker. "Don't take this the wrong way, ma'am, but I sure wish you weren't here right now."

Since she felt the same way, she didn't mind him saying that in the slightest. "What are we going to do?"

"There is no 'we,' Jamie. You are going to sit as quietly as you can while I do the talking."

"Will—"

He just kept talking as if she hadn't said a thing. "Then, you are going to do your best to act like you're not here."

Jamie knew even in her dreams she was never going to forget this day. "I don't know how to do that."

"Then you better figure it out—and soon." His voice hardened. "I don't want you doing anything to attract their notice, do you hear me? Don't speak, and for God's sakes, don't leave my side."

His warning created a new knot of fear inside her. She felt like a fool for even trying to act with bravado. Once again, she was at everyone's mercy. And so far the only man she trusted was over six-feet tall, had muscles on top of muscles, and the type of clear blue eyes that looked like they never warmed up—not even in the middle of July.

"I'll try to do my best."

"Try isn't good enough."

"I will?"

He slowed their horse, clearing his throat impatiently as he did so. "Listen. I know you don't trust me, but you're going to have to believe that those men are probably up to no good. You're going to be safer with me. You'll be safer with me than with just about anyone else on this earth right now."

Her eyes widened; she couldn't help it. Especially since she was feeling the same way. How had that happened? How had she begun to trust her captor so much?

But, as she was coming to learn, Will McMillan didn't leave anything up to doubt. "Do you understand? I don't want to have to worry that you're going to start acting foolish."

She peeked around him. What had been once a cloud of dust was now three shadows. Three large shadows. Three large men. Capable of doing just about anything they wanted.

As her mind spun, her mouth went dry.

Will cursed under his breath. "Jamie?" His voice hardened and became even more gravelly. "Jamie, answer me. What do you need me to explain?"

"Nothing."

"Sure?"

"I understand what you're saying. I promise, I do." She almost snapped right back at him. But then she realized he wasn't being sarcastic. He was dead serious. He was scared for her. And afraid her innocence—and maybe even her stupidity—was going to get her killed. Get *them* killed. "I won't do anything, Will. I'll stay quiet."

His shoulders relaxed. He rolled them for a second before shifting and repositioning his pistols.

The three shadows became men, each one looking more dangerous than the next.

21

*W*ill called himself ten times the fool. Of course, they'd be likely to meet up with all sorts of renegades. He should've been more prepared. As they kept closing the distance between themselves and the approaching riders, Will said a little prayer.

Oh, not for him, that would be selfish. And hopeless anyway. God wasn't going to stick His neck out for Will McMillan anytime soon. He certainly didn't deserve that.

But he did pray for Jamie. Prayed that he'd be strong enough to keep her safe. And that maybe—just maybe—he wasn't going to have to kill three men in front of her in order to do it.

As the men approached, he felt Jamie shift closer to him. He was thankful for that, especially when the one on the left held up a hand.

A greeting? Warning? He wasn't sure. Will slowed the horse and lifted one arm as well.

Fifty feet separated them now. Forty. The faceless men became individuals, each about his age. One wore the remnants of a Confederate officer's jacket—a sure sign that the men were drifters.

His mouth went dry.

At about twenty feet, he pulled up the reins. The gelding stopped then scratched at the snow and brush underneath them impatiently. Behind him, Jamie said nothing. Shoot, he couldn't even hear her breathing.

What little he knew about women made him wish he could turn around and check on her. Maybe she'd gone and fainted?

But then there was no time.

"Afternoon," one of the riders—the one on the left called out.

"Howdy." Will shifted. Though his body tensed, he took care to keep his voice even and steady.

"Where are you headed?"

"Don't see that's any of your business."

The middle man squinted. "Don't recognize you none. You with an outfit?"

Quickly, Will weighed his choices. Letting them know he was with the Walton Gang would immediately garner respect and fear. Everyone knew better than to mess with them. And drifters like these? They'd step aside in a heartbeat.

Probably.

If he told them the absolute truth, that he was a U.S. Marshal, he'd risk dealing with Jamie's incredulousness, and perhaps he'd even lose what little trust she'd placed in him. Then he'd risk losing her and giving away his location.

But telling them he was alone bothered him even more. Men who rode alone were either fools or weaklings. And men who traveled alone with a woman—well they deserved everything they had coming to them; there was no doubt about that.

"Marshals," he finally said.

Pure dismay crossed the three men's faces as behind him Jamie stiffened.

Just as he'd been worried about. Time to talk fast.

"I'm bringing the woman to our main headquarters in St. Louis."

"Heading all the way out to St. Louie? Seems to me you're traveling a little out of the way."

Will forced himself to relax. "That's always the case, ain't it? Nothing's easy." He turned the tables. "Where are you three headed?"

"Nowhere in particular." The blond with the scar on his cheek came closer. "Mister, you mind showing us your star?"

"Why?"

"Not that we'd ever accuse you of lying or nothing, but you'd be surprised about the number of men who make up things out here in the middle of nowhere." Sidling closer, he glanced at Jamie. A slow smile appeared. "Lookit you, sugar. Ain't you a sight for sore eyes."

Will held his breath, wondering how she was going to react.

All she did was shrink closer to him. Perhaps she trusted him more than the drifter.

The scar burned bright on the man's cheek. "Shy? Ain't you sweet. This here your man?"

One beat fell. Two. "Yes," she said softly.

Will cocked his Colt. "I'd be obliged if you took two steps back."

"You afraid of me?"

"I need to get out my badge. Can't do it with you so close. Might spook the horse."

Obligingly, the man moved his horse a few steps backward. However, his two buddies pulled out their six-shooters as Will opened his duster.

Jamie shivered. A tiny gasp escaped her lips, bringing a smile to the blond's eyes.

Methodically, Will opened up his duster, opening the coat wide enough so the three men would have no question as to what he was doing. Then, he reached into the lining, ripped apart a seam, and got out the star. Palming it, he held it out for inspection.

The blond edged closer. "Who are you, exactly?"

"I am Will McMillan. I'm a U.S. Marshal under Sam Edison. And you are?"

The talkative blond stared at the star. Stared at Will. "How come it was hidden like that?"

"It's been my experience that not everyone wants to deal with a Marshal."

"Killing a Marshal is a hanging offense."

"Killing anyone is," he said dryly, though he understood what the man was saying. Gunning down a U.S. Marshal in cold blood was practically an invitation to get strung up from the nearest tree. It was definitely a guarantee that the murderer would be hunted for the rest of his days.

Will sat patiently, waiting. He knew without a doubt he could hit at least two of them before they could get in a shot. But it was that third one that worried him. If he couldn't place the bullet on target the first time, he could be leaving Jamie at their mercy. That would be a shame.

Actually, it would be far better to kill her himself than to leave her at their mercy. Drifters could be merciless with a woman, especially a woman of worth like Jamie.

Keeping his eyes fastened on the men, he sat. Waiting. On edge.

"We'll be leaving you to it, then," the leader said. "Ma'am," he continued, tipping his hat.

Will said nothing as they moved away and then picked up speed. He merely motioned the horse forward, keeping it at a slow and steady pace.

Only when the men were out of sight and he couldn't spy an inkling of more company did he dare to pull up the horse next to a trio of pines.

His body feeling stiff, he dismounted before turning to assist Jamie. "I don't mind telling you that I'm in no hurry to go through that again," he said with a smile.

Then he noticed Jamie was shivering. Her eyes were watering. No, not watering, crying. She was crying for all she was worth.

Though she still hadn't said a word to him, the look she gave him told him everything he needed to know. He opened his arms and drew her into an embrace.

She practically collapsed against him, holding on to his arms like he was her lifeline to heaven.

He raised a hand tentatively. Unsure where to put his hands, unsure what touch she'd accept from him, he finally stopped thinking.

With a sigh, he wrapped his arms around her and held her close. "It's all right," he murmured. "You're okay. Nothing happened."

"I . . . I was so afraid," she cried.

"I know."

"Those men," she gasped. "I was so, so sure . . ." Her voice drifted off as the shock of what had almost happened took ahold of her hard.

He closed his eyes and felt her pain. "I know."

"Do you?"

He cuddled her closer even though he had no right. Pressed his lips against her brow even though he shouldn't. And when she lifted her head and looked at him with those eyes, those lovely caramel-colored eyes that looked like they had the world trapped inside them, he did what he'd wanted to do for some time.

He pressed his lips over hers and gently kissed her. Right there. In the middle of the plains.

When he raised his head, he stared at her, seeking to memorize the moment and keep it close to his heart. After all, he had so very few nice memories.

The vision he saw in front of him was worth everything. Jamilyn's lips, so beautifully formed, so incredibly soft, parted.

His breath caught.

Looking up at him, she blinked.

He steeled himself for her tears. For her to berate him for his lies. For her to turn away in shame. But instead, wonder of wonders, she raised her chin, lifted a hand and pressed it against his shoulder, and kissed him again.

The ache in his heart was almost crippling. The longing he felt for her touch was fierce, and strong, and so very sweet. But instead of running away from the feeling, he wrapped his hands around her and tasted her lips again.

And again.

And when he finally lifted his head, breathing hard and almost out of breath, he knew he'd never been more scared in his entire life.

Because right then, at that very moment, he wanted nothing more than to hold her close and never let her go.

22

$\mathcal{H}$is lips were soft. That's the first thing that crossed Jamie's mind when she felt his mouth brush against hers. His lips were dry and firm but surprisingly gentle.

No, the kiss wasn't punishing; the kiss wasn't rough. It wasn't anything she would have imagined it being.

Instead, his touch was featherlight and twice as kind. So much so, that she found herself melting just a little. Just enough to drop her guard a very small bit and let her emotions take over. To simply feel.

Which, of course, was a dangerous thing.

For a moment she was tempted to move closer to him. Of course, if she did that, she'd smell more of his pure male scent. She'd feel more of his warmth and get another dose of that curious feeling of comfort she got whenever she was near him.

And though she didn't have much experience with kissing, suddenly Jamie knew what was going to happen next. He'd hold her close. She'd curve her hands around his neck, close her eyes, and hope for one more very sweet, very gentle kiss.

She'd be transported to somewhere better than she'd ever been before and start believing in things that she knew didn't exist. Things like fairy tales and happy endings.

When she felt Will's hand graze her waist and tighten, she slipped her hands up his chest. Felt those hard muscles.

And then pushed. Hard. He let her go instantly.

Now eight mere inches separated the two of them. Her breath came out in a rush and she felt like she'd just run for miles. As she found herself glancing at his lips, she closed her eyes and blinked.

Then couldn't help herself and stared at this stranger of a man once again. Oh, what in the world had she just done? It seemed that she hardly knew herself anymore.

To her surprise, he didn't look angry or even all that offended by her push. Looking at her with those unwavering cool blue eyes, his mouth slid into a straight, tight line. "Jamilyn, are you okay?"

His voice was gravelly. More gravelly than she'd heard it before. And still, his gaze hadn't eased. If anything, he was looking at her with even more concentration, just like he was attempting to memorize every freckle on her face.

"I don't know if I'm okay or not."

"I'm sorry if I frightened you. I didn't mean for that to happen."

Instinctively, she knew that. And no matter how alone and confused she felt, she wasn't ready to put all the blame on his shoulders for their kiss. She'd wanted that kiss.

She'd wanted to feel close to someone, even if it had been just for a minute.

"You didn't frighten me. Your kiss didn't frighten me at all."

Something new flared in his eyes, and for the first time in their acquaintance, his gaze turned warm.

Then she had to ask the obvious. "Are you really a U.S. Marshal and not a member of the Walton Gang?"

"Yes."

"Why? What?" She sputtered on her questions, not knowing what to ask. Not trusting how she felt.

"I've been pretending for almost two years to be something I wasn't." Taking off his hat, he tossed it to the ground and rubbed a hand through his hair. "I've been with the Walton Gang for so long that sometimes I forget that everything I've been doing has been a lie."

His matter-of-fact attitude was disconcerting. So was the fact that he didn't look the least bit contrite. "Why didn't you tell me?" she blurted, letting her anger and frustrations come alive.

In a blink, all the warmth that she thought she'd spied became absent again. "Because too much was at stake. If you'd even hinted that you thought I was only playing a role, your life would have been in more danger than it was."

She couldn't imagine that things could have been worse. "I doubt that."

"You shouldn't. You should take every word I'm saying and treat it as gospel." His voice hardened and a hand shot out and gripped her arm. "Listen to me. If James Walton even guessed that I wasn't who I said I was, he would hunt you down."

"Why me? I'm the innocent one. I was taken hostage, remember?" With a shake, she pulled her arm from his grip. Though his grip hadn't been painful, she was finding his touch to be horrible. Oh, but she was horrified to think that she'd ever trusted him.

When her arm was free, he looked at his hand before lifting his eyes. Seconds passed as they stared at each other.

She began to wonder if he was ever going to answer her question.

The muscle in his jaw worked.

Finally he sighed. "Why you? Why you, Jamilyn Ellis? Because he and every person on that train had to have known one thing for certain: that there was one surefire way to get me to talk, to get me to do anything."

"And what is that?" she asked, letting the sarcasm in her voice fall forward. She was tired of being lied to, tired of being scared and afraid.

But most of all, she was tired of feeling guilty for her feelings.

Will closed his eyes. When he opened them, his expression was completely blank. His eyes looking like they were soulless. "I'm going to take you to my boss's office in St. Louis," he murmured. "Once you get there, you're going to feel safer. I promise you that."

She stepped forward. "Oh, no you don't. You're going to be honest with me. For once. Will McMillan, why would James Walton want to hurt me in order to hurt you?"

"Because it's obvious to just about everyone on this earth that I've begun to care for you," he spit out, looking just about as mad about it as a man could look. "That's why." He held up one impatient hand, paired it with a glare, and continued, his voice even more raspy than usual. "Because, Jamie, any man with two eyes is going to know that there is just about nothing I wouldn't do to see you safe and happy. Even if it means getting hurt. Even if it means selling my soul. Again."

Jamie stared at him, stunned. Had anyone ever felt like that about her? Maybe her parents? She couldn't remember things between them very clearly, not since the war had taken away her father's mind and her mother's soul.

But still . . . it sure didn't seem likely.

He laughed, the sound self-deprecating. "Yeah, I figured you'd be real pleased to hear that. I'm not what any woman would call a catch."

And with that, he turned away, leaving her staring and out of breath and without of a single word available in her mind.

It seemed Will McMillan had affected her more than either had imagined.

And neither of them had any idea of what to do about it.

23

$\mathcal{I}$t hadn't taken Scout long to figure out that he'd made a giant mistake when he'd elected to save Kitty from herself. That big revelation had happened sometime during the middle of their first night together. He'd heard a furtive shifting, had opened one eye and felt for his gun, and then realized the girl had gotten up on her feet and was staring out the window.

She'd must have been as aware of him as he'd been of her, because she'd turned and looked directly at him. Obviously, she'd been ready for him to yell at her.

Or maybe something worse.

He'd ended up softening his voice and had attempted to calm her down.

Neither were things he'd had much experience with.

Now, here they were, heading toward nowhere because he was supposed to be looking for Will McMillan and a woman he hoped he would never see again.

Time was running out. He needed to do something—and soon. One didn't just leave James Walton hanging.

Especially not if you were Scout Proffitt.

"Mr. Proffitt?" Kitty asked that evening as they were camped out in front of a pitiful excuse for a fire, trying to get warm and not having all that much success.

"What?"

"Do you ever recall making the wrong choice?" she asked, her voice high-pitched and eager.

"I don't know what you're talkin' about."

"Really?" She leveled her gaze on him. "You never had a choice between two evils and you chose the wrong one?"

Instead of examining his past—which he had no intention of ever doing—he countered with a question of his own. "If there're two evils, it's not a matter of making the right choice. Right? They're both wrong."

"No." She tilted her head to one side, looking impossibly young. "Once, I had a choice between lying or stealing. Both were wrong, but I had to choose one."

"And why was that?" Against his will, he leaned forward a bit. Just in case he was really interested.

"Well, my sister and me had no food and she was hungry. So I went to the mercantile and pretended I was shopping. Then, when no one was looking, I stole some eggs."

Kitty might as well have been talking in Portuguese. "Eggs?"

"Melissa liked eggs something awful."

"Well, don't keep me in suspense, girl. What happened? You get caught?"

"Nope."

"So you cooked her up some eggs?"

"No." She looked at her fingernails. "I was in such a hurry to get out of there and get on home that I broke two of them on the way back."

Imagining how she must have felt, a wide variety of expletives came to mind. Mindful of her age, he tempered his reaction. "Shoot."

She nodded. "Turned out, it didn't matter anyway."

"And why was that?"

"'Cause Melissa was dead."

The stark news hit him like a wet slap. Unable to stop himself this time, he cursed. When Kitty flinched, he felt his cheeks heat and apologized. "Sorry."

"Oh, it's fine." She chewed on her bottom lip for a second. "I mean, don't worry about it. Ain't nothing I haven't heard before."

"Why did you tell me that story?" Personally, he'd found it more than a little disconcerting. After all, he hadn't given her any sign that he wanted to hear about her bad stuff.

'Cause he sure wasn't going to start sharing his regrets.

"I only meant to tell you in case, you know, you were regretting taking me on."

"I don't follow."

"I just mean . . ." she shrugged weakly. "I think I was one of your bad ideas. And if I was, well, I don't want ya to feel obligated to stay with me."

"What? You think I'm just gonna up and leave you somewhere?" He looked around at their makeshift camp in the middle of nowhere. "Here?"

"Maybe. I mean, you're Scout Proffitt. You've probably got a lot of other things to do than help me out."

"What do you think I do all day? Just sit around and shoot people?"

"The newspapers make it sound like that's all you do." She eyed him warily. "They make it sound like it keeps you real busy."

"I do other things besides commit murder." Because she was looking at him with such interest, he tried to think of something to tell her that was even halfway true. He was so tired of lying. "I eat."

The minutes passed between them, and Kitty stared at his face. He felt like a fool again. That's right. He killed and ate. What a prize he was.

And then, to his surprise, she chuckled. "Oh, Mr. Proffitt. You make me laugh; you surely do."

Before he knew it, Scout started to smile, not even sure why he was doing so. Inside of him, a certain warmth filtered, mending lesions he hadn't even known existed.

Making him feel almost human. Almost decent.

"We should finish setting up camp," he said.

"You're going to keep me a little longer?"

"Yep. Don't fret, Kitty. Maybe I even rest sometimes too."

"Everyone needs to rest sometimes, don'tcha think?"

He didn't know. All he did know was that he was more content than he could ever remember being in his whole life.

And contentment was surely not something he'd ever had much experience with. Taking a chance, he tried it on for size.

To his surprise, it almost felt good.

�❧

After four days of traveling together, Jamie found she and Will had settled into a routine of sorts. First thing in the morning, Will would bank their fire and if possible scout the premises. Once, they'd camped right next to a creek, which had allowed Jamie to wash her hands and face.

While Will did those things, it was Jamie's job to gather their things together and see to the horse. She would never come close to being as efficient as Will was, but she liked to think that her efforts weren't completely hindering him.

And though he hadn't come close to complimenting her, she'd caught a flash of amusement in his eyes every now and then like she'd maybe been able to surprise him.

Jamie certainly hoped she had, because she sure was finding herself shocked by Will. Ever since he'd told her the truth about his identity, she'd gone between feeling profound relief and feeling anger. None of it made sense.

She was still struggling with the fact that she didn't feel all that much better in the company of Will McMillan, U.S. Marshal, than she did with Will McMillan, notorious outlaw.

In fact, if she were being completely honest with herself, she would have to say that she was having a bit of trouble coming to terms with the idea that Will was an expert in subterfuge. She'd been somewhat relieved to think that he was no more or no less than what he was.

Just as she.

"Jamie, is the horse ready to go?" Will asked as he approached, rifle in his hand.

"I believe so."

His eyes smiled. "I walked over to the top of that crest and spied a town. Looks like we're near civilization after all."

"What does that mean?" Oh, please don't let it mean that they were going to part ways already.

"It means maybe we'll get lucky and find a room tonight."

"But not a Marshal's office?"

He took a long look at her before shaking his head. "I'm sorry, no. I've been so entrenched in the gang, the only man I report to is in St. Louis."

"And that's a ways away."

"It is. But don't fret. I won't harm you."

He said that all the time. As if being harmed was the worst thing that could happen to her.

No, the worst thing would be to be abandoned. Again.

24

*W*ill knew the room he'd found for them was nothing special. Actually, it was barely a step above a boarding house. But he'd stayed there from time to time and knew the owner was a circumspect man. Calvin Hollis wasn't going to talk to anyone about who was staying there. Ever.

His business depended on it.

With Jamie safely tucked in the room, Will paused outside the manager's office. Once again, he weighed his choices back and forth. It was obvious that he needed help, and it was obvious that he had few people to ask.

He needed the strength and support of men he could trust. More important, Jamie did. No way was he going to save her from the Walton Gang just to have her get injured or ravished at the hands of some renegade.

It was time to trust the man a little more, even though doing so was likely going to be the biggest mistake of his life.

But it seemed he had no choice. He needed an ally, and that meant he needed to contact his boss. Making the decision, he rapped on the man's door.

It flew open almost immediately. "Yeah?"

Will noticed the man looked to be nursing a glass of bourbon, and had been for some time. "You sober?"

"Sober enough." Staring at Will curiously, he said, "Need anything?" He asked surely out of habit and not because he actually intended to do anything for Will or make any changes.

Will wouldn't have expected anything less. Calvin Hollis wasn't known for hospitality; he was known for discretion. It usually worked out well for most of the inn's guests. People stayed there not because they wanted service but because they wanted to be left alone.

"Hollis, I need to send a telegram."

"When?"

"Soon. Now."

Calvin's eyes narrowed. "You know I don't have no telegraph machine in here. But I can show you where the office is. If you need me to," he added grudgingly.

Will almost smiled. He did so enjoy the innkeeper's lazy nature. "I can't be seen. I need you to go there for me."

Calvin stared at him hard, then threw the last of the bourbon down his throat. "I don't believe in doing favors."

"I know." Rolling off a few bills, he set them on the counter. "However, I also know that you like to eat." He paused. "And drink. I can make it worth your while."

Calvin eyed the bills for a good long time before flickering his gaze back to Will. Out of habit, he picked up the glass, then stared at it in confusion when he saw it was empty.

He stared at the bills again. "Just the telegram?"

Will nodded.

"All right. Tell me what you need."

Looking around, Will grabbed a pen and an envelope and plainly printed his message. Then, he handed it over.

Calvin gripped it hard and read it aloud. "Mission broken. Stop. Meeting requested. Stop. Dodge City. Stop." Raising his eyes to Will's, he said, "This it?"

"Yes."

"We're not going to be making a habit of this, are we?"

"No."

"If you don't hear from me, it went off without a hitch."

"I'm paying you enough for there to be no problems," Will said.

Calvin Hollis grabbed his hat, stuffed it on his head, and left without looking back.

That was just fine with Will. He didn't need the man's companionship, just his word.

Once he saw that Hollis was definitely walking toward the telegraph office, Will left and headed back to the room. Knocking softly twice—his code for Jamie—he rolled back on his heels and waited.

But she didn't open the door.

A slow band of worry started to line his stomach and he cursed himself. He rapped the door again. Twice.

Listened for some kind of response. Listened for her footsteps. Nothing.

After looking right and left, and seeing the coast was clear, he leaned closer to the old wooden door. "Jamie? Open up."

Nothing.

Worry and doubt hit him hard. Had she skipped off while he was downstairs? Or worse, had someone taken her?

A thousand scenarios hit him hard. Perhaps Kent or Scout had been following them and he'd been too focused on Jamie's needs to notice.

Maybe she was in the room, bleeding. Hurt. Dead.

He knocked again a little louder, cursing himself. Why hadn't he brought the key with him?

He tried the door handle, jiggling it a few times on the off chance that the lock was so pitiful he could force it open. Of course, he had no luck. If there was one thing Calvin Hollis did well besides keep a secret, it was invest in decent locks.

"Jamie?" he called out again, hating the idea that anyone nearby could hear her name but feeling like he had no choice. "Jamilyn?"

Breaking the door down wasn't an option. Going downstairs and grabbing the key from Hollis was the only choice. Of course, that meant that Hollis would be coming upstairs too. No way was that man going to trust any guest in the place with the master keys.

After halfheartedly rapping on the door one last time, he was just about to pivot and turn when he heard a shuffling on the other side. Then heard the lock slide to the right and saw the door handle turn.

He pulled out his Colt. Cocked it and waited.

The door opened.

There was Jamie, hair down, skin pale, and sporting a glassy sheen in her eyes. "Will?" she asked. "Sorry, I didn't hear you. I was asleep."

He ushered her in, his irritation sliding back quickly. Well, she had to be exhausted. "It's okay. I was just worried." Talk about an understatement!

"I don't know what happened." She shook her head and winced. "I had the most horrible headache. Then I got so sleepy . . ." her voice drifted off.

"I know you're tired. Why don't you go lie down again?"

She stepped forward, then stumbled. He reached for her, wrapping a hand around her shoulders to steady her. Along the way, his knuckles brushed her cheek.

And then he stilled.

Things had just gone from bad to much, much worse.

25

$\mathcal{T}$here were a lot of things Scout Proffitt didn't believe in. He didn't believe in privilege, entitlement, or inheritance. By his way of thinking, nothing that you didn't have to sweat, bleed, or fight over was worth a plumb nickel.

He didn't believe in being tired, and he didn't believe in being lazy. Scout had never met a lazy man he respected, and it stood to reason his opinion wasn't going to change anytime soon. Actually, he took real care to distance himself from men who shied away from breaking a sweat.

Luckily, that wasn't a difficult thing to do. There were a lot of people who didn't mind working really hard at killing and thieving.

But most of all, Scout didn't believe in fate. Too many bad things had happened in his life for him to want to accept that even a tiny portion had been meant to be—no matter what. Surely it hadn't been some kind of twisted divine decision that his being born had killed his momma?

It would be a real disappointment to realize that he'd come into the world with a mess of misfortunes awaiting him.

Scout figured God had given him a fine brain and had intended for him to put it to good use. Therefore, it was likely that most of his troubles had come from his own sorry decisions. Fact was, he didn't cotton to the idea of somebody benefitting from his misfortune.

Which was why, now that he was sitting in front of a fire next to a sleeping beat-up girl named Kitty, things seemed terribly dismal indeed.

The truth of the matter was that she was in poor shape, and he was too.

Attempting to save a woman wasn't like him. Pitying her was a foreign emotion too. In his business—such as it was—feeling sorry for folk kind of went against his job description. He killed people. He didn't wonder about their feelings.

But ever since he'd picked up Kitty, he'd found himself thinking about her, wishing he could make things better. And because he did, because he'd all of a sudden decided to have a momentary surge of weakness, he cursed his very bad decision.

Though he wished he could have blamed it all on whiskey, he'd been in a sober state when he'd decided to save her. It didn't make sense, and now, as he sat next to the flames, he didn't understand how a hardworking, self-made, sorry no-good man like himself had managed to get saddled with a gal like her—a gal who kept looking at him like he was something special. He wasn't anything close to being a hero. And he was nothing close to being the kind of man who women turned to for help, especially eighteen-year-old little things like the slip of a girl by his side.

She was unlike the women he usually kept company with. And she was nothing like the women he'd ever dreamed of spending time with when he settled down. Well, if he got the chance to settle before he filled a pine coffin.

Kitty had the kind of skinny figure most women would curse, and the kind of scars marring her skin that most people would cry themselves to sleep over.

Never mind her hopeless home situation.

But instead of letting her misfortune get her down, she'd been willing to seek help, ride nonstop, and do whatever it took to survive.

Usually, Scout appreciated that kind of attitude. She would have been a good addition to the Walton Gang if she had been able to shoot a Winchester, had another hundred pounds on her frame, and, well, if she hadn't been a woman.

As if she knew he was looking her way, she opened one sleepy eye. "What?" She muttered the word slightly slurred, dizzy with sleep.

Against his will, a twinge of softness overcame him. "Nothing. I was just watching you sleep."

Time drifted as she carefully shifted. Eventually, she propped herself up on her elbows. "How come? Do I snore or drool or something?"

"Not that I'm aware of." He cleared his throat. Moved a couple of inches away from her. "Sorry I woke you. Go back to sleep."

As if he'd actually given good advice, she lay back down. Breathed deeply. Flopped to her side.

He relaxed—thinking maybe they were done talking— when she spoke again. "Mister? Why did you save me?"

"I don't know."

"You sure? I thought it was because, you know . . ." her voice drifted off, almost like she was embarrassed. But surely she'd lived through too much to feel shame.

"I told you I wouldn't."

"People lie."

"That is true. But I didn't." He felt his cheeks heating. When had been the last time he'd spoken like that to anyone? Usually he didn't mind calling a spade a spade. He certainly never spoke in flowery language. Especially never so vaguely. Never with a woman.

"Do you want me now?"

He flinched. Honestly, why couldn't she just have stayed asleep?

"Mr. Proffitt?" Her voice became bolder and so clear that if it was more than just air, she'd be able to bring forth all the stars in the sky. "Uh, Mr. Proffitt, do you want to lie with me now?"

Well, at least one of them wasn't afraid to speak plainly. "I do not. You're too young and you've been through too much," he added quickly, before she could start asking that confounded "why" word again.

Through veiled eyes, Scout watched the girl process that. His heart broke for her lack of innocence. Not just for hers, but maybe for the many girls like her—girls who didn't expect much from the world and had given up on even the idea of people looking out for them.

Little by little, her body relaxed again. When it did, his settled too. He truly was starting to like her a whole lot better asleep.

"If you don't want me, I don't know who will."

Now he was the one who was tongue-tied. "You're finding fault because I don't want to lie with you? That's foolish."

"My stepfather said that was all I was good for."

"He was wrong." Aching for some help, he leaned to his side, dug into the bottom of his saddlebag, and pulled out a cheroot. After lighting the end, he inhaled deeply.

Then glanced her way. Oh, heck. She was looking at him with those hound-dog eyes, silently asking for an explanation. "You're worth more than that," he finally added.

"How can you be sure?"

He didn't know. How did people know that they were destined for something good sometime in their life? That they were worth more than they'd been to led to believe at a young age? Gradually, a small, quiet voice filled his brain and reminded him of his own demons. Though most folk were sure his only worth was his trigger-happy hand, every so often he kind of hoped they were wrong.

"I can't be sure about what your future holds, but I'm telling you, I have a good feeling about it," he said finally.

She scoffed. "Feelings don't count."

"They sure as heck do." At one time, he'd even believed that too. Scrambling for her sanity, and maybe for himself, he blurted, "Girl, haven't you ever heard of faith?"

"Faith in what?"

"Faith that there's something better around the corner than we know about. There's got to be. And that God is watching over us. Otherwise life is just too hard."

Kitty was looking at him like he'd sprouted antlers and was fixin' to hightail it out of the wilderness. "Trust me on this," he said, though anyone who'd ever known him would bet their last dollar that he couldn't be trusted to hold onto his skin.

"Listen, what you need to do is stop thinking. Stop thinking and let me do it. I'm obviously much better at thinking than you'll ever be."

"Hey, now . . ." she sputtered.

But he just kept going like he was a one-man locomotive. "Here's what we're gonna do: real soon, I'm going to find you a safe place."

Even in the dim glow of the firelight, he could tell her expression was skeptical. "What kind of place is that?"

"Somewhere good."

"There ain't no place like that for me."

"There is. There is, and I tell you, I'm gonna find it," he promised, making up lies just as fast as a carpetbagger in Atlanta. "I'm gonna find you a place where you can be happy."

"I don't think I remember how to be happy," she whispered, as if she were revealing yet another flaw.

"Yeah?" he asked, before he remembered to tell her not to think.

Lowering her voice, she murmured, "Mr. Proffitt, for girls like me, happiness don't count for much. All that really counts is getting a meal in your belly and maybe being warm for a little bit. And while all that feels good, it doesn't solve much or change a thing. All it really does is make you numb for a little while."

She was right, though he wasn't in any hurry to tell her. It felt too cruel. No one had room in their life for fools. Most folks understood that walking around like an advertisement for hope only made people want to stay clear of them.

A spark flew up from the fire. Leaning forward, he grabbed a stick and poked at the embers. When the flames finally expanded, emanating a fresh burst of heat, he leaned back again. "Warm enough?" he asked.

When she nodded, he poked the fire again. For a moment, he was happy just to be watching the sparks fly into the night air, looking almost like stars in the sky. The fire sent off the sweet smell of wood burning, hiding behind it the scent of freshness and home.

"Kitty . . . how about this?" he drawled. "How about I just find you someplace where you can be dry. And maybe eat, too? Maybe that way you'll be numb for a good long while."

When she didn't reply, he shrugged.

He supposed she thought he was teasing her, but he wasn't being flippant. There'd been more than one day when he'd ached to be a little numb. That was what bourbon was for, right?

As the dancing flames warmed his neck and sent off more sparks, and the wind changed direction and the scent of smoke blew toward them again, he waited for her answer. "Kitty? What do you think?"

Still no answer.

Suspicious, he glanced her way, wondering what in the world was causing the cat to grab her tongue now.

When one moment stretched to two, then three, he craned his neck a bit. Ah. She was asleep again. Her eyes were closed tight, her lips were pursed. Body tense.

She was lost in the uneasy rest of the exhausted, but never the innocent.

Or perhaps she was just a touch innocent still?

And though he supposed Kitty would never believe it, Scout reckoned that was what the girl beside him was—innocent. In the way soldiers were. Or gamblers. Slaves. Prisoners. Unspoiled by goodness and tender care.

Innocent to easy words and kindness. To gifts and prayer and love.

Funny how he knew goodness existed—in spite of everything that he was and everything he'd done.

Right then and there, he decided to find her at least a little bit of happiness. Because he was that kind of man. He wasn't lazy; he believed in sweat and hard work and tough decisions.

He didn't believe in fate.

No, he was the type of man to take the future in his hands, pull at it really hard, and then run with it just as long and fast as he could.

26

"Try to drink this broth. Just a few sips. Come on now."

Vaguely, Jamie was aware of Will's hand on her back and his voice in her ear, coaxing and pleading. But his presence next to her felt elusive. As though he were just on the other side of a fog bank and no matter how hard she tried, she wasn't going to be able to reach him.

Maybe because of that, eating anything felt like too much of an effort. Speaking felt too hard as well.

So she gave in to her body's wishes and simply shook her head.

"No, Jamilyn," Will's voice replied, hard and uncompromising. "That paltry head shake of yours isn't good enough. Now open your mouth."

There went his hand again, pressing at the back of her head. "Do it," he ordered.

Warily, she opened her eyes.

Those too-beautiful eyes warmed. "Ah. You are awake. Now be a good girl and open your mouth. You need to sip some broth."

"Not hungry."

"That doesn't matter. Open up."

The order was so harsh she opened her mouth. But before she could change her mind, he stuck a spoon in. Straight away, hot beef broth slid past her tongue and slipped down her throat.

With a cough, she closed her mouth and glared.

But Will just shook his head. "You're not getting out of this, Jamilyn. Getting this broth from the café down the street was more trouble than I care to repeat. You're going to drink every bit of it if I have to force your mouth open. Now open those lips. Immediately."

Stunned by his horrible words, she opened.

He smiled and stuck that spoon in her mouth again.

She'd never tell him, but this spoonful of warm broth felt easier going down. She opened her lips again.

"Good girl," he murmured, sounding so sweet and gentle. She swallowed and let him continue.

And so it went on for what seemed like forever. Open. Swallow. Coax. Again.

At last, Will set the cup and spoon down and nodded. "You did good, Jamilyn. Real good. Now sit up for a second so I can help you with your hair."

She couldn't fathom why he wanted to fuss with her hair. The offer felt strange and out of character. "My hair?"

"Yeah, your hair." He frowned. "It's all stuck to your brow and neck."

Automatically she pulled her hands up, trying to smooth the strands. But just as she brushed her cheek, Will's hand stopped her. "Stop now. Let me do that for you. Besides, I need to wash your face, too."

There he went again, making a command that made no sense. "Why?" she muttered, her voice sounding more raspy than she'd ever imagined it could.

"You've been sick for days, honey," he said as he dipped the corner of a kerchief into the basin against the far wall. "You had a fever 'cause you got Mrs. Clark's influenza."

She understood being sick. And she understood the fever. But she didn't understand his need to help her. "No, why?" she asked, the words becoming easier—no doubt thanks to that broth he'd had to beg and borrow for. "Why would you want to help?"

He tilted his head to one side like he couldn't quite understand what she meant. "Honey, are you asking me why I'd want to help you specifically?"

When she nodded, he came forward with a damp cloth and sat right beside her again. After a pause, he gently swabbed her left cheek, his fingers trailing a moist path along her skin, the water cooling it for a brief moment before evaporating.

She closed her eyes in relief.

Will paused, dampened the cloth again, then brushed along her brow. Finally, he leaned a little closer in order to reach her other cheek. Then ran the cold cotton over her heated skin.

When she opened her eyes, she met his gaze. His expression was touching. Worried.

Yet he remained silent all the while.

She'd just given up any hope of him answering her—not that his answer mattered—when he set the cloth down and leaned back. "How could I not help you?" he finally asked. "You need help. You're very ill."

But being helped hadn't been her experience. Before, her parents had looked to her to be the caretaker. To be strong. Weakness wasn't seen as anything other than a reason to be pushed away.

However, she was too embarrassed to say such a thing. It wasn't easy to admit to her failings.

He spoke again. "Anyway, Jamilyn, it's my fault you're here. And it's my fault you got sick. If we hadn't stayed with the Clarks . . ." His voice drifted off as he shook his head. He was obviously biting his tongue so he wouldn't say anything more.

She was flabbergasted. For him to think he'd brought her to danger instead of saving her life? That he found fault with rescuing her instead of leaving her to be manhandled and eventually shot by James Walton's gang?

As she studied his posture and noticed that he was visibly trying hard to not meet her gaze, she knew she had to make things right. "This . . . this is not your fault, Will."

"It is. It sure as heck is."

"You saved me." Her throat was parched. In pain. Each word felt like it was being forced out a sieve, little by little.

"I . . . could have done better." He swallowed hard. "Hush now."

Obediently, she closed her mouth. Closed her eyes as well.

Minutes passed as he set the bowl of water and the towel farther away. He shifted then finally propped his back against the headboard.

She hoped he'd stay. Why, she didn't want to contemplate. He was nothing to her. She should fear him.

But against all odds, and against everything that made sense, she ached for him to stay by her side. Please, she prayed to the Lord. Please let him keep near me. Just for a little while. The worst thing in the world would be to feel even more alone.

Then, hesitantly, he touched her hair.

She stiffened. Then struggled not to show any emotion as he proceeded to finger comb her hair. Oh, it had been so long since anyone had touched her. Had cared for her.

With the death of her brothers, her parents had become even less demonstrative than they'd been when they'd all lived together as a family. It had been her middle brother, George, who had given her love and affection. Travis, to some extent, had been there for her too, but rarely enfolded her in a bear hug.

Then, of course, her brothers had died in battle and had become icons in her house. And she'd been forgotten.

For far too long, she'd made do caring for herself. Learned to get along without anyone offering sweet words or reassuring hugs.

She closed her eyes as she reluctantly gave in to the feeling of peace that floated over her as Will's fingers ran through her hair. Tried to ignore his scent, the faint scent of evergreen and leather that seemed to permeate his skin.

She tried to ignore the vision she suddenly had of his arms enfolding, wrapping her around in her a slow, warm hug.

It shamed her to realize how little she now asked for. Just warm words and comforting hugs. Shouldn't she want more by now?

As competently as a lady's maid, he plaited her hair. Then he moved away just as if her proximity had been catching him off guard as well.

"How did you learn to braid hair?"

"My sister Bonnie, remember?"

"I didn't know men could do such things."

"Plaiting hair ain't against the law, Jamie," he commented, humor sliding along the edge of his voice. "Men do what's expected and needed, right? My mother only had two hands. After a bit, I got real good at fussing with Bonnie's hair." He tugged on the end of her braid for emphasis.

Not for the first time, she wondered what kind of man Will McMillan was when he wasn't on a train or on the run.

She'd never imagined another person—let alone a man, a soldier, a Marshal—would ever touch her hair. Or braid it.

Of course, she would have never imagined that he would have been feeding her broth either.

What constituted a person? She wondered. At the end of the day, what made up their character? Was it their occupation or their family?

Was it their relationship with their friends?

Or was it their walk with God?

Suddenly, it all seemed too much to contemplate. She had no answers, only more questions. Her energy was failing when Will moved to face her again. "I'm tired," she mumbled. "I'm sorry," she added as she sank back to the pillows. Giving thanks that her eyelids felt like they had weights in them, she gave in to temptation and let herself venture back into oblivion.

❦

"It's all right. You just sleep," Will murmured, though he was pretty sure she didn't hear him.

When she didn't move for another few minutes, he let himself look at her. She was such a pretty thing. So delicate.

He clenched a fist, remembering how smooth her skin had felt against his rough palm. How silky her hair had felt.

When he was around her, he wanted to be the type of man she needed. A man who was stable. Who wasn't likely to get shot sooner than later. But that said, what was he going to do when he'd found a safe place for her to stay?

How was he going to let her go to some farmer sod-busting coward who had avoided the war for personal reasons and who had to find a woman through a letter-writing campaign?

How was he going to allow her go to a man like that? Most likely, if he let her go, it would be condemning her to a life of drudgery. Before long, she'd no doubt be having too many children and working too hard to take care of them. Day after day would pass. And with each one, she'd probably begin to get worn and skinny and tired and bitter. Just the thought of her living like that made his skin burn.

And then he remembered the obvious. Oh, yeah. He was going to let her go to a man like that because it wasn't his call. She wasn't his woman, and she never would be. She'd been his hostage.

And though he didn't know a whole lot about romance and relationships, even he knew the cold hard truth.

Hostages did not all of a sudden start liking their captors. Not when they almost died at their hands. Not when they lived too many days in fear.

Those things could never be forgotten. And if they did fade a bit, they wouldn't fade enough to make a lick of difference. Not really.

Certainly not enough to ever marry their captors.

As Jamie slept on and the sun shifted the shadows rushing through the curtains, Will made himself face the facts.

Women like her didn't ever end up with men like him. Not ever. That was as it should be.

But it still was terribly hard to come to terms with at night, when the sun sank low and old fears resurfaced with wild abandon.

27

*T*wo days after sipping that first spoonful of broth, Jamie was on her feet and putting herself to rights. She'd just rinsed out her chemise and one of her petticoats when a hard rap interrupted her thoughts.

"Jamilyn? You decent?"

Gazing down at herself, at how odd the dress looked without the usual layer of petticoats propping it out, she shrugged. No matter how bad she looked, or how inappropriate her outfit was in mixed company, there was little that could be done about things or changed at the moment.

Besides, Will had seen her in less.

"I'm decent." She was just about to go to the door when she heard Will jimmy the lock and turn the knob.

He stopped in the doorway almost hesitantly. "I guess you're feeling better?"

"Much. I'm well enough to get dressed and do a little bit of laundry."

His gaze warmed. "So I see."

Oh, those eyes. Even after everything they'd been through, there was something about a warm look from him that made her insides feel like melting.

Though she would have given a whole lot for a clean calico instead of her torn traveling dress, she was determined not to fuss about it. After all, she was alive, thanks to him. He'd not only saved her life by getting her off the train, but he'd also nursed her through the influenza. Her debt to him was insurmountable.

Not that he wanted to be reminded of that. Attempting to smile, she said, "So, did you find out any news?"

"I did." Looking at the half-crumpled paper in his hand, he said, "We finally got word. My boss is going to meet us here within twelve hours."

The idea that the ordeal could be over in hours felt shocking. "Truly? And then we'll go to Kansas City?"

"Not exactly. Sam thinks that taking you much farther on my own would be a mistake."

"I'm afraid I don't understand. We're all going together?"

"I mean that when Mr. Edison arrives, I'll be telling you good-bye."

She was still having a hard time getting the words to make sense in her head. "Forever?"

"Of course."

She shook her head in protest. "Will, I don't want to go anywhere with a strange man, especially not on a train." Getting on a locomotive again was going to be hard enough. Being accompanied by a strange man would send every fear fostered at the hands of Kent to come tumbling back. "Can't we come up with another plan?"

"There is no other option."

"But can't we come up with something else?" She hated the whine and the high-pitched tremor, but she also couldn't help herself. "Maybe you can write him back—"

"That's not how this works, Jamie. You know that." His voice turned more fluid. "Now, I know Sam is unfamiliar to you, but I promise you that there's nothing to be worried about. He's a very upstanding man. A true gentleman. In his company, you won't feel afraid."

"But he won't be you."

"He's better; he's my boss." He looked at the sheet of paper again. "He's made his decision, Jamie. He thinks it best that he takes you the rest of the way to your aunts."

"Why?"

"He feels it would be safer for you." He cleared his throat. "He . . . Mr. Edison, he's a formidable man, Jamie. No harm will come to you in his company."

That might be true, but to her nothing sounded more frightening than being alone with another man. Struggling to control the tremor in her voice, she shook her head. "I'm afraid I can't do that. Please tell him no."

"That's not how this works. When I get orders, they are expected to be followed."

"Well, I'm not a Marshal," she countered, full of bravado. "Therefore, I don't think I should have to follow your directives."

Leaning back against her door, Jamie noticed that he had both palms pressed against the wood behind him like he was making sure his exit hadn't disappeared. "You're not going to get your way," he said, his voice hard. "I have to follow orders."

But weren't there some things more important than work orders? What about private promises? What about promises made in the dark of the night? Or when they were alone in a room and she was so sick she wished she could die?

"But you promised me that you'd see me through. I thought you were a man of honor. I thought you kept your promises."

"I promised I'd keep you *safe*," he corrected. "I did that. Handing you over to Mr. Edison's protection will keep you even safer. I have not gone back on my word."

She heard the hurt in his voice and immediately became embarrassed. It wasn't right to speak to him that way; it wasn't right for her to use guilt in order to get her way.

It was time she stopped fighting the one man who didn't deserve her arguments.

So she nodded, though it took everything she had not to shake her head or cry or complain. Turning her back to him, she yearned—not for the first time—that things could be different.

She wished she had some options, that something would finally be in her control, because it sure seemed as if just about everything in her life was conspiring against her.

Or was just expecting her to go along with things.

Thinking about that, a burst of anger tore through her. "I do wish someone would one day ask me what I thought."

Crossing the room, he touched her shoulder and turned her around. "Jamie, don't you understand? It doesn't matter what you want. It doesn't matter what I want. All that matters is surviving."

"When will our wishes matter?"

He blinked. "Maybe they will matter when you're safe and settled. It will matter when I know you're settled in Kansas City with your aunts." After a swallow, he added, "When you are seeing your letter-writing man."

She couldn't believe Will had dared to bring up Randall. "Really?" she retorted. "You're really going to bring up the man who for days you've been teasing me about writing to?"

"I meant no disrespect. I am sure the two of you will have a good future together."

"A good future? Do you think he'll even still want me?"

"If he doesn't, I'll set him straight."

"And how will you do that? You'll be long gone." Though her voice cracked, she continued. "But I guess that's just fine and dandy with you."

"I didn't say that."

"What you said was close enough."

They were facing each other. Standing chest-to-chest. Eyes glaring. Tempers and heat rising between them. She was angry, and felt torn enough to want to lash out at him.

Their breathing accelerated. The tension between them heightened.

Then it seemed as if they were definitely out of choices. Someone's anger was going to be stopped. Someone had to give in.

And because she felt she had no choice, it might as well be her. "Will, are you really going to hand me over to some stranger?"

"It's my boss. Sam Edison. He's a man of impeccable character. A man who commands respect. With Sam, you'll be in good hands."

She eyed his face. Ached for some kind of reaction from him, something to tell her his feelings. "But what if something happens? What if I won't be in good hands?" Unspoken were her greatest fears. What if the man wasn't honorable like Will said but more like the Marshals who'd surrounded the train?

His face went blank. "Jamie, you'll be in better hands with him than you would be with me. He will take care of you. He has a lot of influence. He'll get you on another train or a stage or something. He will find a way to get you out of this mess."

She noticed Will was only talking about what *she* was going to be doing. "What about you?" she asked.

"What?"

"What's going to happen to you? Where does your boss want you to go?"

He opened his mouth. Swallowed. "Sam intends for me to go back to the Walton Gang."

"But they'll kill you."

"Sam's heard Scout Proffitt has been on our trail. He's close by. Real close. All I have to do is let him find me."

"If he finds you, he'll kill you."

"Maybe not. I know for a fact that he didn't want to kill an innocent woman. I might be able to use that to my advantage." Crossing his arms over his broad chest, he said, "I can't continue running, Jamilyn. I can't run forever. Sooner or later I've got to stop."

Sooner or later they all had to stop. That was true.

A lifetime of experiences had taught her that it was fool-hardy to run, foolhardy to try to forget her problems or to attempt to push them aside.

Feeling deflated, she nodded. After all, the decision had been made. There really was nothing left for her to do.

It would be easier on Will if she were to accept graciously.

And if not graciously, then to at least finally give in.

$\mathcal{L}$

The previous night, after Kitty had gone to sleep in their miserable room in the miserable boardinghouse, Scout Proffitt had gone down to the bar.

There, in that dark, cramped saloon that looked and smelled like a hundred other drinking establishments, he'd finally found the inforrmation he was looking for.

Ironically, the discovery hadn't done anything except make him even more weary.

When he'd first arrived, he'd fallen into conversation with a puny-looking weasel of a man who had hopes of one day cheating large groups of men out of their life savings. Eager to gain approval from an infamous outlaw in black, he'd given just enough information for Scout to garner a place at the lead card table, such that it was.

Four consecutive games of five-card draw led to him an off-hand comment about the sighting of a stalwart six-foot-tall ex-soldier who still clung to a military bearing and who was in in the company of a woman with lovely blond hair and a somewhat worn-out black taffeta gown.

He'd leapt on that information like a tick on a dog. Further conversation—and the exchange of both threats and money—yielded their location: the Mainstreet Hotel, just a block away.

Tonight, he was armed and ready and more than a little tired of the whole experience. He was tired of hunting and murdering.

And more than a little put out that Will McMillan hadn't been a whole lot harder to track down.

But, such was life. Not everyone gave him what he needed. Not everyone gave him much at all. A real man learned to do his best and keep silent. Because, of course, nothing got done by complaining.

That said, he was in no hurry to complete the job.

"Scout, you going out again tonight?"

He turned to Kitty who was sprawled out on the bed in a fearsome combination of innocence and heat. For a split second Scout wondered if she was attempting in some clumsy way to entice him, but almost immediately he disregarded that thought.

She might not be truly innocent, but he aimed to help get her that way—or at least something close to it.

"Yep," he finally answered.

"Did you find who you were lookin' for?"

He weighed the pros and cons of telling her the truth, then threw caution to the wind and nodded. "I believe I did."

Sitting up, the gal stared at him with those eyes of hers that had seen too much.

Scout looked right back, half waiting for her to ask more questions. Shoot, maybe she even was going to try to give him a conscience.

"So your journey is over."

"Pretty much." He was tempted to add that he still had to figure out what to do with her, but he didn't dare. It wouldn't do for him to think about anything except his orders. Thinking about personal things on the job only created problems.

Her lips pursed as if she'd finally come to a decision. "All right, then."

He exhaled, realizing suddenly that he was disappointed by her reaction. He'd hoped for panic or arguments or even recriminations.

Yes, he surely would've appreciated a healthy dose of guilt. He'd wanted to imagine that she cared for human life more than he did. Surely someone on this earth still considered murder a sin.

Standing at the foot of the bed, he said, "I'll be back later."

"Think you'll be gone long?"

"Don't know. Few hours, most likely. Then we'll need to move on."

She turned away from him before he was tempted to give her more information, which would have been a foolhardy thing, of course.

He paused again and almost asked her if she needed something. But what was he going to do? Murder and then bring her back a meal?

Disgusted with himself, he turned and walked out the door.

Purposefully, he didn't warn her to lock the door. That would mean he cared. Or could do something about her circumstances.

Instead, he kept his head down as his boots pattered over the wooden steps. He passed a pair of soldiers standing by a settee and walked around a whore and her man in the shadows of the lobby.

He walked out the front door, turned left, and headed to the hotel that had once seen better days and now was only biding its time until it fell into complete disrepair.

He checked his Colt.

And prepared to kill a man who could have been his friend —and a woman who he could have loved.

If he'd been of the mind to be the kind of man who'd made friends or had been lovable.

28

*W*ith the greatest reluctance Will left Jamie in the room. Without his protection, she would be vulnerable to anyone who could come near. What's more, he reckoned there was a very good chance she would be lulled by her own ingenuousness, finding hope in the false security of a locked door.

Though he didn't fault her goodness, he wished she was a bit more experienced, a little bit more worldly.

Anyone who'd been double-crossed or reduced to real hardship would never feel secure in a room at a public inn. Experience would have proved that the pitiful lock of a pine door was little defense against anyone intent on doing harm.

He knew how flimsy those doors were. Because, of late, he'd been the one pushing his way into rooms.

Will regretted leaving Jamie's side, but he knew he had no choice. Sometimes keeping her as safe as possible at all costs meant doing things he wasn't comfortable doing. He couldn't hide out with her, no matter how much he yearned to keep the rest of the world at bay.

Yes, this was for her own good. After all, he feared her getting sicker. A relapse could bring on pneumonia or a fever or any other sort of illness or disease.

He'd kept her locked in the room for another reason too. Her questions about Calvin had planted a seed of doubt, and Will wanted to be sure that Calvin was still the man he'd believed him to be since the last time he'd seen him.

If he wasn't, then Will needed to know. One way or another he was going to have to find a solution.

As he took the stairs slowly—half expecting to hear Jamilyn's cough through the paper-thin walls—he figured his reasonings were justified. People changed. People turned and became hard or addled or ruined.

Life had surely taught him that. During the war, he'd seen strong law-abiding men become so weak it had shamed all of them. He'd seen brave men become so scared that they'd run from a battle or had turned their backs on women and children—even if it meant they would be leaving them to certain death.

Sometimes, he realized with a burst of consciousness, those men had been his own comrades. The sharp pain of fear often encouraged the most stalwart to save their own skins. Even if it was just for a little bit longer.

'Course, he'd also seen the meekest of men become sadistic killers—and master interrogators. Pain inflicted and suffered could do that to a person.

So had the constant wear and tear and worry that war had brought on. When so many died, many began to care little for the sanctity of human life. And even less for the people who still walked on the earth.

Of course, all hadn't been lost.

There were those blessed few who'd miraculously become stronger. In spite of the greatest of odds, they'd risen out of the ashes of destruction like phoenixes. And before everyone's eyes, they had become better men.

He was one of those men. Well, he'd liked to believe he was. Surely his year and a half in the company of the Walton Gang hadn't ruined him yet.

Certainly he still knew what was right and wrong. He wasn't just imagining he knew those things instead of merely looking at life in various shades of gray.

Though perhaps only at dawn did men truly feel the hands of angels on their shoulders. Guiding them toward divine justice.

The poetic turn of phrase caught him off guard. Those weren't his words.

It had been what Clayton had said. Clayton.

Lord, he hadn't thought of him in months.

With some surprise, memories of that steadfast man rushed back, as clear as if Will had just left his side and not Jamilyn's. In an instant, he could feel the man's presence. Strong and silent. Ever just.

Clayton Proffitt.

It was somewhat ironic that Clayton—the most upstanding man he'd ever met—shared the same last name as the notorious gunslinger. God surely had a sense of humor. Without a doubt, Clayton had been one of the few men who had been a role model for everyone else. Will hadn't been alone in this opinion. Though Clay had been younger than almost everyone else, he'd had a way about him that had inspired loyalty. He'd had dark eyes and a square jaw and an innate dignity about him that inspired others—even in the middle of the smell of death and sulfur—to believe in something better.

Will could hardly recall an infantryman or cavalry officer who hadn't decided Clayton Proffitt's word was as solid as the word of God.

He remembered a time when they'd been in Georgia and had stopped at a pitiful farm. The owner had looked so frantic he had been likely to try to kill them with a pitchfork. Will felt the same pain that he had that afternoon.

The couple were starving. Their skin hung on their frames as if by sheer will, and the vacant expression in their eyes told too many stories. Obviously they'd seen too much.

Even to Will's eyes, it was evident that they had literally nothing to give a band of soldiers besides shelter from the storm that was raging outside. Though he believed in pity at the end of the war, he'd ached to turn around and leave. Surely there'd been no need to take even the couple's dignity?

Beside him, others of their ragtag band had felt the same way. They were grubby and dirty and injured and suffering. But the time had come to draw a line.

But Clayton Proffitt had been in charge. He'd gazed at the man, not a trace of pity or remorse in his eyes. Then he had stepped forward led them all inside that ramshackle home.

For a second Will had been tempted to protest, but one quiet look in Clayton's eyes had said it all. The truth was, that shelter had been enough. All of them had been so cold and wet for so long that they'd hardly remembered what it had felt like to not have wrinkly skin and sores on their feet from walking in wet boots.

The men had stumbled in. Smelly and embarrassed. Strangely subdued.

And that man—that down-at-the-heels farmer—he'd gazed at them all with such pain in his eyes that it had almost felt tangible.

"All we want is to be dry for twenty-four hours," Clayton had said. "That's all."

The man retreated until he was standing against the wall. "I don't got anything for you. I swear I don't."

"I don't want anything else," Clayton promised.

"And your men?"

"My men want what I tell them to want."

Will hadn't even flinched at the information. Because, well, it was true. They all did without hesitation whatever Clayton Proffitt wanted. Because he was their captain and because he was who he was.

However, the owner hadn't known that. "That's what the others said. But they lied."

Will and a couple of other men had been cold enough to want to yell at the man and ask him to just stand aside. But Clayton had merely stared at him, rain dripping from the brim of his hat. "I'm not like the others. Neither are my men."

And Will, right there with the other men, had slowly grown taller. Just as if they'd been worth something.

Stepping a little closer, Clayton raised his voice so every one of them wouldn't be mistaken about what he said. So no one else in the house would misunderstand. "I know you don't believe me, but that's the truth."

The man started to shake. "I don't have nothing—"

"You have your pride and your woman. I understand that," Clayton said quietly. "That's enough. I have a bleeding man and a band of soaking wet soldiers who are exhausted. You need to let us sleep here before my man dies."

Will had felt more than saw the nervous man glance over at Robert Shaw.

"He's a good man, mister," Clayton had whispered. "Too good to die on your front porch. Too good to have on your conscience."

Miraculously, the man had moved to the side. "Come in," he'd said, defeat in his voice.

They'd set up camp in what had once been a library but now had only a few dozen books. Not even looking over his shoulder, Clayton had tossed four of them in the fireplace and set them on fire. As sparks ignited the worn books' pages, an aura of heat enveloped them all.

Heat had never felt so good. Not even on an August day.

The house's owner had protested. "I was saving those! You have no right."

"I'm afraid I do. Sir, I'm obliged to you. If these books weren't here, we'd be in a sorry state for sure."

He'd sputtered some more. "But—"

"He's going to die if I don't treat his wound." Clayton's voice had brooked no argument. "And listen to me good," he added, glaring at him with piercing slate-gray eyes. "I do not intend to bury him."

Others had gotten water and found a pot of some sort and put it on the flames.

And then they'd pulled off poor Robert's shirt. Ribs showed where healthy muscles and sinew used to be. Among an array of scratches and sores and chill bumps lay an almost five-inch wound on the man's side. It was festered and angry.

When the owner saw it, his eyes practically bugged out of his head. "That from a bayonet?" he whispered.

Clayton never looked away from Robert. He'd just sat there on his haunches, as steady as ever. "Imagine so. Hard to tell after all this time."

As the water heated, the wound was inspected again. Swollen and red and putrid, the infection was visibly spreading. Robert had hissed in sharp pain when Clayton gently pressed two fingers against it.

"Get over here, Will," Clayton had said. "Hold on to him while I wash him up."

"I can do it, Captain." It hadn't felt right for their great hero to lower himself like that.

"I'm proud to tend to him," Clayton had murmured, then had bent down and had begun to gently wash Robert's pale skin. Over and over, Clayton had put the cloth in the scorching hot water, wrung it out, and carefully bathed him.

Behind them, he'd felt rather than heard the man's wife appear. "Henry?" she said timidly.

"Go back to your room, Katherine," Henry had commanded, his eyes still where the rest of theirs were—resting on the captain's hands gently bathing the soldier who was so close to dying he probably already had one foot in heaven.

Clayton never looked up.

As his wife shrunk against the wall, her husband swallowed hard. "Dear Lord in heaven."

"Hallowed be thy name," Clayton said with a half-smile. Looking Will's way, Clayton pulled out a knife and plunged the tip in the nearly boiling water. "Will, are you ready?"

"Yes sir," he'd said. Not because he was ready, but because no other response would do.

"Good enough. Here we go."

"Clay?" Robert had asked, his voice raspy, his eyes blurry. "Clay, what are you—"

Without saying another word, Clayton took that heated knife and lanced the wound. Robert screamed, his cries mixing in with the woman's cries. The other men in the room looked away with discomfort.

But Will held himself firm. Just as his captain had asked.

As expected, the wound's sordid contents seeped out in a sluggish rush. Clayton brought the knife to the cut, slicing a little deeper, bringing forth more sickness and a smattering of red blood.

Robert cried out again, the cries so harsh and so full of agony that everyone in that room knew they'd be as marked by the occasion as much as Robert would ever be.

"Easy now," Clayton murmured, right before he motioned for someone to bring over the water, liberally soaked a square of cloth pilfered from the house's bed sheets, and then cleaned the wound.

Robert screamed again, flinching and jerking. They all knew he was in terrible agony. Five minutes later, he gave in and shamed himself by crying. His shoulders shook as the tremors came.

Then the most miraculous thing had happened. The farmer's wife had come forward. Her husband had stood still as she'd slid through their ranks.

And as they'd all looked on, she'd gone down on her knees and had sat next to Robert. "It's okay, honey," she murmured. Looking up to Will, she whispered, "What is his name?"

"Robert."

With a nod, she leaned a little closer. Still murmuring sweet things, she ignored her husband's blustering and their shock and had taken Robert Shaw's dirty hand and held it tenderly between her own. "Oh, Robert. I know. I know you hurt. I know," she murmured.

Her husband looked like he was about to have a conniption. "Katherine!"

However, she ignored him completely. Instead, she leaned a little closer and spoke to their comrade softly. "Robert dear, you're going to be fine," she said over and over again, soothing the man in her arms.

Soothing the rest of them.

When his crying settled, she said, "Do you have a sweetheart?"

"Ann Marie," he rasped after what felt like forever.

"That's a lovely name," she said. Just as if they'd been at a church social. "Rest now, Robert. Rest and close your eyes and think of Anne Marie, waiting for you at home."

"But—"

"Don't tell me you're not going to survive this, soldier," Clayton had interrupted, his voice as harsh as if they'd been in the middle of a battlefield. "You will get better. If not for Ann Marie, then for me."

The woman holding Robert's hand had stared at him in shock. "You think you matter to him more than his sweetheart?"

"I know I do today. She might hold his heart, but I'm the one who's going to keep him alive." And then, right then and there, Clayton Proffitt had smiled.

And what was amazing was that right then, right there, they had all believed it. Without a doubt in their minds. Forevermore.

Back in the frozen streets of Dodge, Will blinked. As the memories grew faint, he forced himself to remember the last of it. The woman had turned his way. "And what is your name, soldier?" she'd asked, even though it wasn't any of her business, and he wasn't used to talking to women.

"Will McMillan," he'd said. "My name is Will."

"And do you trust your captain with your life too?"

"Always." With a strong of satisfaction, he'd know that he'd just been able to give her the easiest answer he'd ever given in his entire life.

Coming back to the present, Will shook his head as his eyes adjusted to the light around him.

Will couldn't believe he still remembered every single detail of that moment. More important, he couldn't believe that he didn't feel the immense sense of sorrow that always stayed with him when he thought of Robert.

Because indeed Robert Shaw had survived.

And they'd all left that broken-down farmhouse two days later when the rain had abated and they had orders. Not one week later, they'd been ambushed by a band of Yankee scouts.

Before it was all over, Robert had taken a bullet in his side—in almost the very same spot where the saber had cut him. And where Clayton had almost healed him.

In front of them all, Robert fell to his feet and died.

And it had felt inconceivably cruel to Will.

He'd dragged Robert's body off to their camp and had buried him. And then had stood over his grave and had cried.

He hated that he'd cried in front of their captain. He hated that he'd cried like a baby, tearing up for the waste of yet another good man. Crying because life was hard and it wasn't getting any easier.

And because for a brief, minute amount of time, Clayton Proffitt had encouraged them all to believe in miracles. Then God had shown them all that such things, if they existed, didn't last for long.

"Will?" Calvin called out from the doorway of the inn. "Will, you're just standing there like a durn bump on a log. You need something?"

As he looked at Calvin, Will was tempted to ignore him. Though the memories from his past were sharp and hurtful, they at least had a definite ending.

This journey he was currently on did not.

"I don't need a thing," he said. "Just taking a breather." Then he walked on down the street. It was time to move forward. To get some fresh clothes. To get ready to say good-bye to Jamie.

To get ready to begin again.

Yet again.

29

Scout wasn't having much success deciphering the mind of the woman in his company. Ever since they'd had their big talk, Kitty had been a bit more reserved. Almost uneasy. Almost stiff.

Which, of course, meant nothing and made no sense.

As the days passed and they had gotten closer to Dodge, Scout cursed his luck and cursed her skittishness. It was getting on his nerves, and he never had been one for putting up with nonsense.

Along the way, he'd decided he was surely the best thing she was ever going to find. He'd taken to putting her needs before his. He'd kept her warm in front of the fire and had taken her to the shelter of an old barn during a snowstorm.

And he'd found some old corn and had made corncakes just two nights ago. He'd bought an ugly blanket off a toothless old Indian so she'd have something better than cold hard dirt to lie on top of at night.

And above all that, he hadn't touched her in a single inappropriate way. Not even once.

Hadn't even come close. Actually, he'd almost been acting like a gentleman, which, come to think of it, was a pretty amazing achievement.

To his way of thinking, Kitty should be smiling at him like the sun. She should be driving him crazy with inane chatter and useless information.

Instead, as the miles accumulated behind them, she just got quieter.

And then they pulled into Dodge City.

After arranging for the horse to be sheltered at the livery, he'd taken her to a not quite respectable-looking boardinghouse and secured two rooms. The owner was a deaf old woman nearing eighty. Her eyes were cloudy with cataracts as she'd signed in Nate Lawrence and his sister Louise, handed them two keys, and pointed with one knobby hand swollen with arthritis to a scuffed-up stairwell.

Scout had thanked her with a nod, then led the still-silent Kitty up the stairs. When she continued to poke along, he began to get aggravated. "Come on, *Louise*. I know you're tired, but if you go much slower you might as well be going backward."

When they stopped in front of her door, she finally spoke. "Scout, don't make me go in there."

Grabbing her shoulder, he fought to refresh her memory. "It's *Nate*, honey. Don't you forget that."

Her shoulder trembled under his touch. "Nate, please . . . don't make me go in there."

It was official. He was confused. "Go where?"

"In that room." She was pointing at the door like a rattler was curled around the handle.

"You're not making a lick of sense. This is the first almost decent place we've bedded down in days. Now, go on in and stop fussing. You're going to have your own room. Some privacy too."

When she still looked scared, he lowered his voice. "I'm trying to save your reputation here."

"That don't matter. I don't want a room of my own."

"I may be an outlaw, but even I know how a woman is supposed to be treated."

"But the woman below thinks I'm your sister."

"She might, but most people will realize right away that we don't look a thing alike." Tired of her foolishness, he stepped away. "Now listen. I need to go see if I can find someone. Go on in there and lock the door. I'll come back to get you at supper time."

"Scout, please . . . locks don't help," she whispered.

Her eyes were filled with so much pain that he didn't even chide her for using the wrong name. However, there was a reason he was still alive instead of strung up under the bough of some oak.

Duty and survival always came first.

"After you get in that room, lock it. Then push a chair in front of the door and forget about leaving."

"But—"

"If there's no chair in there, push the dresser."

"But—"

"You can't come with me. Not to where I'm going."

"I won't get in the way."

"I don't want you with me."

"Then tonight . . . tonight, can I sleep with you?"

Her begging was making even him forget their pretend names. "Kitty—"

"I won't sleep if I'm alone. I'll just stare at the door and remember."

"I'm not sticking you in a bed with me tonight. It ain't gonna happen."

When her eyes filled with tears, he hardened his heart. "Come on, girl. This is what you are going to have to get used to. Wherever I leave you—and I will, I promise you that—you're going to be on your own again."

Looking like he'd beaten her down instead of giving her some trust and freedom, she took the key he'd handed her, slipped through the doorway, and closed it directly behind herself.

Next, the steady screech of the dresser sliding across the floor echoed through the wall, followed by the unmistakable sound of despair as she began to cry.

And before he could slide even further into guilt and confusion, he ignored her cries and walked out of the boardinghouse. Lord have mercy, he needed to find Will McMillan and Jamie Ellis and shoot them dead.

The sooner he got his work completed, the sooner he'd be able to move on with his life.

❧

Jamie had woken up in an empty room. At first she'd been fearful, not quite certain where she was. But then as her heart settled down and her brain cleared, she began to tally what she knew.

They were in Dodge City. In a small, rundown hotel that had curiously ornate woodwork framing each doorway. She'd been terribly ill. And Will—the man she used to fear but who now was pretty much the only person she completely trusted—had taken care of her.

Vaguely, snippets of the last five days rushed forward, each scene played out quickly with barely enough time to absorb all that had happened between the two of them. All she knew for sure was that when she'd been feverish, Will had bathed her brow with a cool cloth.

When she hadn't been able to walk, he'd carried her.

When she couldn't eat, he had fed her broth, cajoling and bullying her until she'd consumed enough sustenance to continue fighting the influenza. His gaze had been kind; his manner had been a true combination of patience and control.

Somehow, in the middle of the fever and the broth and his touch, the last of her fear of him subsided. Little by little, it had ebbed and transformed itself into something else entirely. Gratitude? Or was it perhaps friendship?

In the quiet peace of her rented room, she knew for certain it was most certainly not that. Because she was not his friend. They had no common ground. He was taller, stronger, and more forceful. Only he knew where they were going, and only he knew the people he needed to talk to.

From the moment their paths had crossed on that dangerous train, she'd been forced to rely on him and her faith, hoping against hope that she could learn to trust what he said and that one day he would actually do what he said he would do. He would return her to another Marshal who would in turn help her board a train to Kansas City. Afterward, she'd live with her aunts and get to know the elusive Randall—the man who would most likely be her future.

Even thinking about her future seemed hard. After everything that she and Will had been through, she was now dreading the moment when he would prove himself to be a man of honor.

And she would dread it, she knew. Because though he was so much more than she was, and though they had little in common except a shared desire to survive, she had fallen in love with the man.

Not that she was ever going to tell him that.

She was nothing to him except a burden that was costing him just about everything he was.

How could she ever meet his expectations? How could she ever be enough of a woman to be worthy of such a man?

The answer was simple: she couldn't.

Two knocks and Will's reassuring voice brought her to the door. She still double-checked, however. "Will?"

"It's me. Let me in, Jamilyn."

During her illness, when she'd been too sick to open her eyes, she'd become used to its gravelly tone. She now realized that low timbre was almost more familiar when it was hidden by the wood between them than when he was standing by her side.

Two clicks released the locks. When she opened the door and he crossed the threshold, she felt overwhelmed by the looks of him. To her surprise, he'd bathed and now sported new denims, broadcloth, and kerchief. The fine lines of his cheeks and jaw had been shaved close. He smelled vaguely of soap and the sharp, fresh scent of brand-new cotton and wool.

The clothes, his scent, his all-encompassing form made her catch her breath. "You changed."

"I did." Looking curiously self-conscious, he ran one hand down over the pure white fabric covering his chest. "I thought perhaps I should make myself presentable for my boss. Sam Edison doesn't appreciate mess or dirt."

"Would he be upset with you for something so small?" The idea that his boss would find flaw with Will dragging her across the state in dirty clothes felt harsh.

After bolting the door behind him, he faced her and shook his head wryly. "The fresh clothes are probably my doing more than his expectation. I . . . I like being clean. Being in the

Walton Gang doesn't lend itself to a whole lot of opportunities for a man to get his laundry done." Crossing the room, he checked and double-checked his pistols. Even took the time to make sure his Winchester was at the ready.

The actions looked so deliberate, a bit of a knot tightened inside of her. "Are you expecting trouble?"

"Beyond the normal? No."

Like a sharp freeze, the reality of her situation bore down on her again. Her illness, combined with the room they were in, had given her a false sense of security. "Do you think Mr. Proffitt is still looking for us?"

He hesitated, then finally nodded. "Absolutely."

"Do you think he knows we're here?"

"Word is out that a man matching his description has been seen hereabouts. But I'm not completely certain it's him."

"Why is that?" Scout Proffitt's penchant for wearing entirely black, combined with his deadly black-as-night eyes, was a hard thing to miss.

A dry chuckle erupted from Will. "The people who claim they've seen him are saying he's with a girl."

"A woman?" She was innocent, but not ignorant. "Why does that seem so hard to believe?"

"Because people are going out of their way to say it's not a woman. It's a girl. A young one. And he's acting proprietarily toward her." He rolled his eyes. "Rumor has it he's acting like a guardian."

Jamie didn't understand the derision in Will's voice. "Why does that surprise you? Couldn't he have a sister or something?"

"No. Scout doesn't seem to have a family."

"Are you sure? Sometimes family is a person's only weakness."

"Point taken." Pain flickered in his eyes, reminding Jamie of the conversation they'd shared about his sister Bonnie.

He cleared his throat as he crossed the room and pushed back the thick curtains. "Anyway, Scout doesn't have a family. Not one I've ever heard about. That's why these rumors about him taking care of a girl have to be false. Scout Proffitt doesn't tarry with women. He doesn't accompany them places. He doesn't look out for them, and he definitely doesn't do good deeds."

"What does he do with them?" she blurted before she could think better of her words. Because, of course, there was only one thing a man like Scout would be doing with a young woman who was not a family member. Knowing her face was blusing red as a rose, she said, "Please forget I asked that."

From his position next to the window, Will smiled. "As it happens, I was thinking the same thing. But, at the risk of shocking you terribly, I have to say that squiring a lovebird ain't Scout Proffitt's way either. Scout spends small amounts of time with women. Then he moves on. He doesn't have attachments. And he sure wouldn't risk his life by looking out for anyone else."

"So it's not him." Her body trembled as she thought of the other men who also had been on the train. If one of the others were nearby, she knew she'd be in big trouble.

Since Will looked determined to stand next to the window and look out of it every few seconds, she sat down on the edge of the bed. "When will we see your boss?"

"He's making his way here as we speak."

"And then he'll take me away?"

"Yes. He'll make sure you're safe."

"And what will you do then?"

After scanning the street below them for a solid minute, he turned back to her. "Just what I told you I'd do. I'll continue to do what I get paid for." He paused, then added, "Maybe I'll go see if I can get back in James Walton's good graces."

She knew without even looking at him that his words of comfort really were nothing at all. He wasn't going to be allowed back in. Most likely they'd shoot him in the back.

And his real job didn't hold a whole lot of promise either. Jamie figured there was a real possibility that he might even be kicked out of the Marshals. She seemed to be his failure.

"I hope things get better for you," she said.

"You know, I almost think you mean it."

"I do. I feel terrible to be so grateful for something that hurt you so much. You've put your life on the line for my benefit. Saving me has cost you a great deal."

"Jamilyn, saving your life might have been the best thing I've ever done in my sorry life. Getting killed for that wouldn't be a bad thing."

"Don't say such things!"

"Why shouldn't I?" he drawled. "At the end of the day, your welfare is all that matters."

"That's not—"

He cut her off. "You matter more to me than you could ever imagine."

His sweet words, spoken so quietly and without inflection, took her breath away. Was it possible he'd been falling in love with her too?

She had to know if she was worth more to him than just a victim. Because of that, even though it was unseemly, she pushed him. She needed to use every moment of these last few precious moments together to get the truth.

"Why?" she asked. Quietly. Her voice coming out hardly anything more than a harsh whisper.

With a weary sigh, he pushed himself away from the wall. His blue eyes looked tired and his expression was drawn. "You know why."

She got to her feet as he walked toward her. She clenched her hands into fists as she watched a myriad of emotions cross his face—almost as though he'd had enough of fighting himself. Or maybe his internal struggles matched hers.

There was so much inside of herself that was warring between what she'd always known and what she'd imagined things could be, that it was almost an impossible struggle to give in to the inevitability of it.

Then he stepped forward. Closer. So close his shirt was almost brushing against the sleeves of her gown. Clean cotton rustled against frayed taffeta.

Her dirty black dress looked odd next to his clean clothes. The gown hung on her now, and its dusty black sheen paled next to the crisp white cotton.

Suddenly, she was aware of the weight she'd lost. And her sickness. And everything that life had thrown at her.

And then he took her hand. Once, twice, he brushed the tip of one calloused finger against her knuckle.

She shivered.

Will noticed. "Am I scaring you, Jamie?"

Mouth dry, she shook her head. "No," she said aloud, just in case he didn't see.

His hands turned hers over. That same thumb brushed a path along the inside of her palm, then traced a path along her wrist, lightly caressing the blue lines of her veins.

She trembled again. But this time, Will didn't look distressed. Instead, his lips curved slightly.

Confusing her.

"What are you doing?" she asked.

"Nothing too terrible. Just feeling you."

"That's it?" She raised her eyes.

"Truth?"

"Yes."

"I'm trying to get up the nerve to kiss you." His fingers pressed on her skin, then stopped, as if he were half waiting for her to gasp or cry out. Perhaps he was even half hoping for it?

If so, he was out of luck.

Life was hard. More than that, life was precarious. There was still a very good chance they were going to get caught. A very good chance she was going to die sooner than later.

And so she looked at him directly and silently begged him to stop postponing the inevitable.

The tension between them dissipated as if he'd finally come to a dangerous decision.

Will McMillan leaned closer, brushed his lips against her cheek, seemed to breathe in her scent, and closed his eyes. And then, right there and then, he kissed her.

His lips were smooth and firm. Slightly parted. His touch was languid and slow, like they were under stars during a warm summer evening.

So much so that all her senses fixated only on him. He smelled good, his touch was everything, and suddenly nothing else seemed to matter in the world.

Part of her ached to open her eyes and meet his gaze. To reach out and grasp the arms that held her loosely and pull him closer.

To pester him with questions, just to figure out what he was feeling. And just as important, attempt to understand what she was feeling too.

30

*J*ust when he'd been sure he couldn't be any more of a fool than he was, Will McMillan managed to surprise himself again. Since he'd already apologized, he gazed into Jamie's eyes and wondered if he was ever going to forget this moment. After all, he needed to.

But as her hopeful expression penetrated his defenses, and his body responded in kind, he realized something was very apparent: he was now an even bigger fool than he'd thought.

Had he really thought he was going to be able to forget this moment? Forget being so close to Jamie, tasting her? Feeling closer to her than just about anyone else in his life?

He cleared his throat, a hundred apologies and excuses running through his brain. But all of his words dissipated into nothing when he looked into her eyes.

Looking shell-shocked, Jamie stared at him, her mouth agape. As if seconds were minutes, her lips closed. "My," she whispered, just as if that word was the very last of her coherent vocabulary.

"Jamie," he murmured in return, to show her that he too could speak eons with just one word.

As the minutes marched on, their situation—and the mismatched pairing—brought them back to reality. They did not have a relationship. They were two people who were very close for terrible reasons for a short period of time.

Someone pounded on the door.

Jamie gasped.

"Don't move," Will ordered as he clasped a Colt in his left hand and stepped closer. "Who's there?"

"Calvin, Marshal."

Grudgingly, he opened the door. "What do you need?"

Calvin rolled his eyes, his scraggly, thinning hair making an exclamation point to his expression. "I'm here to summon you."

"Because?"

"Because a Mr. Edison is here. That mean anything to you?"

"It does. Thank you."

He stepped back, intent on closing the door right away and focusing back on Jamie. But the inkeeper's hand grasped the door in a firm grip. "He's downstairs. Waiting."

"Please tell him I'll be there shortly." What he didn't say but which lingered between them was that he wasn't the type of man to be given orders. Or told to rush.

"Will, what's the problem?" He attempted to crane his head around Will's form. Attempted to look at Jamie.

Will easily sidestepped so Calvin didn't have that ability. "There's no problem."

When the door closed, he locked it.

And then turned right around and leaned back against it again. "Ready? It's time to go down."

She bit her lip—that beautiful ripe-raspberry-colored lip that he had finally tasted. "Already?"

"Only you would say that, sugar. This has been a long time coming."

"When I see Mr. Edison, what will happen then?"

Will knew his heart would break. That's what would happen. "What's going to happen is you're going to be just fine, Jamilyn. When you're in Mr. Edison's company, you'll finally be safe."

"And he'll send me home?"

His heart broke, because now he knew she was like him. She didn't have a home. All she had was the vision of what one was supposed to be like. But painful memories weren't for sissies, and especially not for the likes of them.

Playing along, he nodded. "Yes."

When Jamie nodded, then stood up, her whole demeanor looked as if she was off to the gallows.

Funny. That was how he felt too.

✍

Sam Edison was short. In his boots, he was still barely taller than Jamie. But that was the only area in which one might find him lacking. Everything about him—from his light gray eyes to his thick mustache to his long, elegant fingers to the way he stood so calm and still—radiated power and authority.

It was no small wonder Mr. Hollis had wanted Will to bring her to Mr. Edison right away. Jamie doubted anyone disobeyed the formidable man's directives more than once.

He stood straight and proud as Will walked her down the stairs and moved toward him. As they approached, Mr. Edison's face seemed made of steel. It didn't look like he moved a single muscle until Will stopped in front of them.

"Sam, thank you for coming," Will said. "I'm obliged."

"The bureaucracy in St. Louis was nearly driving me plumb crazy, McMillan. I was glad for an excuse to leave it for a bit." Turning to Jamie, his eyes softened. "Miss Ellis, I'm truly sorry for your recent unpleasantness. I hope this event won't harm you too much?"

His voice was so gracious, so formal yet very kind, that tears pricked her eyes. He was the first man who she felt like she could be weak with—almost like he counted on the opportunity to coddle the opposite sex.

With Will, she had done her best to be strong because she hadn't wanted to make things harder on him than they already had been. "I . . . I am sure I will prevail, sir."

"I will hope and pray that is the case." As her tears welled again, Mr. Edison pulled out a neatly starched, white handkerchief from a hidden pocket in his well-tailored black suit. "Here you go, dear."

She held it up to her face and smelled the faint tart scent of lemons. "Thank you, sir." She dabbed her eyes and looked warily at Will. Was he embarrassed by her burst of weakness?

Will met her gaze, his look softening with something that looked like a true mixture of longing and regret.

A lump filled her throat.

Then, he held out an arm. "Jamilyn, perhaps you'd like to sit down while I speak to Sam for a moment?"

It wasn't really a question, more like a sweetly worded request. But she took his arm just same and let him escort her across the small lobby and seat her on a lumpy scarlet-colored couch.

But instead of leaving her immediately, he crouched on his heels in front of her. "You okay?" When she nodded, he almost smiled. "Good girl."

He turned away then, walking with a purposeful stride toward his boss.

Jamie couldn't have stopped watching him if she'd even wanted to. At first, she tried to concentrate on only breathing slowly and easily. To give praise to the Lord that she'd made it through the ordeal.

But her eyes kept fighting her. Across the way, she watched Will swab at his cheek with his hand. Just like he'd done time and again when he had been trying his hardest to see the best in an awful situation. Moments later, he nodded and the faintest of smiles appeared before it was carefully hidden.

Just like he'd done countless times with her.

Shame curled in her stomach. What in the world was she doing? She should be so happy to be leaving this man's side. But instead, all she was doing was wishing they'd had more time together.

Surely even one more day would have helped.

She scrambled to her feet when the men approached. "Miss Ellis, they're holding the train for us. We should probably not inconvenience the rails too much longer. Are you ready, ma'am?"

"Yes, sir." Steeling her spine, she held out her hand to Will. "Mr. McMillan . . . thank you. Thank you for everything."

Just as formally, he gently enfolded her hand in his, then bowed slightly at his waist. "It was my pleasure."

"Will I ever see you again?"

He stilled. Will glanced at Mr. Edison, then, like each word was being torn from his insides, said, "If you need me, contact the U.S. Marshals' office. It might take time, but they'll find me."

"Promise?"

"On my honor."

She relaxed. His honor was everything. Meant everything to her. And it couldn't be faulted.

He wiped his hands on his jeans before holding one palm toward her. "All right then. I guess this is goodbye."

The moment she placed her palm in his, she felt the same electricity that always flowed through her whenever they touched. But it wasn't enough. Releasing his hand, she flung herself toward him, aching to feel one last embrace.

He caught her to him easily, wrapping his arms around her and holding her even closer. Spurred by his actions, she pressed her face toward his chest and breathed deep. Closed her eyes and hoped she'd never forget his scent.

Knew she'd never forget the feeling of comfort and security she only seemed to find in his arms.

And then, just as quickly, he stepped away. His posture became stiff and solid. "Good-bye, Miss Ellis."

It felt too hard to tell him good-bye; her feelings were too mixed up and felt too fragile. Instead, she turned to Mr. Edison. "I'm ready now."

"Let's be on our way then." And with that, Mr. Edison turned away and walked toward the front door of the hotel, not really looking behind him, just assuming, Jamie supposed, that she would follow.

And so she did. She followed the gentleman out into the bright sunlight and away from the dim lobby lights. Out toward her future and away from the too many questions that surrounded both her feelings for Will and her past.

"It's just up the road, ma'am," Mr. Edison said. "Will you be able to walk the distance?"

"Yes, sir. I have a feeling I can handle that just fine."

And that was the last either of them said until they were on the train, in their own private compartment, sipping tea when the train pulled out of Dodge and taking them far away.

31

*G*oing back to the room was out of the question. So was standing in the street, looking like the worst sort of pitiful fool. Will decided to compromise by going into the lobby and sitting on one of the chairs near the fireplace.

Calvin Hollis, seeing he had returned, took a few steps toward him, but he must have been frightened by Will's scowl because he immediately backed off. That was the good news.

The bad news was that there was nothing to distract Will from the train's whistle as it left the station. He sat as still as possible and tried to pretend he wasn't listening for its echo long past when it couldn't be heard.

When it couldn't be heard, except in his memories.

Though he'd given up liquor after the war, not liking how it didn't help his stress but only clouded his ability to deal with it, he felt that he would give good money for a shot of bourbon at the moment.

'Course, chances were good that not even whiskey was going to make a dent in the pain. The sharp sting of whiskey was not going to relieve the ache that had settled in his throat.

He was going to miss Jamilyn Ellis terribly.

No, that wasn't true. He already did miss her. What was going to happen was the hole in his heart was going to expand and become festered. It was going to hurt and ache and burn until he got used to it.

Because the missing wasn't going to go away. And he had no other choice. He'd saved Jamie to give her the life she deserved—and it sure wasn't a life beside a man who made a living pretending to be someone he wasn't, doing things that no one should witness, let alone doing them over and over.

And he had done just that.

Through lowered eyelids, he watched a couple enter the hotel and approach the registration desk. Calvin handed them the guestbook to fill out.

Life went on. Even in times of pain and frustration, that was the underlying quality that lay behind it. People came and went about their business. Calvin there could probably tell him more about that than anyone.

Will needed to remember that and stand up and get on his way.

He was just contemplating how to do that when the door opened again and Scout Proffitt sauntered in. His movements were easy and steady. Confident. Just as if he circulated around Dodge all day. He was dressed in black, as usual. His Stetson looked new, his boots spit polished.

But beyond all that, there was something different about him. It seemed to cloud his movements. Make things about him harsher. A worry, maybe?

Or maybe—like himself—time and aggravation had gotten the best of him.

Scout recognized him and tensed. Will could see he thought about reaching for his ever-present Colt, then disregarded the impulse. Will was glad of that. No one could outdraw Scout

Proffitt, and Will was in no hurry to try, especially seeing that they were in the middle of a lobby and Will was still sitting down.

But even more important than that, he had no desire to harm the outlaw. Under all the layers, Scout was a good man, a decent man, though most likely everyone who mattered would be shocked to hear that.

After a pause, Scout walked forward. "Where's the woman?"

Just to rile him up, Will tipped his hat. "Good to see you too, Proffitt."

Scout's dark eyes narrowed in confusion. "You know our paths didn't meet by chance. I'm only here for one reason. I need the woman back."

"And me?"

"I have orders."

"Are you going to follow them?"

"Until this minute, I had planned on it."

"But now?"

"Now, I just need you to answer the question." But still, a faint sheen of embarrassment burned his cheeks. "Where is she?"

"Once I give her to you, what are you going to do? Shoot me here?"

"Not here."

"Too crowded?"

He shrugged. "I need some answers first." After surveying the area, he turned with a jerky pause, walked a little closer, then joined Will on the couch. "So, where is she?"

"She's gone."

Scout looked poleaxed. "What happened to her? She dead?"

For a moment, Will thought about not answering, but there didn't seem to be much reason to ignore the question. Jamie was safe now and not likely to ever run into Scout or a member of the Walton Gang for the rest of her life. "U.S. Marshals took her from me. She's in their care now."

"When?"

"An hour or so ago." Had it only been that long? It already felt like a lifetime had passed.

Scout winced. Then sighed. "I can't believe I missed her."

"Believe it." He glanced at Scout, then saw to his surprise that the man didn't look all that perturbed by the announcement. No, if anything, he looked relieved. "You going to go after her?"

Scout pursed his lips. "No. I'm not going to take on the U.S. Marshals for a decent woman. I'm bad, but not *that* bad. Shoot, I never thought killing her was a good idea anyway."

"And me?"

"I don't know." He stretched his legs out in front of him, looking almost glum. "Things have changed for me since I got my orders."

"I heard you're traveling with a woman. Is that true?"

"True enough."

"You fall in love?"

"Me? No. Not at all. This gal, she's young." Frowning, his throat worked a bit before he spit out another word. "Damaged."

Weren't they all? "She here in town with you?"

"She is." Scout glanced at him for a good long time, then spoke again. "Here's the thing. For some reason I'm not even sure about anymore, I got saddled with her. Now she's my responsibility, and I've been dragging her around the prairie. It's been cold as all get-out."

Will stared at him in shock. "I'm trying to picture you as a caretaker."

"Well, don't think about it too hard, 'cause what I've been doing ain't been pretty. Never have I felt less like a guardian and more like a scoundrel. She needs a whole lot more than I can give her."

"You should lose her. And I mean this in the best sense."

"Doing that won't be easy. She's clinging to me like I'm worthy of her trust. She expects things from me I didn't know I could give."

"And have you given them?"

"Yes," he muttered. "I've been better to this poor little thing with no hope and no sense of worth than I've been to most of the rest of the world. It makes no sense." Tossing his hat onto his knees, he ran a hand through his hair harshly. "With her, I'm better." He cleared his throat. "And I'm not exaggerating, Will."

Knowing his future was out of his hands, Will kept asking questions. "Where's the gang now?"

"North to Nebraska, I believe." After a time, Scout lowered his voice. "What do you think happens to men like us? Do we ever change? Do things ever get better for us? Or are we as damaged as the little thing I've been traveling with?"

"I'd like to think we can change. I don't know though. Maybe it's just a pipe dream. Men do things that are difficult to make amends for."

Scout's expression turned bleak. "I have a feeling you're right." After a sigh, he got to his feet. "What would you say if I told you that I'm feeling like I want to forget I ever saw you?"

"I'd say I was obliged. But I wouldn't believe you."

"That's fair."

"You might feel like forgetting me if you knew the truth."

"And what is that?"

"I am really a Marshal. I was only with there to collect information." Will paused, whether to make a point or because he wasn't sure how the truth would be taken, he didn't know.

Scout looked taken aback. "Maybe now I should be the one askin' if you're intending to kill."

"If we didn't see each other, and you never returned to the gang, you'd be forgotten, don't you think?"

"If that's the case, then forgetting about each other might just have merit."

"It might. If forgetting is even possible," Will allowed.

"Could we do that?"

"Do you aim to rejoin them?"

"No. I'm going to take care of this girl, put her somewhere safe, and then start over." His voice turning wistful, he added, "Even if I don't get very far, I've got an inkling to give it a try. Even just for a little bit."

Getting to his feet, Will held out a hand. "I'm game if you are. Scout Proffitt, I hope I never see you again."

Scout nodded as he shook his hand. "You won't. You're a good man, Will McMillan. Better than most."

"I'll take the compliment, but I have to think that it only seems that way because you've known some of the worst men around."

With a wary smile, Scout tipped his hat, then turned and left. As soon as he left through the front door, Will turned to go back up the grand staircase.

"Hey Will," Calvin called out as he rushed forward. "Who was that man? Who were you talking to?"

"Can't see how it matters."

"It's just, well, that man looked just like Scout Proffitt."

"Who?"

"You know. The outlaw. He always wears black and he's supposed to be as dangerous as all get-out. The man looked like all the 'wanted' posters."

Will forced himself to laugh. "I'm sorry to disappoint you, but that wasn't Scout Proffitt. I don't associate with outlaws. He's just a man I used to fight with. Back in the war."

Calvin looked crushed. "That is too bad. Seeing him would have been something, you know? Knowing a man like that? I wouldn't hardly forget it easily."

"No, I imagine not," he said in parting. Walking up the stairs, Will thought about what a strange bedfellow fate was. Here he'd been on the run for days, fighting fevers and struggling with his emotions. And now, in the space of thirty minutes, the two people who had been at the forefront of his mind had made an appearance.

Scout was gone, and, well, Jamie was gone too. A better man would be relieved that he'd seen the last of them both.

Unfortunately, Will could only find it in his soul to be grateful for the loss of one of those people. The other one?

Leaving her had nearly broken his heart.

32

"Kitty, I'm back," Scout said as he inserted the key into their room's lock. "You decent?" He paused for a moment. Not only did he not want to catch her bathing, but he also had to prepare himself to offer an apology. He'd left her frightened and in tears, and he'd felt bad about that.

'Course, most likely, she'd simply sass his apology, laugh off her worries. He was half counting on that. That girl had a mouth on her like no other, which both confounded and amused him to no end.

But when no sound passed through the door, he grew concerned. "Kitty?" he called out while he turned the doorknob and slipped the key into his duster's pocket.

The room was dim. Only the glow from the moon shimmered through the muslin curtains barely covering the pane of glass. Stepping in, he looked toward the bed, certain she was asleep.

And sure enough, there she was, lying on her stomach, dead to the world. And here it was only seven o'clock in the evening.

He paused, uncertain whether to leave and let her have her privacy or to stay in the room. But remembering her panic and cries when he'd left, he thought the better of it.

Kitty had been in such a state, it would be far better for her to wake up to find him sitting on the rickety lone chair in the room, watching her and waiting. Even though he'd sworn up and down that he wasn't going to share a room with her.

Decision made, he strode to the door, locked it firmly, took off his duster, then prepared to get good and uncomfortable in that chair. "Kitty, you're killing me," he muttered under his breath as he crossed the room.

Which was when he noticed she hadn't made even the slightest movement. It was unlike her. Kitty was a restless sleeper. She talked; she mumbled; she twitched and shifted. All of it had irritated him when they were sleeping outside on the hard ground and his body had been begging for more than a measly handful of hours of sleep.

"Kitty? You okay?"

When he leaned closer, his nose caught the unmistakable scent of blood. Metallic and pungent, it was one smell he knew he'd always recognize. After all, he'd made more men bleed than he could count. But never before had the sight of it thrown him into such a state of worry.

Instantly, his body went on alert. Before he even realized what he was doing, his Colt was in his right hand and he was looking in every corner of their small rented room.

No longer caring about Kitty's nap, he opened the dresser's doors and pulled back the drapes, half expecting at any moment to be attacked.

Then he saw the pool of blood covering the floor on the opposite side of the bed. Closer inspection showed that it was dripping from the girl.

He choked. Oh, dear Lord. What had happened?

Dropping the gun on the mattress, he rushed to Kitty's side. Hands trembling, he brushed back the hair from her cheek, his eyes examining every inch of her face.

Had she been shot? Attacked? Confusion warred with panic inside of him as he tried to figure out what could have happened. "Kitty," he said again, rubbing her back.

Her back was warm but rigid—telling him all he needed to know.

But he couldn't believe it. "Kitty? Kitty, wake up now. I need to see you. See what's wrong."

Staring at her face, he waited for her eyes to drift open, for her to sleepily smile and cuss at him. But of course, she didn't.

Tears stung his eyes as pain and worry and a curious premonition coursed through him. With a new resolve, he rolled her over. After pressing two fingers to her neck and feeling nothing, he began a frantic search. Eyes skimming over her plain, modest calico, he looked for bullet holes. Looked for the telltale stain of red.

All the while blaming himself and his past for what happened.

The truth was, he had more enemies than most people had freckles—not only people who he'd damaged, but also their relatives. And then, of course, there were all the people who were hoping of making a name for themselves by shooting him.

Or, perhaps, shooting someone they suspected he cared about.

Blinking hard, he roughly maneuvered her body, still searching for the injury. Only as a last resort did he let himself look at her wrist and come to terms with the awful truth.

Kitty's wrist was neatly sliced with a knife. She'd obviously sliced through the tender skin with care, intent on her goal: death.

As he held her arm, her precious blood stained his hands, soiled his fingers, ran down to his leg, and joined the puddle at the floor. As he stared at the blood on the floor, he caught sight of a silver blade half-under the bed. Scout's trembling grew worse as he knelt and picked it up.

Bright red blood soaked and slicked his hands as he stared at the knife, recognizing it as one of his own. Kitty must have pilfered it when he'd begun to let his guard down around her.

As he came to terms with the fact that it was his weapon that had done her damage, the rest of his body seemed to have no other choice but to freeze up. In protest, a burst of pain shot through his head, making him ache to close his eyes and shy away from the rest of the world.

Kitty had sliced her wrists with his knife.

Just after she'd begged him not to leave her alone in an empty bedroom because it reminded her too much of being afraid at home.

Scout squeezed his eyes hard and tried to stop the tears that were forming. But just like the rest of him, his eyes had given up on listening to his deceitful brain.

Fact was, he was a murderer and a criminal. And though he'd tried to help a girl, he hadn't been good at it. If anything, he'd managed to make her life worse.

Because while it was true she'd been misused and abused at home, at least then she'd had hope. Before he'd come into her life, she'd dreamed of someone good coming into her life to take her away.

But all she'd gotten was him. In his company—under his care—she'd lost the illusion that things could one day be better. Death had become more welcome than another day of living.

The tears that he hadn't asked for fell harder. Sliding down his cheeks, dripping onto the cotton of his shirt. Falling onto his denims. Mixing with her blood. Little by little, his body gave up its need to stay still. First his shoulders began to shake, then his chest. His eyes squeezed shut, desperate to block out the scene in front of him, the reality of his memories.

Finally, he gave in to the inevitable and pressed his palms to his face and let out a cry of despair. He cried hard. Cried like a baby. Sobbed and bawled like he hadn't since he'd been small.

He cried for the waste of a life, and cried for all the hurting in the world. Only a long time later, when he'd clumsily wiped his face with the sleeve of his shirt, did he wonder what to do with her body. And realized it was the first dead body in his life that he'd ever thought about burying. Usually, he simply shot then moved on. Quickly.

Which, of course, made him feel sick all over again.

"Mr. Lawrence?" A light, feminine voice called out from the other side of the door. "The hot water you requested is here."

The words confused him. His mouth opened, but he couldn't think of a thing to say.

"Mr. Lawrence? Are you in there?"

Old habits of self-preservation kicked in. Standing up, he forced himself to speak clearly. "Just set it outside the door," he ordered. "I'll get to it in a moment."

"You sure? 'Cause I'm supposed to bring it on in."

"Leave it," he barked back, hardly recognizing the husky, strained chords in his voice.

A clamber and a smothered exclamation told him his orders were followed. As her footsteps fell away, Scout sighed in relief. He was in no condition to leave the room—but of course he had no choice. He was going to need to bury Kitty, not leave her.

But a suicide would bring questions and the possibility that many of the good folk of Dodge wouldn't take kindly to a sinner's body on their sacred ground.

His options were fading fast.

Then slowly the answer came to him. It was as unexpected and as difficult to accept as it was perfect. He was going to need to go back to the hotel and locate Will McMillan.

Now that he knew he was actually a lawman, Scout knew Will had the force of the U.S. Marshals behind him. His position trumped any doubts or questions a small-town sheriff might bring up.

It even trumped the usual fear that Scout Proffitt's name brought to most people. Taking one last lingering look at Kitty's body, he turned away, then caught sight of a slip of paper under one of the forgotten pillows.

It had been under her—obviously she'd placed it there for him to find. He didn't want to read it. He didn't want to know why she'd ended her life. Didn't want to feel even guiltier than he did.

But life had never been easy, and taking the easy road had never been his goal. With heavy steps, he crossed back to the bed and carefully unfolded the carefully arranged note.

There were only a few lines. Each word was neatly printed and phrased.

> Scout, I'm sorry for doing this to you. I just couldn't see a way out. For a woman scarred and used like me, there aren't many choices. One of them can't be me being alone.

Being alone is worse than just about anything.

But please know I'm grateful for you, and grateful for the last few days. Though I'd never believed in God, you showed me that maybe, just maybe, He exists after all.

If he does . . . now wouldn't that be something?

Kitty

The words rang in Scout's ears through the night as he stared at the note and prayed to a Lord who had surely given up on him long ago.

When morning came, he grabbed the pitcher of water from outside his door and hastily cleaned up. Then, before he found a way to delay further, he picked up his Colt and holstered it, shrugged back into his duster, and left the room again after taking care to lock up the room securely behind him.

He kept his head down as he walked out the back stairs and into the early light. With some surprise, he realized that more than two hours had passed since he'd entered the room.

Worried now that he'd waited too long to seek assistance, he picked up his pace, making it to the hotel in half the time it had taken him before.

When the man at the front saw him, his eyes grew wide. "Yes?"

"I need to see Will McMillan. He still here?"

It was obvious the man didn't want to tell him anything, but Scout stood tall and straight, almost forcing the man to tell him something he didn't want to hear.

"I'll go see," he said finally. When he left, Scout walked to the corner of the room. There he could keep an eye on things while being unobserved by most.

But then he noticed that his sleeve was soaked with blood. Torn between the new flood of despair that besieged him and the old habit of needing to stay unobtrusive and hidden at all times, he stared at the sleeve until he sensed Will coming his way.

In his own way, the lawman's face looked as haggard and ruined as Scout felt inside.

"You looking for me?" he asked without preamble.

Though it killed him, he nodded. "I need your help."

"You sure about that?"

"It's a personal matter." Feeling that the skinny guy behind the counter was aching to listen, he motioned toward the door. "Can we go talk outside?"

Will glanced at the door warily. His eyes were hard when he turned to Scout again. "You fixin' to kill me?"

"No." Hurt washed through him as he realized that if he'd nodded, Will wouldn't have been surprised.

That was what everyone knew him to be: a killer. A bad man. The kind who would call on a man for help and then turn on him like a snake. That reputation fit him like a kid glove that was too tight.

Though almost all the bitterness in his life choked his words, he responded. "Like I said, this is personal."

After another measured glance, Will turned and started walking. Scout eased from his position at the door and followed. Once they were away from a family standing idle near the front entrance, Will turned to him and waited. "Well?"

There was no way to make his words easier to say. "The girl I was with killed herself while I was seeing you. I've gotta bury her decent."

Will's stoic response was impressive. The only sign that he was taken aback was a muscle jumping in his jaw. "You sure?"

"Am I sure what? Sure that she's dead, or sure that I want to bury her decent?"

Will raised a hand to wave off Scout's wrath. "Don't get riled up. I'm not your enemy here."

Scout was stunned speechless. His world wasn't filled with shades of gray, not really anyway. Men were either good or bad, and for as long as he could remember, he'd been firmly in the bad category. Now that he knew Will was a U.S. Marshal, Scout never expected Will to think of him as anything less than his enemy.

"I want to bury her decent. She deserves at least that, though I have a feeling Kitty wouldn't think she'd be worthy of even that much."

"All right then. Let's go deal with it."

"That's it? No questions?"

Will's gaze slid over him. "Even pushing aside the fact that if you'd killed her you wouldn't be standing here . . . I believe you. And I agree with you too. I've left my share of bodies littering the ground—and it's a tough thing to come to terms with. I've come to believe that everyone deserves a decent burial, especially a woman, don't you think?"

Scout's teeth clenched as he absorbed the other man's words. He wasn't so sure about everyone deserving something decent. He sure didn't.

But that was okay. "Obliged," he said tightly as he started walking toward the run-down boarding house, dreading the sight of Kitty's lifeless body as much as he was dreading Will McMillan's reaction to it.

But it had to be done.

Life wasn't for cowards or sissies. He'd never been either. But today was proving to him that maybe he needed to become something more than he was.

Even if he wasn't sure it was possible.

33

Their journey to Kansas City hadn't been grueling, but it had been fraught with a sadness in Jamie Ellis's heart. A sadness that wasn't easily pushed to one side.

After they'd boarded the train, the elegant Mr. Edison had given her his orders. "I procured a private compartment for you, Miss. But I'd appreciate your company for the meal this evening. I have some questions about your time with the Walton Gang that I'd like to have answered before our arrival in Kansas City. If it won't be too much of an inconvenience."

Though the request had been delivered in dulcet tones and with the utmost respect, there was no doubt about the order. Mr. Edison was ordering her to dine with him and was giving her fair warning that he expected information in exchange for his retrieving her.

Perhaps that shouldn't have been a surprise.

"I'd be honored to dine with you, Mr. Edison," she said just as formally.

He bowed slightly. "I'll be at your door to escort you to supper."

"Thank you."

He'd left her side then, and she'd entered her compartment alone. Oh, it had been so very civil.

And her compartment was as pretty as anything she'd ever seen. Fine linens covered the slim mattress. Mahogany wood framed the small writing table.

The chair was upholstered in a plush burgundy velvet and situated by the lone, wide window, giving Jamie an excellent view of the snowy landscape outside. In short, it was everything a first-class compartment was reputed to be and twice as lovely as she imagined.

Gingerly, she sat down and looked out the window, watching the endless trail of white horizon. And only to herself she admitted the cold hard truth: she would've given almost anything to feel the icy snow against her skin, to feel the wind brush against her cheeks. To breathe in the frigid frost, so cold and harsh that with each breath her lungs would feel as if they were about to explode.

She ached to be on horseback, an animal's muscles mixing with her own. Smelling the leather and the dust. Feeling the warmth of the horse's pelt under her fingers.

But most of all, Jamie ached for Will McMillan with such a fierce longing it almost took her breath away.

Will was the first man in her life she had trusted. The first man who'd put her needs before his. The first man of honor.

But she didn't idolize him. No, instead of only feeling grateful to him, she ached for him as a companion. He was serious but not without humor. Easygoing but never one to be lazy or taken advantage of.

But most of all, Will had a way about him that had inspired her to reach a little bit deeper into her soul and imagine a better life than she'd ever hoped for. He'd made her think of people differently. For that matter, he'd made her think of herself differently . . . for a little while, she'd begun to believe that she was worth more than she'd ever imagined. For that, she'd always be grateful.

Yes, he'd become dear to her. And, she realized, he felt the same way toward her, at least to some extent.

As she watched the barren landscape slide by, Jamie knew she'd be lying to herself if she neglected to think about their romantic connection. There was something sweet and true between them—a beautiful romance, laced with a tingly, warm desire that was intoxicating.

Feeling the longing toward him was a revelation. She was also woman enough to know that it hadn't been one-sided. Yes, they'd had a connection of sorts—the two them. Their whole relationship hadn't been only of captor and hostage or guardian and victim.

No, somehow in the middle of things, they'd become more than mere labels to each other. They'd become man and woman. They'd become Jamilyn and Will. A couple of a sort.

But, of course, their relationship had never been meant to be. And it certainly hadn't ever been meant to last.

Minutes passed, floating into hours. A steward came by offering warm towels and hot water and a neatly wrapped box.

"What's this?" she asked in confusion.

"The gentleman you are traveling with asked me to give it to, Miss. He thought a change of clothing might be appreciated."

"Oh. Yes. Yes, thank you." She felt awkward, having Mr. Edison buy her clothing, but she was enough of a realist to realize that she was going to need more than one dress in her future.

Inside the box, the dress that greeted her was lovely. The fabric was taffeta; the color an interesting shade between brown and gold. It shimmered in the light. It was cut rather plainly, with a minimum of pleats and buttons and lace. Underneath it lay fresh pantaloons, a snowy white chemise, and a thin pair of petticoats.

It all was beautiful, too lovely for her to be embarrassed that he'd felt the need to buy her a new dress and underthings. She was simply very grateful for it all.

Anxious to change, she shook out the dress and stepped out of the dress she was wearing. Then she did her best to transform the rest of herself.

With the aid of the small mirror in her compartment, she took down her hair, combed it with her fingers as well as she could, then spent double the time neatly pinning it up.

After, she luxuriated in the feel of warm water against her neck and face. Using both the towels and the basin, she did her best to set herself to rights. She probably hadn't spent so long on her toilet in years, but she didn't mind it. Fussing with her skin and hair kept her hands busy and made the time go by.

Finally, she put on the new gown and was able to fasten all the buttons save for two. She was just wondering how to tackle them when a brief knock sounded at her door.

"Miss Ellis? May I escort you to supper?"

"I'm almost ready," she said, opening the door just a crack.

Immediately, Mr. Edison's hand reached for the door, opening it a little farther. "Why, look at you," he said with a smile. "You look pretty as a picture."

"Thank you." She stepped back. "I'll be out in a moment, sir."

"Not now? What else do you need to do?"

Presenting her back to him, she said, "I'm still trying to find a way to fasten two of these buttons."

For the first time in their brief acquaintance, the Marshal looked flustered. "I apologize. I should have realized those buttons would be difficult for you to reach."

"I'm grateful for the gown, sir. It's truly the finest I've ever owned."

"If you would like, I could fasten it for you. I do have some experience—I had a wife and four daughters."

"Four daughters? No wonder you are such a brave man," she teased—just as she noticed his use of the past tense. Had he lost them all?

Eager to leave the awkward situation, she spoke. "If you would be so kind, I would be forever grateful."

She stepped back so he could enter. Then, without another word, she presented her back to him. In the mirror in front of her, she watched him pause, his hands hovering above her skin like he was reluctant to touch her.

His face void of expression, he fastened both buttons. Immediately afterward, he stepped backward, looking anxious to end the intimate task.

"There you are, ma'am," he said as he strode to the compartment's entrance. "Are you ready for dinner now?"

"I am indeed, Mr. Edison." She closed her door and followed him down the gently swaying hallway of the train.

They stepped through two other cars, passing dozens of people along the way, all in various forms of rest or sleep. A few glanced her way when she passed, making her shiver.

As she scanned their faces, Jamie felt a curious sense of déjà vu as she followed Mr. Edison. She hadn't thought she would be so affected by being back on a train, but she was. Suddenly, everyone seemed like a prospective bandit, ready to take them hostage and do harm.

Only when they entered the ornate dining car did she finally breathe easier.

Mr. Edison, in that curiously acute way of his, squeezed lightly on her elbow. "Have strength, my dear. This is a different time and place."

"You know what I'm fearing?"

"I guessed," he said lightly. before turning to the nattily dressed steward waiting by the doorway. "Good evening, Jeremy."

He steward bowed deferentially. "Mr. Edison, we are honored to see you."

Mr. Edison waved off the bow. "I hope our table is ready and that it has a bit of privacy."

"Oh yes, sir. We've saved the table at the very end of the car for you, sir. This has worked well for you in the past. Will it be sufficient this evening?"

"It should be acceptable. Thank you."

Jamie followed Mr. Edison with a sinking feeling. The man was everything proper and charming, but she was quickly realizing that he was perceptive too.

His lovely manners and gentlemanly ways seemed to be merely covering a hard and calculating man underneath. He seemed very much used to getting his way, and used to getting answers—no matter what the cost.

With more than a bit of trepidation, Jamie sat across from Mr. Edison and prepared to be interrogated.

However, he didn't seem to be in any hurry to ask questions. For a good ten minutes, he studied the menu, then ordered steak for them both. He refused the offer of whiskey and instead asked for coffee for both of them.

Little by little, Jamie relaxed. The man's company was easy to be around. His deep, smooth voice was addictive sounding, his polished manners and language a balm on her nerves after being around the rough men of the Walton Gang.

After two bowls of beef consommé arrived and they'd both had a few exploratory sips, he leaned back. "And so, Miss Ellis, I suppose it is time to discuss your captivity and escape."

She swallowed. "Yes, sir."

"Tell me what happened. How did you get to be taken hostage? The only female hostage?"

She tried not to feel as if he was finding fault with her surviving. "When the Walton Gang made themselves known, it was as if a beehive had broken up, there was so much confusion."

"Explain yourself."

"Well, first everyone was just sitting, reading, sleeping . . . as everyone is wont to do during train travel." She paused, then looked at him for agreement.

But instead of nodding, his expression was carefully blank. "And then?"

"And then the train slowed, the Walton Gang showed up, and pandemonium broke out. Women were screaming and fainting; men got still or leapt to their feet." She closed her eyes, remembering. "It was terrible."

Once again, images of the armed men taking over the train besieged her. The memories, combined with the all-too-familiar rocking of the train, made it seem like she'd stepped back in time and was going through the whole experience all over again. As tremors coursed through her, Jamie sipped her coffee in an awful attempt to calm her nerves, but it seemed to do no good.

Mr. Edison's gaze seemed to acknowledge her every tremor. Then he continued, his voice emotionless and quiet. "How did you come to be in their custody?"

After the waiter removed their soup bowls, she did her best to explain. "The train stopped. People were running around, then were gathered and told to step forward. I was at the back of the car, and so I ended up standing next to Kent." She shivered at the memory. "He grabbed my arm and told me to stay with him."

One eyebrow rose. "And you did?"

She didn't know if he found fault with her actions or simply wanted clarification. "I had no choice, sir. He had a gun and was gripping my arm." Remembering the scene, she said, "Moments after that, the Walton men started making people get off."

"And people did without a fight?"

"From what I could see, they did. I was still held by Kent."

"And then?"

"And then I found out later that one of the gang members had pulled six men to one side. Will—I mean, Mr. McMillan—tried to let them go, but Scout shook his head, saying Mr. Walton himself wanted hostages in case they needed collateral."

"Scout, as in Scout Proffitt, yes?"

"Yes, sir." She stopped when their steaks were delivered. But instead of motioning her to eat, Mr. Edison gestured for her to continue.

Pushing aside the present, she nodded and sank right back into the memory. "Right about then, Kent pulled me forward and asked what he was supposed to do with me."

"And what did Scout say?"

"He got mad because the train had started moving again." With apprehension, Jamie glanced at Mr. Edison. When he nodded, she continued, vowing to do her best to describe how confusing and horrific the situation had been. "See, everyone else thought all the women and children were gone."

"But obviously that was not the case. You were there."

She nodded slowly. "They kept me. Will ordered Kent to put me on one of the benches, and that's where I sat until Mr. Walton arrived."

Almost delicately, Mr. Edison picked up his knife and fork and cut off a small bite of the beef. After a moment's pause, he placed it in his mouth and chewed while she continued to tell her story.

On and on it went. Mr. Edison cut his steak and asked pertinent questions, and she sat, hands in her lap, nervously recounting the longest week of her life.

The recounting seemed to take forever. In no time at all, his plate was clean. And still she talked.

Only when she finally got to the part where he'd taken custody of her did he lean back. "Thank you, Miss Ellis. Your account has been most illuminating. I'm very sorry to have taken you from your meal. Please enjoy it."

And then he got up.

She turned. "Mr. Edison, you're not going to stay?"

He paused in midstride. "I'm afraid not, my dear. I rarely keep company with women anymore. Jeremy here will look out for you though. You mustn't be afraid."

Remembering his use of the past tense, she took a chance. "Your wife and daughters . . . are any of them left?"

His face froze for a brief second before it looked as if he thawed himself with only great effort. "No." After a deep breath, he knocked his knuckles on the table. "Please don't forget to eat your dessert, Miss Ellis. The hummingbird cake is not to be missed."

"No, sir, I won't," she murmured to his back. Because he'd already moved on, his posture straight and stalwart.

Feeling more overwhelmed than ever before, she picked up her knife and fork and finally began eating her steak. She didn't care that it was rather cold.

Twenty minutes later, as she carefully slid her fork through creamy icing, she had to agree that indeed, the hummingbird cake was very delicious.

It was a shame that she was unable to enjoy it.

34

The woman had been as bad off as Scout had insinuated. Though he'd never seen her before, Will felt a sharp lump lodge in his throat as he watched Scout stoically roll the girl in the bedspread and gently carry her out to the funeral director.

When he'd offered to help, Scout had simply glared.

Together, they walked side by side on the streets of Dodge, Will glaring at all who dared to stare, Scout carrying the body in an ivory blanket stained with blood. Neither spoke. No words were necessary—and none would do the situation justice.

When they entered the undertaker's shop, Will had been prepared to use the weight of the U.S. Marshals to induce the elderly man to bury the gal. However, it turned out that no threats were necessary.

All it had taken was a decent amount of money. Scout unrolled bills, one after the other, each one assuring that the undertaker would prepare her body for burial and ask no questions. A few more dollars spent enabled the girl to be buried in the church cemetery immediately, though it would have been far preferable to stow the girl until the spring thaw came.

However, that was the benefit of being Scout Proffitt, Will supposed. There were some people one never refused. A pastor was usually one of them. Notorious outlaws surely came as close seconds.

"Sir, perhaps you'd like to come back in a few hours?" the undertaker asked nervously. "By then I'll have prepared the . . . uh . . . box."

"No, I want to wait."

"Sir, it might take a bit." He ran a hand over his scalp, smoothing the few remaining hairs on it. "Are you sure?"

"Very sure," Scout said, sitting on the one lone chair.

Wringing his hands, the undertaker nodded, and finally approached the girl's body. As Scout watched with eagle eyes, the man lifted the girl off the table, struggled for a brief moment with her weight, then finally carried her out of the room.

When they were alone, Will cleared his throat. "Want me to wait with you?"

"I'd rather be alone, if you don't mind."

"I don't."

Shifting, Scout looked his way. "Are you still willing to go to the preacher?"

"That's where I'm headed now."

"Do whatever it takes, you hear me?"

"I always do," he said. Will waited a moment for Scout to acknowledge him, then turned away when he realized that Scout wasn't with him anymore.

Instead, he was staring off in the distance, looking somewhere else. Lost in thought.

The church was located just one block from the undertaker. Whitewashed and with its several windows, it looked like the beacon of hope and light that it was.

When Will opened the door, the fresh scent of incense and lemon oil infused his senses, bringing him back in time to Houston, Texas, and the church he'd attended with his parents.

That one had been far bigger but had smelled much the same.

Immediately, his heart felt heavy. It had been far too long since he'd been able to be in a place of worship.

On the back pew, he'd found a man in black. Looking younger though no less as haggard and worn-down as the undertaker, the holy man got to his feet when Will approached.

"May I help you, son?"

"I hope so, Pastor. My friend and I have a girl being readied for burial over at the undertaker's. We need you to say some words over her."

"Now? The ground's nearly frozen solid."

"I realize that, but my friend and I will take care of that. My friend doesn't want to leave town without us doing the proper thing for this girl. He wants her buried right."

The pastor smiled slightly. "For him to go to so much trouble, she must be a special woman. Was she your friend's sister or sweetheart?"

Will almost let that slide, then realized that wasn't fair to the girl, to Scout, or to the preacher. The gal was what she was, and from what little Scout had said, it wasn't all of her doing.

"I'm not going to lie to you. I can't lie to a man of the cloth."

"I appreciate that . . . what is the truth?"

"Fact was, this gal, she wasn't much. My friend was only helping her escape a painful situation. But I'm afraid he got there too late." Knowing how pitiful it sounded, and how terribly sorry he was for Kitty, Will breathed deep and spit out the rest. "Preacher, the fact is . . . she died by her own hand."

A line formed between the preacher's brows. "A suicide?"

"I'm afraid so."

"Some would say she doesn't deserve a Christian burial."

"Some would say what happened to her didn't leave her much choice. Others might say what happened to her wasn't too Christian either."

The preacher's gray eyes looked Will up and down. "What was she? A harlot?"

"She wasn't old enough to be anything. All she really was, was a girl on the losing end of a very bad streak of hard luck and pain. Today, it just got to be too much."

Swallowing, the preacher nodded. "She's in good company, then." Getting to his feet, he cleared his rheumy throat and then shuffled toward the door. "Don't just stand there, son."

Will was stunned. He'd been fully prepared to argue with the man, to cajole and beg and threaten.

And now, it was being done.

"How much is it going to cost to ensure she gets buried?"

The shuffling stopped. "I don't recall asking for a thing, son."

"I'll pay."

"Not necessary. It seems to me this young girl has already paid enough, don't you think?" The preacher didn't wait for an answer as he stopped at a coatrack near the door, slipped a heavy black coat over his shoulders, placed a hat on his head, and then led Will outside to the undertaker.

As they walked, Will watched the man limp slightly. "You okay?" he asked, gesturing toward the preacher's leg.

"It's nothing. Just an old hurt I can't seem to get rid of."

Will reckoned he had a few of those.

✐

So that was how the four of them ended up digging a hole in the frozen ground together. Pickaxes were taken out when shovels didn't do the trick. Sweat poured off their skin. One by one, jackets were discarded. Vests followed. Faces became flushed. An hour passed. Then two.

Then, just as the sun started to set and the wind picked up, the men made a grave. The six-foot hole was anything but smooth and symmetrical.

But it would do.

Ropes were used to lower the pine casket that had been clumsily nailed together while an outlaw watched and waited and paced.

When the box was in the ground, the four of them stood at the edges of the grave in silence as their bodies cooled.

After a time, the undertaker spoke. "This is where you come in, Stewart."

The preacher cleared his throat. "The Lord is my shepherd," he said, his voice slowly becoming sharper and clearer with each verse.

As the psalm continued, Will glanced Scout's way. The younger man, now dressed only in a wrinkled and dirty black shirt and black trousers, stood motionless in the cold. His piercing gaze—the one that had inspired fear in the hearts of countless men over the years—never drifted from that pine box.

After a somewhat anemic "Amen," the preacher cleared his throat. "Mister, would you like to add anything?"

Scout lifted his head and looked at the holy man. A thousand questions lit his eyes, his expression fierce enough to make Will wonder if he was about to say too much.

But after a moment's pause, Scout shook his head. "Forgive me, but I can't think of another thing to say. Is that wrong?"

Instead of speaking, the preacher reached out and gently squeezed Scout's shoulder.

Will watched in amazement. Never before had he seen another man reach out to touch the notorious gunslinger. He'd certainly never expected that Scout would accept the touch so easily.

After clearing his throat, the preacher spoke again. "In times like these, I don't think we happen to need many words. The Lord already knows enough to get the deed done. She'll go to heaven. Don't you fret about that."

Slowly, Scout turned to the preacher. "You sound sure of yourself."

"It's my calling to be sure."

"And me?" A slight, derisive smile curved his lips, almost as if Scout was aching to be told he was worthless. "Do we all go to heaven?"

"Heaven is open to us all, I think. For those who believe . . . and for those who repent." And then, without bothering to explain, the preacher picked up his coat, slipped it on, then turned and started hobbling away. His limp was more pronounced, but otherwise his posture was straight and true.

When the preacher was almost inside the church, the rest of them picked up the shovels and tossed the rest of the dirt back in the hole.

While they worked, it was almost easy to pretend they didn't see Scout Proffitt's tears.

35

$\mathcal{S}$omehow, Mr. Edison had located Jamie's two aunts and had encouraged them to come to the station to collect her. Jamie spied the two ladies when the train pulled into the station at Kansas City. Clad completely in black, they were standing close together and were looking at the train with pinched expressions.

They looked far different from her memories of them. Jamie vaguely recalled elegant women with refined voices and gentle natures. There was little that was gentle-looking about these ladies, however. Stark and plain, the pair looked like twin crows coming to nest.

"You close to your kin?" Mr. Edison asked from behind her shoulder.

Knowing he was seeing the same things she was, Jamie fought to keep her voice easy. "No, sir. I haven't seen them in over ten years."

As he motioned her forward in order to join the line of people exiting the locomotive, Mr. Edison cleared his throat. "People change. They might be real different from what you remember."

She was different too. "I'm sure we'll get along fine. It was kind of them to offer to take me in," she said when she stopped by his side.

"Indeed. Yes, family is a blessing, to be sure."

A tingling rippled up her spine. He sounded almost sarcastic, but surely not? "Yes, sir."

The line of people in front of them edged forward. Holding her old dress in her arms, she felt vaguely like she was jumping out of a burning building into a deep pool of water.

"Scared?" he asked.

"Not at all," she lied. After all, what good would happen if she were frightened? She had no other place to go and no other family to take her in.

"Oh. Well, that is good. I suppose little would cause you worry after the ordeal you've been through."

They'd almost reached the exit. Through the portal, Jamie noticed the two ladies edge closer together, becoming a wall of taffeta. Were they nervous to see her too?

"Ma'am, please allow me," Mr. Edison murmured as he somehow found a way to inch by her side and support her elbow as they stepped onto the platform. Ten more steps brought them to the side of her only living relatives.

Upon her approach, the two ladies looked her over in unison. Dark eyes examined her from head to toe. Not a line of emotion appeared on their faces, reminding Jamie of precious china dolls she'd spied at a general store outside of Denver.

Feeling terribly awkward, Jamie stepped forward and held out a hand. "Aunt Millicent? Aunt Francis? It's me, Jamie. I mean, Jamilyn."

"Ah," Aunt Millicent said as she inclined her head. "We wondered if that was you."

Jamie's hand fell back to her side. So, there was going to be no warm embrace or sweet reunion—nothing except continued disapproval and distrust.

Beside her Mr. Edison stood silent and still. A coolness emanated from him that she'd never felt before—not even when he'd been asking her all those questions about being at the mercy of the Walton Gang.

Face flaming, she turned to him and tried to ease the tension. "Mr. Edison, may I present Misses Millicent and Francis Lowe?"

He inclined his head, mimicking Aunt Millicent's cool gesture. "A pleasure."

His perfect manners, contrasting mightily with her kin's rudeness, spurred a fresh wave of embarrassment. Jamie bit her lip, unsure of how to make things better.

After a long moment, Aunt Francis stepped forward. Without a spare glance Jamie's way, she looked intently at Mr. Edison. "You said she's been held hostage by the Walton Gang? Then lived alone for a full week with one of your agents?"

There was a tremor in the lady's voice. Seeking to reassure her, Jamie said, "Aunt Francis, please don't worry. I'm fine. I'll tell you all about it after we let Mr. Edison get on his way."

However, all her words of reassurance fell on deaf ears. Neither aunt acknowledged her. Instead, their attention fixated on the man by her side, whose demeanor seemed to become chillier by the second. "Mr. Edison, is what we heard true?"

"It is."

Millicent and Francis exchanged glances. "We wanted to meet you at the train to hear the story from your lips. But if that is the truth, I'm afraid we won't be able to take her in."

"You are refusing to take in your niece?" Mr. Edison asked.

"She's ruined. And she'll surely ruin our reputation as well."

As Mr. Edison silently stared at the women, Jamie felt her throat closing. "None of what happened was my fault," she protested. "I almost died."

Aunt Francis finally deigned to meet her gaze. "Jamilyn, you must understand our point of view. After everything you've been through and most likely done, there's nothing we can say or do to change things. The fact of the matter is your parents would expect no less from us. We have our reputations to consider."

"But what about Randall?" Jamie sputtered. "We've been writing to each other. I thought he was anxious to meet me."

"Certainly not any longer."

"But—"

"After you've spent so much time in the company of such nefarious men? You're used goods." Aunt Francis turned chillier. "No man of worth would ever even want to be seen with you now."

Even when her dress had been ripped and torn, when her hair had been sweaty and dirt and dust had attempted to fill her every pore, Jamie had never felt so unclean. Tears pricked her eyes as panic rose sharply.

What was she going to do? If her aunts weren't willing to even acknowledge her, she now had nothing.

Her world began to spin. Her knees grew weak. She began to sink—until a strong hand grabbed her waist and held on tight. "Easy, Jamilyn," Mr. Edison murmured. "I've got you."

As she struggled to keep what was left of her composure intact, he turned to her aunts who were once again standing together like twin birds of prey.

"Good day, ladies, and good-bye. I must say that your words have been truly illuminating," Mr. Edison added before guiding

Jamie away from her two aunts, who were staring with horrified expressions.

After motioning a rail worker to collect his luggage, the elegant man leaned close. "Chin up, dear. Don't you dare pass out on me. We are not going to give those biddies the satisfaction."

Jamie was beyond embarrassed. She'd become numb. Stumbling next to the famed Marshal, she kept her chin up until they exited the terminal. Then, as the cool air fanned her cheeks, the awful reality of her situation hit her hard. Once again, she was alone.

The feeling was as frightening as the gun had been next to her temple.

"Can't say I've ever met two more disappointing individuals, Miss Ellis," he said with a grimace. "I thought I'd seen it all, but those women proved that was certainly not the case."

"I don't know what to say, sir, except that I'm sorry."

"For what? Having the misfortune of being on a train with the Walton Gang?"

"For dragging you all this way," she countered. "I'm embarrassed to have caused you so much trouble." Even as she said the words, she scanned the area, half hoping her luck wasn't completely used up. "If you could direct me to an employment office, I'll get out of your way."

"You truly imagine that I would simply drop you off here?"

She was too frazzled to take anything for granted anymore. "You should. I know you're a very busy man, and I'm not your responsibility."

"You are. Until I know you're safe and settled, you are." After pulling out his pocket watch, he said, "I seem to remember a rather decent inn not too far from here. Let's spend the evening there. We can do some thinking, then discuss your options."

Relief coursed through her, though she wasn't eager to let him know just how desperate she was. "Thank you," she finally said after mentally debating what to say. "I'd be most grateful for your assistance."

Her words seemed to spark a bit of amusement within him. His mustache twitched. "Miss Ellis, you do beat all," he murmured before stepping in front of her and hailing a hackney coach.

As she'd come to expect, Mr. Edison's will always won out. Within seconds of him raising his hand, a driver approached. Two minutes later, they were on their way.

As they traveled, Jamie used the time to look around Kansas City, and was instantly charmed. It was bustling and busy, and both the women and men looked rather dapper in their city clothes. Many of the buildings were made of brick instead of the pine they used out in Colorado. Buggies and horses traveled along the wide streets. Every so often they passed beautiful homes in fine condition. All in all, it was so different from what she'd known in Colorado, that it took her breath away. She felt even more insignificant than ever.

All too soon, their ride ended. After helping her alight, Mr. Edison led the way into a fashionable red brick building three stories tall. Inside the foyer, richly polished wood floors were covered with multi-colored Oriental rugs. Above them, a gas chandelier glowed, illuminating shining surfaces of fine cherry furniture and ornately fashioned lamps.

Far more striking than any of that was the woman who greeted them. Her blond hair shone like spun gold. Her blue eyes sparkled behind dark eyelashes. And Jamie was sure she'd never seen a day dress as beautiful as the peacock blue silk she was wearing.

"Sam Edison? What a delightful surprise," she said as she held out one slim, smooth hand.

"Rebecca. It's a pleasure. May I present Miss Jamilyn Ellis? She's been my traveling companion for the past two days. Jamie, this is Mrs. Rebecca Bergoren, proprietress of the Trumpeter Inn."

Jamie smiled politely as she felt herself being examined by the statuesque woman. "How do you do, ma'am?"

"Very well, thank you." She smiled, then turned to Mr. Edison, correctly assuming that he had all her answers. "You need some rooms this evening?"

"We do."

"We happen to have one room available. Will that do?"

"It will not. Please let Jamie have it though. I'll sleep on the couch in the parlor."

"I couldn't let you do that, Mr. Edison," Jamie said. Turning to Rebecca, she said, "Do you happen to have any servants' rooms available? I would be perfectly happy there."

"Servants?" With one eyebrow arched, Rebecca glanced Sam's way.

But Jamie wasn't ready to make the poor man do more for her than he already had. "Mrs. Bergoren, Mr. Edison has been very kind to escort me to Kansas City, but I find myself in need of employment. I'd be happy to work off my room and board here, if it would be at all possible."

"Doing what?"

"Just about anything. I can cook. Wash dishes. Do laundry."

The lady glanced toward Mr. Edison again. "Sam?"

"I can vouch for her character, though I admit to never having seen her cook or clean. If you could give her a chance, I'd be obliged."

The innkeeper looked at Jamie again.

Feeling somewhat like a horse at market, Jamie pulled her shoulders back and stood as straight and tall as her petite size would allow her. There was no shame in working or earning her keep. And though her aunts thought far differently, she was beginning to realize that she had nothing to be ashamed of. She'd done the best she could her whole life and she was still standing.

From her point of view, that said a lot.

"Jamie, I might call myself crazy in the morning, but today I'm in the mood to give you a try. You've got just enough gumption to spark my interest. Stay here a minute while I walk Sam to his room. Then you and I will get acquainted."

She'd done it! She'd found herself a job.

Mr. Edison shook his head before he followed Rebecca up the carved staircase. "You sure about this, dear? Working here is not the same as being a guest. I'm afraid the work will not be easy."

"I'm not afraid of hard work."

"But perhaps nothing too hard? If we put our heads together, I'm sure we could come up with an alternative."

"There is no need for that. It's time I stood on my own two feet. If Mrs. Bergoren will give me a chance, that's enough."

"All right then." He turned away and walked up the stairs without another look in her direction, making Jamie suddenly feel like he'd already crossed her from his mind.

Until she heard his voice trickle down to her ears.

"That girl is exceptional, Rebecca. She's been through an ordeal and has carried herself through it better than most men of my acquaintance."

"You sound taken with her."

"I'm taken with anyone of character," he said. "You should know that by now."

Jamie couldn't help but smile. She didn't know what her future had in store for her, but she knew where she'd been.

And that history had proved to her that she should never take anything for granted.

And never to worry too much about the future.

Right that minute, things in her life were better. She was safe, she had shelter, and she had a way of continuing her life.

For now, that was more than enough.

36

$\mathscr{D}$odge City, Kansas, was dirty and smelled to high heaven, and Will McMillan was stuck there until further notice. Holding in his hand the latest telegram he had received, he was tempted to crumble it in disgust. But if the war and his experiences of working undercover for the U.S. Marshals had taught him anything, it was that that patience wasn't just a virtue—it was a necessary part of success in his life.

Therefore, because Sam Edison wanted him to stay put a little longer, he would. Not because he liked the idea, but because it was his job.

Across from him, Calvin leveraged his elbows on the counter. "You don't look too happy about your latest directives."

It was too late to pretend Calvin wasn't completely entrenched in his business, so Will didn't even try. "I'm not."

"What are you going to do then?"

"What I'm supposed to do. I'm going to sit tight and wait."

"You be wantin' supper? I could probably rustle something up if you really wanted me to."

Leave it to Calvin to get back to business. "Nah. I'm going over to the restaurant in a bit." Will turned away before Calvin asked if he wanted company.

Still not eager to sit in his empty room, he walked back out onto the main street and took a good look around. Not much had changed in the overgrown cow town since a few hours before.

Which was too bad, really. He was itching for action. Shoot, he'd even pay good money to get involved in a decent fight if he could.

"Uh-oh, I know that look and it ain't good," Scout said from a few feet away.

Will jerked his head to his left. "Didn't see you there," he said, then cursed for even admitting such a thing.

"I just got here. Don't worry, you haven't lost your touch." Scout stepped a little bit closer, then mirrored Will's stance, lazily propping his shoulders against the building behind him, looking straight ahead.

"How are you doing? Thought you'd be long gone by now."

Scout's lips thinned. After a pause, he shrugged. "I'm not ready to move on."

"That girl's death hit you hard, I reckon."

"It did." As if the words were perfectly painful to admit, Scout added, "I can't help that. She was too young to die."

Will figured that was true at just about any age, but he kept the thought to himself. His friend was hurting. "I was going down the road and get some supper. Feel like joining me?"

"Will that be a problem? We're on the opposite sides of the law now."

Scout had a point. If Sam Edison had been in their midst, the man would've had Scout hog-tied six ways 'til Sunday by now. But, like Scout, he was having trouble moving on.

Escorting Jamie to the train and out of his life had been one of the most difficult things he could recall doing in some time.

"Here's the deal," he said finally. "I'm worn out and tired of second-guessing myself. As far as I know, you haven't killed a man since we've been in Dodge . . . have you?"

"No, I have not." He had the gall to look offended. "Honestly, McMillan, is that what you think of me? As nothing more than a killer?"

"At times, that's all you've been."

"You don't know me. You don't know *all* of me."

"Then be more than what I do know," Will bit out, his patience with the world at an end. "I rode by your side for more than a year. I've watched you kill people without blinking an eye. And what's more, I'm sure that's what you will be going back to."

"I'm not going back to Walton."

"Can't say that I blame you. But he wasn't the only reason you are the man you are. Somewhere along the way, you made your choice."

"Maybe we don't all have choices."

"Maybe we don't. But, if life has taught me anything, it's that sometimes you have more choices than you think."

"So that's why you let Miss Jamilyn Ellis go on her way?" His voice was cold, full of derision.

Scout's jibe hit Will hard, not because it was mean-spirited, but because it was true.

Not that he was going to admit that. "What happened with her is none of your business."

"That's where you're wrong, Marshal. You might have watched me slowly make my way to hell over the last two years, but I watched you with that woman. She got under your skin."

He couldn't deny it. But knowing he'd been so transparent didn't sit easy. "It was better for her to go."

"To go where? To live in a big small town town with a pair of elderly aunts she doesn't know?" He scoffed. "She's completely alone, and she looked at you like you hung the stars and the moon."

"She did not—"

"Oh, she did, and what's more, you knew it. Come on, Will. Do you think you're the only man in the world who doesn't lie to himself at times? She loved you, you felt the same, and you pushed her away. You'd rather she be alone or marry somebody else than be brave enough to risk your heart."

"You're out of line."

"Well, it wouldn't be the first time."

Pushing away from the wall, Scout turned in the opposite direction. "Good-bye, McMillan. Just so you know, I'll be leaving tonight. With luck, you'll never see me again."

"If you ever change . . . and you need something . . . find me."

Scout stopped. "Do you mean that?"

Will nodded. "I do. We may be different people, and at different places in our lives, but I think we have more in common than one might imagine. Besides, underneath all that black, I know you're a good man."

But instead of accepting the compliment like Will had hoped, Scout laughed off the comment. "I'm telling you what, Marshal . . . there's some days I'm not sure at all how they let you into law enforcement. You've got the softest heart of any man I've known."

And with that, he started walking down the sidewalk, his pace slow, his head straight ahead, his aura menacing. A pair of women stepped off the sidewalk, choosing to muddy their skirts instead of risk touching him.

If Scout minded, Will would never know.

Turning the opposite direction, Will headed toward Lucy's and finally allowed himself to review Scout's words about Jamilyn and admit that the man's words were true. He'd fallen in love with the girl, and he'd been too afraid to do anything about it.

Showing that Scout Proffitt had nothing on him in cataloging sins.

Rebecca Bergoran was a perfectionist and a natural-born leader. Jamie learned that after only a few hours in her company. The woman had never met a speck of dust that she could abide or a discarded newspaper on a table that she could ignore. Or a person she didn't think needed direction.

Jamie, however, was especially good at keeping her opinions to herself, which most likely meant they would get along together just fine.

"Everything has its place," Rebecca said for about the fifth time that morning as Jamie followed her around the roomy parlor on the main floor of the inn. "These rooms are our guests' first impressions and if there's dirt or debris around, it might be the only impression they get."

"Yes, ma'am," Jamie said obediently. Again.

When the tour stopped in the expansive dining room, Mrs. Bergoran pointed to the figurines in the china cabinet. "Dinner is in four hours. Before then, I want you to give everything in here a good rubbing."

"All right."

"Do you have any questions?"

"No, ma'am."

More quietly, Rebecca asked, "Were you able to sleep last night, dear?"

Jamie's room was small and sparse. It was also deliciously warm and outfitted with a narrow bed that had been surprisingly comfortable. "Very well, ma'am. From the moment my head hit the pillow, I was asleep."

"Good." Mrs. Bergoran paused, looking as if she wanted to say something more, but then she shook her head and left.

Happy for the solitude, Jamie picked up a dust rag and opened the china cabinet doors. Carefully she pulled out the array of vases, glasses, and plates that were stacked on the top shelf. After wiping down the shelf, she began returning each item one by one, giving each one a careful swipe as she did so.

She didn't mind the mindless task. Actually, she was grateful for it. Now that she wasn't so exhausted, and stunned by her aunts' behavior, her mind was eager to replay the events of the last few weeks.

That couldn't be done, of course. If she'd learned anything in her twenty years, it was that pain and disappointment were a part of life. No good ever came from reliving it—or from doubting her past decisions.

Picking up another plate, she rubbed it carefully.

"Looks like you've got the hang of dusting just fine."

Startled, Jamie almost dropped the piece of china. With shaking hands, she hastily set it down then turned. "Mr. Edison, you scared me half to death! I almost dropped that plate."

"I noticed." His mustache twitched. "Sorry I startled you. I only wanted to tell you good-bye."

Crossing the room, she held out her hand. "That was kind of you. Thank you for everything, Mr. Edison."

He squeezed her hand for a fraction of a second before dropping it. "Do you think you'll be all right here?" He looked skeptical as he glanced around the room.

"I hope I will. I mean, I'm sure I will be just fine."

Looking ill at ease, he clasped his hands behind his back. "Jamilyn, I hope you won't take the wrong way what I'm about to say. But I think I'd be remiss if I didn't speak my mind."

"Yes?"

He cleared his throat before he began to talk, his voice uncharacteristically husky. "I've found, during my life, that unforeseen events can have a profound effect on a person's mental health." He glanced at her before continuing. "This kidnapping and abduction, if you remember nothing else, please know that it was not your fault."

Her heart started beating faster. "Sir?"

"Those men were killers, Jamilyn," he said slowly, with a somber, knowing look. "They would have killed you if you'd stayed. They had planned on it, you mark my words. Will McMillan's quick thinking saved you—as did your bravery."

His praise embarrassed her. "Yes, sir."

"What I'm trying to say is you've done nothing to be ashamed of. You survived, and any man will tell you that that's quite enough sometimes."

Oh, the conversation was getting awkward. It was achingly apparent that Mr. Edison wasn't happy with the way his words were sounding. It was also terribly apparent there was little else he could say. He might have been the head of the Marshals, but he wasn't an orator by any stretch of the imagination.

"Thank you, Mr. Edison. I'll remember your words."

He brightened. "I'm glad." Then, fishing in a pocket, he pulled out a small piece of paper. "This is how to get a hold of me. If you contact me, I will do everything in my power to help you out."

"That's very kind of you."

"It would be an honor." His eyes watered slightly. "Good-bye, Miss Ellis. Jamie."

Before she could say good-bye, he turned and left.

After carefully placing the paper he left into a pocket, she walked slowly back to the china cabinet and took out another stack of dishes, afraid once again to dwell on the past.

37

$\mathcal{T}$he missive was short and to the point: MEET ME IN KANSAS CITY (STOP). TWO DAYS TIME (STOP). REGARDS, S.E. (STOP).

Will folded it neatly and pocketed it while he walked to the station to see when the next train was leaving.

Yes, that's what he needed to think about—the train schedule. He definitely shouldn't be thinking about hidden meanings behind the telegram.

Mr. Edison had his next orders and there was little he could do about them. A man didn't question Sam Edison. Ever.

But boy, if he'd ever had an urge to do so, now was the time. He didn't want to receive his next orders. He was bone tired. Tired of being on guard, tired of looking over his shoulder.

Tired of most everything in his life.

Not that it mattered.

All that really mattered was that he did what was asked of him. And that, today, was to get on a train to Kansas City.

Feeling wearier than ever, Will approached the ticket counter. "I need to get to Kansas City," he said simply.

After peering at him through a dirty pane of glass, the ticket agent looked back down at a sheaf of papers in front of him. "You're in luck," he said with a toothy smile. "Next train is in two hours."

"One ticket, then."

After paying the money and accepting his stub, Will walked back to the hotel. It was time to move forward, even if he didn't want to. Mr. Edison was counting on him, and that was enough.

After sending a telegram back to Edison, he bathed and ate. And then prepared to do his duty. Which, by his way of thinking, was about the only thing of value he had left in his life.

He hoped it was enough to see him through the day.

⌇

To his surprise, his boss was waiting for him when he finally reached Kansas City.

"Sir," Will said, by way of greeting. "I didn't expect to see you here."

"I don't imagine you did. Greeting trains isn't something I have much practice with, to tell you the truth."

Will's heart sank. Whatever Sam had in mind for him must be terribly urgent. With a true sense of inevitability, he hoped it was a case far away from Missouri or Colorado. At least then the terrible memories that plagued him might have a chance of subsiding.

Of course, the U.S. Marshals didn't take job requests. It wasn't their job to coddle the men who worked for them, and each one knew it.

Will also knew that Sam had never been the type of man to put up with men pestering him with questions. So he held his tongue and followed the older man to a clean-looking supper house four blocks from the terminal.

After they were seated, Sam leaned back against the cushion of his chair and gazed at Will directly. "I appreciate you coming out here so quickly."

"I'm glad the train's schedule fit your timeline."

"Coffee?" a waitress in a worn-looking calico dress asked.

"Two," Sam said without looking at Will.

After coffee was delivered, Will sat still and stoic, waiting for news. Any moment now, he would be getting his new directives. After that, it would be his job to accept the work with the danger and to plan accordingly. Within hours, he would be adopting a new identity and traveling again.

And though it was hard to accept, Will knew he had no choice. A man didn't refuse orders.

After taking a few fortifying sips of extremely hot coffee, Sam leaned back and folded his hands on the table. "Funny thing happened when I delivered Miss Ellis to her aunts," he said.

Will almost choked on his drink. "Sir?"

"You remember Miss Ellis, surely? She's a fetching little thing. Blessed with golden hair and a pair of wide-set caramel-colored eyes that look as though they've seen too much of pretty much everything."

Will knew that was no doubt the case. "I remember her, sir."

His boss tilted his head. "I thought, when I saw the two of you together, that she meant something to you."

"Of course she does. I mean, she did," he amended, feeling more and more uneasy with each passing second.

"But you weren't interested enough to ask about her?"

Ask about Jamie? Ask Sam Edison, one of the most feared men in law enforcement in the country, about a woman he had affection for? "Well . . ." he hedged.

"Well?"

Fighting the urge to loosen his collar, Will tried unsuccessfully to bide for more time. His boss's line of questioning was without preamble, and for the life of him, Will couldn't figure out if the man was genuinely interested in his feelings for the woman or if he was using the line of questioning as a trap. "I didn't ask about her because, well, I didn't see the point."

"How come?"

"If life has taught me anything, it's to not look back," he admitted.

"How far back do you try not to look?"

But for the life of him, Will didn't know what to say anymore. "As far back as I can," he finally admitted. "Life is hard."

"That is true." His boss smiled as the server returned, carrying two plates filled with hot roast beef, mashed potatoes, and rolls. "Thank you."

The food in front of Will smelled wonderful. His mouth watered, and if he'd been alone, he would have already dug in with his knife and fork.

But of course he wasn't alone.

"See, the thing is, I believe Miss Ellis's current situation is a difficult one."

All thoughts of eating left him. "I thought she was going to live with her aunts."

"Her aunts didn't want her." Sam smiled slightly before neatly slicing a corner of the beef and digging in.

"How can that be? She's their family. Plus, she's all alone. She has no one else." Without quite realizing it, his voice rose. "She'd been kidnapped. She almost died back in Dodge."

"I'm aware of that." After a sip of water, his boss switched topics. "I read your report. I've also spoken with the folks at the Kansas Pacific. Because of your testimony, we've found the link between the Walton Gang and the railroad company. At this moment, both James Walton and Mr. Arthur Jackson, former employee of the Kansas Pacific, are being transported to St. Louis. Many are indebted to you, McMillan." As the words sunk in, another neat bite of meat was sliced off and swallowed.

Bitterness coursed through Will as he realized his boss wasn't going to spend another moment talking about Jamie. Perhaps to Sam, she was just one of the many characters in a case that was now closed.

However, Will couldn't settle for that. "What happened to Jamie, Sam? Do you know?"

Sam carefully set his fork down. "Did you really imagine I wouldn't know?"

"I don't know what to think anymore, sir."

His eyes narrowed. "You are trying my good nature, McMillan."

"And you are trying my patience, sir."

In another time and place, Will probably would've immediately apologized. Men who wanted to survive didn't speak that way to Sam Edison. Ever. "Where is she?"

"She's working for a friend of mine. Rebecca Bergoran. She owns a pretty little inn on the outskirts of town."

An inn on the outskirts of town? The worst sort of things flooded Will's mind before he sternly told himself that Sam was an upstanding man. If he called the place an inn, it was just that, not anything worse.

But he still wanted more information. "What, exactly, is she doing there?"

Sam's brows snapped together. "Exactly?"

"I'm only curious."

"Well," Sam drawled. "When I left her, she was dusting the dining room."

Momentarily appeased, Will forced himself to nod. "And she was . . . well?"

"She was surviving," he corrected sharply. "There's a difference, though I suppose you know that. Eat, McMillan. Food's getting cold."

Will did as he was told, but though he was going through the motions, nothing in his actions felt right. He didn't understand why he'd been summoned to arrive in Kansas City right away just to be taken to a dining hall.

He didn't understand why Sam had brought up Jamie but seemed to be bouncing around Will's interest in her and wouldn't give more information as to why he'd even mentioned her in the first place.

It was the type of puzzle that drove a man to speak too sharply and to make mistakes. He dearly didn't want to do that.

Minutes passed as the man across from him seemed to find a lot of pleasure in eating particularly slowly.

Finally, patience shot, Will spoke. "Now that Walton and Jackson are in custody, what job do you have for me? Where do you want me assigned?"

"I didn't bring you here to reassign you, Will," Sam said after yet another too-long pause.

Why then? Was he about to be fired? "Then why did you?"

"So you could finally realize what's important to you."

"I'm not following you."

His boss leaned back, and in a trademark move, crossed his arms over his chest and looked at him levelly. "I've given you your future, son, and her name is Jamie."

Will blinked. Was Jamie his future? He'd been sure she'd been just a dream of his.

With impatience, Sam continued. "You obviously care for her very much. Are you really going to let her dust and mop for the rest of her life in some inn in Kansas City?"

"But what choice do I have?" He hated to sound so weak, but he really had no idea of what to do.

"Quit the Marshals."

Quit? Will had never heard of anyone being allowed to quit. Usually the only way out was death. Unless "quit" was code for something else. "Sir, am I getting fired?"

"I am most definitely not firing you. I'm letting you off the hook, allowing you the chance to do something right for yourself for a change instead of for everybody else in the world. Go do it, son. Go out in the world and get a real job. Find something that lets you go home every night. After all, if you get your girl, she's sure to be a woman who's worth going home to."

Shocked into silence, Will's head began to clear as the choices swam in front of him and spurred his tongue. "I never thought I could do anything except put my life on the line. I never thought I could do more than hold a rifle and shoot to kill."

"It's not your fault you're good at that, McMillan. Your abilities were sorely needed during the war. And they've been put to good use during our war against the outlaws. But surely every man needs a chance to do something for himself."

"Walking away . . ." He blinked hard, unable to fathom it all. "Do you actually think I could do anything else?"

"Always. Will, I've had a good life. At one time I had four girls to go home to. I'd never trade those days for the world. At least I have memories. And, Will, that's a sorry way to live, you hear me? Memories don't warm a bed and they don't comfort a hurt. But the sad thing is you've got even less than that."

It was true. He'd lived his whole life by himself. "Is it even possible?" he asked again. Shoot, he knew he was sounding weaker than a newborn foal, but here Sam was taking a lifetime of his certainties and tossing them on their side.

"If it's not, then not a one of us is worth all that much, I don't think." Reaching out, he grasped Will's hand. "Will McMillan, I am hereby releasing you of your duties with the U.S. Marshals. Thank you for your honorable service."

After shaking his hand, Will stood and gave one of the most upright men he'd ever met a formal salute. "It was a privilege, sir."

Sam saluted right back, then handed Will a packet. "You're going to be needing the contents of this, I think. There's a formal commendation for your honorable service as a U.S. Marshal, a letter of recommendation from me, and some compensation for your services. God be with you."

"Thank you, sir," he said, before turning around and walking out, packet in hand.

For the first time in his life, he was about to do something for himself. Not for his family. Not for his country. He blinked quickly so no one would see the tears welling in his eyes.

38

Shawnee, Oklahoma, wasn't much, but Scout didn't need it to be. All that mattered was that it had a decent saloon, with a couple of desperate men interested in playing high-stakes poker, and that not a single person in the dark, ram-shackle building dared look at him close enough to ask if he really was the infamous Scout Proffitt.

"You playing or posin'?" the drunk across the table from him snarled.

A couple of the men on either side of him flinched, but it had been a long time since he'd been cowed by a greasy old man who couldn't hold his whiskey. "I'm in," he said, tossing a few chips into the center of the poker table.

The game progressed as the hours rolled onward. Two men left at midnight, their spaces taken by fresh blood, cowboys who looked eager to spend their hard-earned cash on high-stakes chances. Whiskey flowed and the flashy women posing in his line of sight got little to no attention.

All while the drunk across from him imbibed more rotgut, lost more money, got angrier, and turned more desperate.

For his part, Scout was winning. He didn't care about the money, only about the time. The longer he was at the table, the less time he'd have to figure out how to sleep at night.

As cards slapped the table, men around him groaned. He had won again.

"You're cheatin'! I know it!" the drunk yelled.

Scout stilled. "I don't cheat."

"Of course you do. Look at you. Dressed in black from head to toe, silver pistols at your side. You look like a bandit."

The men around him gasped.

"Do I?" Scout was getting a little tired of being chewed on. Quietly, he said, "Is that what you really think? That I look like an outlaw? A no-good, lying, cheating outlaw?"

Maybe it was his silent glare, or the way it was obvious he couldn't wait to beat someone to a pulp.

Maybe it was his half-smile. But the man's eyes opened wide and his brow started to sweat.

Around them, the room seemed to grow quiet as each person looked at Scout just a little more closely. Perhaps one or two of them even started to imagine that his black wardrobe and the scar on his cheek looked almost familiar.

Or maybe they were waiting to see just how far a drunkard with half a brain could go.

Seconds passed. Scout leaned back, his hands resting loosely at his side before he was even conscious of it.

But then the drunk cleared his throat. "My mistake," he mumbled. "No offense."

Looking at the others, Scout said, "Are we still playing?"

"We're playing," one said. "Bill, you out?"

It was evident the man had used his last nickel. "No." Grabbing the back of an advertisement tacked to the wall, he held out a hand. "Somebody get me somethin' to write with."

"Bill—"

"Do it."

A pen was pushed into his hands. The man hastily scrawled a message on it. "Okay. I'm in now."

"What is that?" Scout asked.

"Deed to my farm."

One of the men to Scout's right closed his eyes.

But Scout finally felt a glimmer of hope burst up inside him. "Where's your farm?"

"Not here. It's in Texas."

That sounded even better. "Where?"

"West of Texarkana. It ain't much, but it's worth a fair amount."

One of the other men coughed loudly. "Don't you have a family, Bill? Ain't that your homestead?"

"I'm dying. Cancer. They're moving on anyway." Belligerently, he stared at them all. "Y'all in or not?"

Two men left, obviously too high and mighty to risk taking a man's land. Two others quickly took their places though. And then the bidding progressed.

The stakes were high, the cards flying quickly.

And for the first time in his life, Scout was sure that a higher power was on his side. Because one by one he acquired the cards he needed.

Men folded. Another raised.

The drunk, looking pastier by the second, raised the bet.

And then it was time.

Scout presented his set of four aces.

The drunk lumbered to his feet, his eyes wide and his expression full of fire. After emitting a good long stream of profanity, he pointed one bony finger at Scout's chest. "You're a no-good cheater. You're going to pay—"

Slowly, Scout got to his feet. "I didn't cheat. And I'm not going to pay you a dime." With deliberate moves, he gathered the chips and examined the paper. "You need to sign this."

The man's skin turned a grayish-white. "I . . . I can't do that. I can't give you my land."

"It's too late. You bet it, and I want it. You'd best sign it now or I'm going to finally put you out of your misery."

The men around him nodded. Scout might have been scary, but he was right.

Grudgingly the man signed his name as the rest of the men around Scout paid up and got to their feet. But just as the old man handed him the paper, he lifted his chin, showing his last bit of respect. "Who are you? Who have I just given my farm to?"

"Do you really want to know?" Scout said. "Because if you know my name for certain, I will have to kill you."

He turned away then. Not a shot rang out as he left the premises. Scout made sure he didn't turn around because then someone would see his smile.

He was a landowner now. And for a man who'd ached all his life for a home, there was nothing sweeter.

A woman ran after him, her bright red dress standing out like a cardinal in winter. "What's your hurry, honey? Don't you want some company for a while?"

Scout paused. He almost considered it, but then shook his head. "Nope." He was done looking for easy company and temporary relief.

And with that, he left Shawnee, Oklahoma, and the crowded company of worn-down men. Mounting his horse, he headed south to where both his past and his future lay.

He was going home to Texas.

39

*I*roning pillowcases was a thankless job in the afternoon's humidity. Jamie brushed away the few strands of hair that kept sticking to her cheeks and forehead and picked up another iron from the fire.

After smoothing out the pillowcase, she deftly ran the hot iron across the cloth, finding comfort in how the soft cotton instantly smoothed.

Oh, if only life was like that. If only she could grab a hot iron and quickly smooth the wrinkles away and make things even and perfect again.

But, of course, such a thing was never going to be possible. She was now forever marked by her past. And if her daylight hours didn't confirm that, her nightmares surely did.

With a flick of her wrist, she snapped the pillowcase taut, then easily folded it into thirds. For good measure, she ran the iron over the folds one last time.

"It's funny. During all the times I've thought of you, I've never pictured you once doing something so domestic," a voice drawled behind her. "I wonder how come."

Jamie almost burned herself as she set the iron on the plate. To gain herself some time, she picked up the completed pillowcase and added it to the stack. As she did so, Jamie noticed that her hands were shaking.

Most likely, she was not hiding a single thing from the most observant man she'd ever met.

Well, it was probably just as well that she was noticeably trembling—her insides were quavering something awful. "I don't know," she finally answered. "Perhaps you didn't really believe I was a domesticated woman, Mr. McMillan?"

"*Will*. It's Will," he corrected. "Remember? You promised to call me by my Christian name."

"Will," she repeated, his name feeling like both an unexpected treat and a source of sorrow on her lips. If she turned around, what would she see in his eyes?

Afraid to face him, she plucked up another pillowcase. But she didn't have the will to set it on the board. Instead, she only fingered it lightly. And tried to keep her composure.

Her lack of welcome didn't seem to bother him. "As for your ironing, I suppose I should have guessed you could do the chore so well. After all, I knew you were a lady of worth . . . and so much more to me."

There was a new yearning in his voice that was hard to ignore. Husky and deep, he sounded like he was measuring each word carefully before speaking. As though he had so many words floating around in his head that he was worried about the wrong ones spilling out.

She knew what that was like. At the moment, it was her feelings that were leaning in that direction. Or was it her heart?

Even though she'd faced bandits and hunger and shame, she was still afraid to turn around. The sight of him would be too much like her dreams, and she didn't know if she could handle that. "Why are you here?"

"I couldn't stay away."

Her heart clenched. "That's not how you acted when we said good-bye in Dodge City. When I got on the train, you seemed content." Her throat worked, making her continue even though she wasn't sure how to explain herself. "You made it seem like you doubted a future with me."

"I didn't doubt you, ma'am. I doubted myself. I've been in a distant place from anything of worth for a very long time."

"I'm afraid I'd have to disagree, Will. You, I'm sorry to say, are the most honorable man I know."

"Jamie?" Impatience settled in. "Jamie, are you ever going to turn around?"

Her mind worked over the words. Tried to convince her breathing to work with her lips. When it felt as if she finally had control of herself, she admitted her weakness. "I'm afraid to see you."

"Why is that?"

His voice was closer now. So close that she could sense his body behind her. Though she considered reaching a hand out to him, she still waited. Hope and need were sorry companions to disappointment. "Because I'm afraid you won't be who I remember you to be. And . . ." She sucked in a breath and tried to get her bearings right. "And, I'm afraid you'll be disappointed too. Now that we're out of danger, you'll see that all I am is myself. Nothing special, nothing out of the ordinary." Nothing like him.

"Never. You've always been far more than ordinary to me." Now he was close enough that she could smell leather and the underlying scent that belonged to Will McMillan alone.

Her mouth went dry as his hand curved around her shoulder, and gently squeezed. Not hard. Just enough to let her know that he was there. He was present and he wasn't going away.

But it was easy enough to jerk her shoulder out of his grasp if that was what she really wanted. She didn't. "Why are you here?" she repeated.

"Because a very smart man reminded me that here was where I needed to be."

"In Kansas City?" She honestly wasn't sure about how much to hope for.

"I need to be with you, Jamie."

It sounded like there was a smile to his voice now. She could imagine it just as if he were standing in front of her instead of behind. Then with his other hand he gripped her other shoulder, effectively caging her in. Holding her close. When he sighed, she felt his breath cascade against her neck.

But even more powerful than his proximity were his words.

"Jamilyn, when I was with you, I swear it was the hardest time of my life. Not even during the war was I so afraid. Every minute of the day I was terrified I was going to misjudge a situation and get you killed. I was afraid I wouldn't be man enough to protect you, that I wasn't going to be strong enough to help you survive."

"I had no idea you felt that way."

"I didn't know I could admit it," he whispered, his voice sending fresh waves of awareness down her neck.

For the first time, he'd let her feel his weakness. But instead of making her turn away from him, it made her finally turn around. Instantly, his gaze searched hers. Blue irises flared as he silently conveyed everything they were both afraid to verbalize.

As she'd anticipated, his hands dropped when she moved her body. They stayed at his side when she faced him completely.

Chest-to-chest. Hip-to-hip. Little separated them except worries and doubts, unsaid promises and unspoken fears.

But even with all that, there was something far stronger holding them together. Love. "I fell in love with you," she said. Surprise flickered in his eyes before he carefully tamped it down. "Will, back when you were worried about being everything for me, I fell in love with everything you were."

"Was it enough?"

This time, she was the one who reached out. Running a finger along a wrinkle lining the outside of his eye, she tried in vain to ease his lines of worry. But they were too embedded, coming from a lifetime of hard work and living dangerously, to be removed with one soft touch. "Oh Will, don't you understand? All along, you were more than enough. You were more than I'd ever known."

"The hardest thing I ever did was let you go on that train with Edison."

"I got the feeling it was." When a ghost of a smile appeared, she slid her hand lower and brushed her thumb against the curve of his bottom lip.

"What? Was that day at the train station not the hardest day for you?"

"Not at all." When he stared at her in surprise, she chuckled. "Will, letting you go was easy, because it was the right thing to do. I wanted you to feel all right. I wanted you to feel good about yourself."

"Because?"

"Because that's the kind of man you are, Will. You try to do right. And because you are that way, others try to be that way too."

"I want you in my life. I want your hand, Jamilyn. I want your hand and your heart and everything else."

"Are you proposing to me?"

He nodded. "And doing just about the sorriest excuse of a proposal as a man ever has done." He paused, looked around, and then pulled her toward the corner of the room. It was darker there and a little out of sight from almost anyone who happened to be walking by. Then, without another word, he knelt down on one knee and reached out for her hand. "Jamilyn Ellis, I love you. Will you do me the very great honor of marrying me? Of being my wife?"

"Of course," she said, feeling like she'd just mistakenly walked into someone else's life. "If you're sure."

"I've never been more sure."

As she looked in his eyes, she knew he was speaking from his heart. And from her heart too. "Of course I will marry you, Will," she said. "I love you too." Bending forward, she pulled him up to his feet and raised her chin.

Then no other words needed to be said. As had become their custom, a look and a touch said almost everything. So did a kiss and an embrace, she was coming to find out.

A long while later, when he finally stepped away, they were both breathing heavily.

"Jamie, come away with me. Tonight."

"Where will we go?"

"We're going to find a preacher and do whatever it takes to get him to marry us. And then I'm going to saddle up a horse and go back home to Texas. To the hill country. And we're going to find us some land and settle down and live."

She laughed. "Just like that?"

"Just like that. Sam reminded me that while I was living my life as different people, the bank account of Will McMillan was growing bigger. Fact is, I don't know if I'll ever need to work again."

She smiled at that. Not because of the money, but because of who he was. Because of the man he was. "How long do you think you'll stay a man of leisure?"

Eyes shining, he grimaced. "Not long. But I had an idea that I thought I'd play around with for a bit."

"And what is that?"

"I'd like to be the law in a small, sleepy town. And along the way, I want to study the Bible and plow a field. And build a house and raise some horses. I want to make a life with you, and with you by my side, I'm thinking maybe I can help a few other people."

Suddenly looking doubtful, he stilled. "Um . . . what do you think?"

"I think you can do just about anything you set your mind to, Will. And I'd be proud to be by your side."

Her hand clasped in his, Jamie walked out of the room, and after briefly telling Rebecca what she already seemed to know, strode out of the inn.

Into the bright sunlight, into her future, and to a home she'd never seen.

Next to the man who needed her as much as she needed him.

"Jamie," he drawled as he clasped her hand. "You ready?"

When she nodded, they walked forward. And began.

Discussion Questions

1. The epitaph on Wyatt Earp's tombstone reads, "Nothing's so sacred as honor and nothing's so loyal as love." Many of the characters *A Texan's Honor* spend their time contemplating honor. What does honor mean to you? Is it possible to acquire it, or do you think it's an innate part of a person's character?

2. Jamie Ellis begins the novel as a hostage and a victim. She grows stronger during the story and in the end makes her own choices about her future. How do you think her experiences at home before the train robbery played into how she was able to survive the Walton Gang?

3. Will states that saving Jamie is the best thing he's ever done. Do you agree?

4. Psalm 85:10 says, "Mercy and Truth are met together; righteousness and peace have kissed each other." How do you think that mercy and truth go together? What about righteousness and peace?

5. The character of Kitty serves as Scout's redemption. Why do you think he needed a friend like Kitty in order to grow? Or do you think she didn't affect him in a positive way?

6. Scout feels like a failure to Kitty. Is this true? Do you feel Kitty deserved her Christian funeral?

7. Why do you think Scout and Will's friendship works?

8. Several times throughout the novel, Scout compares himself to his brother, Clayton, the hero of *A Texan's Promise*. Scout is always sure he could never be as heroic as Clayton, but are they really all that different? What are some ways their characters are alike?

Be sure to visit Shelley online!

www.shelleyshephardgray.com